GOOD THUNDER

GOOD THUNDER

A NOVEL BY

JOHN SOLENSTEN

State University of New York Press
Albany

Published by State University of New York Press, Albany

©1983 State University of New York

For information, address State University of New York
Press, State University Plaza, Albany, N.Y., 12246

Library of Congress Cataloging in Publication Data

Solensten, John.
  Good Thunder.

1. Dakota Indians—Fiction. I. Title.
PS3569.O54G66   1983   813'.54   83-367
ISBN 0-87395-712-1

10 9 8 7 6 5 4 3

I

Linda Tall Rabbit

The moon track is pale yellow on the river, as the burly black shoulder of a thunderhead pushes southeastward over the high prairie toward Ft. Pierre. Lying on blankets in the back storage room of Rex's Bar, Linda Tall Rabbit is trying to give birth, is trying to push the child's head out and not scream so the men in the front of the bar will hear her. She wishes she could push harder and open wider and that she could stop tearing. It is a lonely and terrible thing even though Listening Grass is there with her.

The head feels like a wet stone bulging out of her own black wells of fainting. In her own mind she swims up toward the light and the air. Each time she does so she fears she will not come out of the dark well again. Linda is tall and rangy. Even heavy with child her body is fat stingy and sinewy. Listening Grass holds Linda's head in her rough brown hands and cries undulating deep cries of encouragement and consolation into Linda's ears. Linda's mouth is wide, with strong lips like a man's and her teeth are big as she bites into the leather thong Listening Grass has pressed into her mouth. Sometimes, when she pushes hard, Linda's bare feet come down plat! plat! beyond the blankets on the linoleum floor by the water heater in the storage room of the bar. Her eyes are brown and soft as a cottontail's, but her body is hard and sinewy as she tries to push the child out of the dark of her womb and into the light where the pain burns at her loins.

Three men standing in the doorway into the bar itself peek in to watch her. With each hard plat! of Linda's feet they swear in a quick chorus of drunken admiration. The bartender's voice tries to call them back. "Come back in here, you guys!" it calls from a region of country western music and smoke and guttural voices rumbling in the April night. The neon sign on top of the bar outside winks on and off: "Rex's Bar," "Rex's Bar." Linda is used to the sign. She has worked in the bar for two years and has slept many nights on the blankets in the storeroom where she is lying and giving birth.

Listening Grass takes more water into her wash basin, draining it directly from the faucet at the side of the water heater. She washes Linda's face, belly, and legs under the blanket while Linda rests from her writhing and heaving. She sees the men watching. She hisses at them and pulls the blanket back up on the ridges of Linda's knees. Then she holds Linda's head in her Hands again, leaning over the twisted face and singing an old song of consolation and encouragement.

"Lord God!" one of the three men exclaims between draws on his spiked beer. "Who ever caught up to her to get her like that?"

"Couldn't catch her even in the cellar. Couldn't get next to her or she would kick your head off with them big feet. Send you right on your ass!"

"She is still kickin'," the first man says, "and it ain't workin'. That kid must be 16 pounds or bigger'n that even!"

Linda screams then—a long bray of a scream—and then high pitched until she finds the leather thong in her mouth again. The beer mugs hang in mid-stride toward the mouths of the three men watching.

"Where's the doctor?" the third man asks. "She ought to have a doc, for Chris' sake!"

"A vet, a vet is what she needs. Tall's a horse."

"Could never mount her."

"Somebody did." A pause. Heavy swallowing and two profound belches.

"Somebody did."

"Who?"

"Not who? No who. Where is what."

The neon sign on the back of the bar winks on and off. Rex's Bar, Rex's Bar. Linda pushes again. Faints. The pink light from the sign flashing in through the back windows on the river makes the men look like they are experiencing flashes of blushing embarrassment—and the stacks of Stohr's beer cases too. Everything pink and blushing.

A white flash of light from the bar as the bartender pushes the door open wider and steps in. "It's near closing," he complains, tying his stained apron in the back as he scowls at the three men. His forearms are thick and powerful. "This ain't right and it's near closing."

"It's near opening," one of them says.

"We got a bet on the time," another says.

"Wise guys," the bartender replies. "You guys are all wise guys."

"Oh yeah!"

The bartender tries to be conciliatory. He enters into the spirit of the occasion. "What's takin' so long?" he asks. He can see the dim outline of Linda pushing. Her face is a mask, her teeth big and white and then neon pink in the light. He can see her feet plap! plap! on the floor as she push-breathes. "What's takin' so long?" he asks again at the florid faces of the three men. They disregard him.

"In a goddam boat!" one of them exclaims.

"A boat." Throats swallow beer and fire-fierce alcohol.

"Was a boat where she couldn't get away—a boat under the dam last fall."

"A boat?"

"Magnus Magnuson, the guide. Bringin' her here to clean up. Had her in the boat. Somebody seen 'em. They was comin' from his place."

"Jesus! In a boat."

"She said she would lie on her back only for the sun if the sun was a man."

"This one?"

"No, the one in the sky, for Chris' sake!"

"A boat?" The three of them are afloat on the idea. Swig on it. Belch on it. Ride a river of dull lust of memory through the long raised legs under the blanket. Listening Grass hisses at them, her eyes wolf yellow through the folds of ancient skin on her face.

Linda hears the cry of a crow through the music and the murkiness of shadows and voices. She pulls her whole body into one movement. The child slides out bloody and webbed in membrane. Linda hears a crow cry. But crows don't cry in the night. She bleeds and her body cools, cools—deep-into-the-bones cooling. Something takes her head in its beak and rises with her, choking her, into the night sky and then drops her into a blackness where her soul lies in the nest of roots in the grass. The roots are cold. It is a place called death. It is the other mother.

The child is a boy. When he first cries out it is nearly two o'clock. The three men clap noisily and cheer. "What's his name?" they call to Listening Grass. But she only bends over moaning and rocking slowly as she washes the child and cuts and ties his cord.

"How about A. O. Smith?" one of the men asks. "How about the name off the water heater. Goin' to be in hot water all his life. And has a little faucet on 'm!"

"A. O. Smith!" they cry out together. Swig and belch.

The bartender comes back in, wiping his hands again on his apron. He sees the stillness under the blanket and the child's crying. "Something's wrong. You boys better go now," he tells them, pushing them with his thick, stubby hands. They resist.

"Why, hell, they're tougher'n that, for Chris' sake!" The one saying this swaggers with winking indignation. The others nod agreement.

"I better call somebody," the bartender says.

"Call Magnuson," one of them laughs. "Tell him to bring his boat."

"This ain't no joke anymore," the bartender says walking gingerly toward the nativity. He leans over Listening Grass and the stillness beneath him frightens him. "You better go," he tells the three of them again. "It's no joke," he says as he pushes them through the doorway back into the bar.

"The kid's all right," one of them yells back at the bartender. "We heard him makin' a war whoop already."

"Get out of here. It's no place for you anymore. I got to call the sheriff or somebody now."

While the bartender is calling in the empty bar, Listening Grass adjusts Linda's body and washes it and cleans up the blood. She slides Linda's body away from the wet place on the floor and wraps it in a blanket. Then she wraps the child in another blanket and hurries out through the bar and toward the street with her bundle.

"Hey! Where you goin'?" the bartender yells, but Listening Grass pretends she doesn't hear him. "Hold it!" he yells walking out as far as the phone cord goes, but Listening Grass pushes the latch and is gone. She walks very fast, pretending she doesn't hear him. Outside, in the gray morning light the wind flaps her long dress and the rain comes down softly through the hard reverberations of thunder in the early morning sky. She knows where she is going. She walks, head down, to the little frame house where Nancy White Cloud grieves after losing her first-born child.

At the door Listening Grass says nothing. She hands the baby over into Nancy's arms. Then she turns back into the street where the rain spottles little gray ghosts of dust on her men's work shoes. She croons softly and walks with long strides toward her place in Indian Town on the edge of the river in Ft. Pierre. Her thick gray dress flaps against her legs when the white and red ambulance sweeps by. Its beacon is turned off and has no pulse because it goes to pick up the dead.

Inside the little brown frame house where the baby has been taken, Nancy White Cloud bends over him, loving him, feeling the wet tug of his mouth down into her toes as he sucks at her nipples. She looks into the morning light and relaxes so the milk flows easily. When the thunder rattles the house, the baby sucks harder. His eyes are wide with pleasure and then begin to close sleepily. The light is kind to their eyes and the morning smells fresh and sharp to Nancy because it is spring and she has a good, long boy-child at her breast.

Her husband, Eddy, watches her from the doorway of the kitchen while she sits at the table nursing the child. His eyes are tight and hard with anger.

"Where did you get it?" he asks.

"You saw her bring it."

"I asked where you got it. I want to be sure."

"You know where. Why are you asking?"

"Tell me again so I can make sure."

"Linda is dead now."

"So?" Eddy is a short stocky man. He is wearing a sheepskin jacket as if he might be going somewhere—even at six o'clock on Sunday morning when nobody goes anywhere in Ft. Pierre, South Dakota except those who deliver things. He waves his hands angrily. His hands are quick and very hard. Nancy is smiling at him, trying to smile through and around his anger. "So?" he asks again.

"So, I have milk and I want a child and this is a boy, don't you see?"

"You in a hurry? We just buried a child out there. What's your hurry?"

"And the doctor—he said there would be no more again and so I wanted this one, don't you see? He could belong to us. He should be tall and strong."

"Then let me put him in a basket on the river . . . Let the people find this tall child of hers and his."

"Oh!" She pulls the baby toward her and locks him in the circle of her arms.

"He's about right for you," Eddy says. "He is half Wasichu. You can have him sit on your desk in some office when you go there to do the paper work. You can give him a vision of college or maybe get him a job in Sioux Falls in a factory. Sometimes I think you are half Wasichu too. You got all the notions."

"Please!"

"Sure. Please. They'll be laughing at me. The old men will say, 'White Cloud is a sparrow and the cowbird has let him hatch a cowbird chick in his nest.' And then some day the kid will go fishing on the river. His uncle will pick him up."

"Please!"

"I have heard too much about everything."

"Linda is dead."

"Too much!" Eddy scowls and walks out of the house toward the truckstop on the highway where the men pass the bottle in their cars.

"I will work and keep him. I won't let him go. This is my chance," she says through the front window at Eddy's retreating figure. When the thunder rattles the house again she stands up and holds the baby in front of the window glass. She is joyously defiant and tired and happy. Eddy looks smaller and smaller as he walks toward the truck stop. "His name is Charlie Good Thunder!" she calls after him. "You don't beat me and win; you beat me and lose!"

At Rex's Bar the men from the coroner's office put Linda Tall Rabbit into a plastic sack. Her body is stiff and sinewy in death. The rain dapples the plastic with silver drops as they carry her to the ambulance.

"Would you believe it?" the bartender cries as he stands in the rain watching them. "Would you believe the old lady walked right out of here with the baby and down the street and left me with this, this whole goddamned mess? Why, hell, that's kidnapping or something, isn't it?"

The rear ambulance door clunks shut.

"It'll be all right," the driver says as he ducks into the driver's side.

"You look like hell," the other attendant says to the bartender.

"No sleep and Jesus what a mess."

"It's wet out here. We got to go."

"I wonder what will happen to that kid."

"It'll be all right. You better get some sleep and get in out of this rain."

"It's a good thing it's Sunday."

"I guess. We got to go now."

The bartender watches the ambulance dip and swing in a curve toward the mortuary ten blocks away. He is wet and chilled tired. Inside the bar he pours himself a half glass of rye whiskey and coughs and waits for his wife to pick him up.

Thunder. Charlie awakens and cries and sucks. The thunder crashes and makes him suck harder. Nancy feels it down into her loins like a quick root as she sits nursing Charlie at the front window. The lightning flashes but the thunder is good for both of them.

Rocking him and humming Nancy prays and thinks inside her head as she nurses and waits to see what will happen next:

When Charlie sucks my breast I forget the empty place inside me where the other one grew and died. The others didn't show me his face. I wish I looked. Now it's too late, too late. Except for Charlie. He sucks and I am a new tree under the rain and I am growing again. My skin is full of noises like leaves in the rain. This man, my husband, he doesn't have a great heart or great head or anything. Why is the circle of love of some men so small? I don't know. This man, my husband, likes to be with other men all the time between crawling on me. The war isn't over for him. What does a date on army discharge papers mean? I thank God for this boy who makes me feel full again and worthy. But why do I need him to make me feel good? I don't know. I am waiting at the window. Go away or come home, Eddy, but I am showing this to all the world. And I will get a better job and even keep him alone. You wait and see.

Nancy stands up again and moves closer to the window. There is a church bell ringing off a white steeple in the town below her. A few children pass in front of the house throwing stones and jostling each other. One of them, a thin tall boy with a tiny mouth and fine high cheekbones like a girl's, points at the window and laughs. Nancy stands there with the child, a picture for the morning to see.

2

The Mother

Charlie lies on the new bathinette Nancy has bought with the money from her new job. He screams and farts and kicks at the light. When Nancy opens his diaper and bends over him he squirts warm urine in her face. She shakes her head. "You boys! You men!" she says. She shakes her head and smiles and wipes her glasses with a diaper. "You boys! You men!" she says. Her husband, Eddy watches her, his eyes full of dark, sinister thoughts. He has been angry for weeks. For one thing he has no job.

"What you bitchin about now?" His voice is tight and threatening through the words. "Maybe you're too tired with a kid and a job."

"Nothing," she says. She is thinking about two things: washing her hair and crying, but she waits. She has to wait.

He moves closer and she can smell the whiskey, rank and rich from his throat. She is almost as tall as he is. She kicks her shoes off slowly and bends over Charlie again, hoping the arc of her warmth will shield them both but knowing it can't.

"How much for the little man's wash table?"

"Not much." His breathing is thick and audible and contemptuous. It is like a wind carrying something that will have to fall to earth someplace.

"It was only 38 dollars."

His hand whacks the plastic pad first and her heart jars as

Charlie screams and begins to kick frantically. When Eddy aims a fist at her screaming, looking over the knuckles like a gun-sight, she steps into the force of it, taking it on the side of her head. It stings terribly, a high hot pain on the ridge above her fear. A silver noise rings through the slanting yellow sunlight in the kitchen. Time stops. Her eyes widen with the punches thud-ding into her shoulders and she staggers, trying to push the bath-inette behind her. Again, she thinks. It is happening again. There is no stopping this because it is happening again.

The bathinette tips and Charlie tilts and slides with a murder-ous whock! down on the slick linoleum kitchen floor. When Nancy turns, the blows catch her arms, her shoulders. Even drunk he is accurate, deadly, cunning. "The bruises. The purple marks. The shame. Long-sleeved dresses. Charlie! Charlie! Are you dead?" Nancy's heart cries.

He smashes the bathinette, chopping it with the side of his hand gleefully. "Here! Here! Here!" he cries. The chrome pieces bend over the brown sinews of his arms and the swelling mus-cles of his legs as he twists them.

But Charlie isn't dead. His face contorts in shrieks of terror. He blubbers under her face and she kneels over him and they both scream, tangling their faces in her hair.

"I told you," she hears Eddy shouting. "I told you a million fucking times no, you hear? I told you a million times no, but you hang on and hang on and I gotta pay and I gotta be laughed at and I got to stand around when that Wasichu comes around later to see his kid in my house!"

Kick. Numb throb. She can see the right cowboy boot under the army pants. Men. Death, she thinks. Men. Death. You men, you death. Boots, she thinks. She has her ear on Charlie's mouth. It is wet and sucks at her ear and screams and she loves it because it is soft and wet and small.

"I told you a million times no kids, no kids. No kid of mine, no kid of yours. I told you a million times to take it back. You think I'm not a proud man? You think I'm not anything any-more so I can take anything? You think I fought a war to come home like this?"

Sobbing, Charlie sobbing short bleaped cries of indignity.

Eddy's voice is weary and sad and terrible above them then. And yet he kicks once more—squarely on the buttock. If you hurt me there, she thinks, thinking of there between her legs, you can't touch me again, if you hurt me there. Her behind is up as she kneels over. It is a position he likes in love and that now he hates.

Somehow through the noise of it all Nancy hears the clock on the refrigerator ticking. Then she knows she has won. And yet she thinks, You men, you kill. Your boots. Her thick brown hair fans over Charlie. His arms thrash into it and tangle in it and bind them together so they are strong under the voice wearying above them.

"I'm going to tell you the last time to get it out of here. If I see that one bastard blue eye of Magnuson's in that face again I'll throw his little ass in the river, do you hear? And don't get no ideas about taking off with him, do you hear? You get rid of him. You take him back to Listening Grass. He's not mine, do you hear? You put him on the river in a basket. You give him to some church. But don't have him here when I get back. You may pay on this house but I got the G.I. loan and I don't want no other man's kid in this house that I know."

She can see the boots again and through the circle of her arms she can see them walk away with the voice. The kitchen screen door flaps open into the June day, then shuts, the spring twanging behind it. She begins to cry. She sits up with Charlie and begins to croon an old song about the circles of the seasons, the sadness of passing things. The little bruise on Charlie's forehead is knotting with blood, and his face frets and his eyes blink fast on the pain.

"No!" she cries. "No! No!"

She gives Charlie his bottle. He falls asleep.

What to do? she wonders. She thinks about the rifle behind the kitchen door, a .22 with a long feeder tube. She can shoot it, can kill a gopher easily at 200 feet. But she can't kill Eddy. He has a stone, a miraculous thing such as Crazy Horse had. And the people would side with him. And her old father—he would say, "You must choose your people and your husband." That's all he would say and she would probably lie to him anyway about

Charlie's father. It would be like bringing something home from a store and lying about the price. And she's very confused since her father has been dead for more than a year and her mother for nine years.

What to do. It's not that the people won't take the child if it is truly an orphan. There are many who would take him. But everyone knows that Magnuson is the father and won't say so. It's all wrong and it's all too late. The money, the bills from Magnuson's pockets—chewed like old cuds of cows—define his fatherhood. Money. A white man defines many things with money —love especially.

Neither one of them can admit—can say, "I am his father" or "I will be his father because someone has to." Pride. Tall boots. Man pride. Race pride. Mothers have no pride. Don't need it. Pride is a boot. Take the old idea—the colors of the four directions of light—black, blue, yellow, red. Pour them together and you have the color of earth. Earth has no pride. Brown.

She has an idea.

The lawyer, she thinks. There is a law, a man's law that is strong too. It costs money but I am working there and maybe it won't cost so much. Cost for what? What will the law do? Can it sit in the kitchen and tell Eddy to leave us alone? Assault is a word, but is it a word for wives? Many wives are beaten—especially on weekends—and no one does anything, so what will the law do?

She has no phone, so she leaves the house, carrying Charlie in a little blanket. Outside on the street she walks stiffly but quickly toward the filling station where she knows there's a phone booth and maybe a telephone book for Pierre and the other towns around there. She passes a few people and they smile or disregard her. They know who she is but they don't stop except to say, "Good morning, Nancy." But they don't stop to ask, "How is the baby, Nancy." They are kind people. Most people are kind people.

The telephone booth is by the Mobil station. A telephone directory hangs in a blue plastic sheath from a chain inside. When she lays Charlie down inside, he begins to cry again. She feels terribly vulnerable standing there. They can see me, she thinks.

They can all see me. It's Saturday and they can all see me going by in their cars if they look.

She dials the office. Nothing. Charlie crying now. She fumbles through the book again and finds Mr. Porter's number: Mr. Todd M. Porter, 224 Sidney, Attorney-at-Law, Residence.

The voice at the other end is calm and friendly and Nancy leans against the glass, relieved a little. "Hello?" the voice says. It's Mr. Porter.

"Hello, this is Nancy from the office. I been working for you six months."

"Yes, Nancy."

"I have trouble and I don't know what to do." She begins to cry then, but his voice is calm and reassuring as he asks, "Can I help you some way?" and then, "Do you want me to come over there?" She sees that people are watching her—really watching. "Oh, please." And the calm voice: "Where are you?" and her answer, "I will be at the Penney's store. I'm afraid to stay here." And the calm voice: "You keep calm if you can. I'll be there in about ten minutes."

The world on the streets as she walks toward the Penney's store is tear-bleared and frightening. Charlie screams but she has the formula bottle and she gives it to him there inside the blanket and he sucks noisily. Her legs throb with new dull pain and her ribs hurt as she breathes hard with the walking.

She waits in the entrance to the store—just inside the revolving door in which Indian children play until the manager chases them away. She waits, aching and weary and desperate. Up the steps inside the store she can see the children's department and a white enameled child's crib, but no bathinettes. She fights the crying again. Families pass by. Families. She fights the crying and rocks her baby.

"So there you are!" It's Porter. She has never seen him in casual dress before. He is wearing a white knit shirt and blue summer slacks. She realizes that he is much younger than she is. His face is tanned and confident and smooth except for wrinkles around the eyes from too much reading or too much sun. "Do you want to go to the office?" he asks, a hand on her elbow.

"No, Eddy will look there right away."

"Your husband? Didn't I meet him one day at the office?" He frowns saying it.

"Yes." The people passing by begin to watch them closely.

"It's not good here," he says. "I think I can see some of the trouble now."

"Some of it?"

"Don't you want to go to the office now?"

In the car he tries to look at Charlie, but he's sleeping and Nancy holds him close to her, the edge of the blanket over his face. The interior of the gray car is rich red velour and very quiet except for a soft ticking somewhere. It reassures her. Law, she thinks. Maybe the law will comfort me.

At the office she goes in ahead of him and stops at her desk to put Charlie down. The office is quiet too and secure. Charlie whimpers softly, his eyes pursing at the pain in his forehead, but they are safe for awhile.

Porter smiles and waits for her to say something.

"My husband doesn't want me to have this child because the father is a white man in town. The mother is dead. Today my husband beat me and said that if the child isn't gone when he comes back he'll kill me."

"So this is the real trouble?"

"This child is what I want even if it means no husband or no house or anything." She is crying again.

"Has this happened before—the beatings I mean?"

"Many times but not so bad. This time he kicked too."

He is very serious then, sitting on the edge of the desk. "He won't understand, your husband. And he will probably think I put you up to it if you take legal action. And, of course, it will all take some time and it won't be easy and he'll probably come after you."

"But can I have this child?"

"I think so, but that will take a month or so. What do you call him?"

"Charlie, Charlie Good Thunder."

He peers in at Charlie, still looking very serious and then even more serious when he sees the bruise on the forehead.

"If you want, you can take a taxi and get a few things and stay at the housekeeping motel, the Crestview it's called. But I warn you that your husband won't give up easily. You'll have to . . ."

"Is there anything the law can do?" she asks.

"I can put him under peace bond. I don't want trouble here either. He may just let you go. Do you think so?"

"Yes," she says, "Put him under a bond. I won't give up my child." She pauses. "And I'll pay for everything."

"You're a good worker here in the office. We won't worry about paying. We'll just worry about you and this child now. One thing at a time."

Nancy sags into a chair behind the desk where she sits and types everyday. The chair feels very good around her. It is as if she is holding herself and in some way comforting herself. She watches Porter dial the telephone. As he waits for it to ring on the other end, he looks over at her, his eyes serious again. Charlie is lying on her desk, the rubber pacifier in his mouth. The office is very quiet.

"Your cab will be here in just a couple of minutes," she hears Porter saying to her as he hangs up.

"Thank you."

"Will you be all right?"

"Yes, and I am going to learn more on this job and be a legal secretary."

Porter smiles then. "I'm sure you will, but all of the rest of it won't be easy," he says, his eyes focusing on Charlie's face as she picks him up in the blanket.

When Porter opens the front door of the office, Nancy cringes at the light. When she steps out into the street she looks both ways. Behind her Porter stands inside the front window of the law office. Through the slats of the venetian blinds he looks striped dark and light, but his presence reassures her.

The taxi comes, a dented and rattling yellow Plymouth with flared rear fins and no grill. The driver is an Indian she has seen somewhere before. He tries to be congenial. "See this belly?" he asks hugging the folds of it over his belt. "Macaroni!" he says, as he opens the back door for them. He leans toward them. "We Indians have to eat macaroni full of starch, so we get a belly." She doesn't know what to say about macaroni so she says nothing.

After the two of them—Charlie and she—are in the back seat and he is ready to go, he reaches over and flips the meter on.

Back at the house the driver is very nervous and doesn't get out while she loads her clothes and a few other things into the back seat. There are other things she wants to take along too but there's no room. She hurries, her head throbbing.

Terror! Eddy standing there in the kitchen as she turns around. Eddy standing there out of nowhere. Why hadn't she heard the door open? She is holding a bottle warmer with one hand; the little potty chair is slung over the other.

But his face is calm, even kind. Behind him stands Running Deer, tall and reproachful, his great bulbous nose florid and puffed and purple from drink, but his eyes kind too. They have been friends a long time and came back from somewhere in the army together. Through the front window she can see Running Deer's big green battered Pontiac. It squats on its springs with the weight of clothes and guns inside.

Eddy's voice breaks the silence first. "You saw the lawyer fella?" he asks.

"We seen you there," Running Deer says.

"Yes." She puts down the potty chair. "I was afraid. You kicked me many times and I was afraid you would maybe kill me too."

"Whew!" Running Deer lets his breath out, looks at Eddy, his eyes a serious question.

"I told you why," Eddy says.

She doesn't want to look at his face so she looks at his boots and they make her brave with anger. "I won't give him up. If I don't get him I never have a child."

"He is not an Indian."

"He is my child and that makes him an Indian."

"No."

"But I say yes."

"Whew!" Running Deer exclaims, " I better go wait outside."

"I'm going now," Nancy says. She bends to pick up the things again.

"You can leave them," Eddy says.

"I need them."

"No, I mean you can have this house. You can make the payments." Eddy is already moving toward the door as he speaks.

"We're going to Rosebud," Running Deer says. " It wasn't my idea at first but I have no woman and I want to get out of this town."

The two men push through the door quickly. Through the window Nancy can see that both of them stagger on unsteady legs, as they lurch toward the car. She can also see the cab driver push down the lock latches on the doors of the cab. Charlie and he are locked inside.

She goes to the door and calls to Eddy. He lurches back to her and stands unsteadily below her on the steps, a little smile on his mouth.

"Aren't you going to say goodbye to him?" she asks.

"Why hell no. I didn't say hello to him either."

"Are you coming back?" Her heart skips a little in her throat as she asks it.

"No, I got to get away from it all and find some pride again."

"Pride?" She finds herself softening a little, but then she feels the bruises hurting too.

"I got to find a war or something. I got to kill myself with something besides liquor. . . . I'll go Rosebud first, then who knows?"

She doesn't reply. She hears the kitchen clock ticking behind her and she feels stronger again. She doesn't touch him either. He seems already gone away to her. *The kicks. The blows.* Stranger, she thinks.

He comes back briefly. "You ride your taxi and tell your lawyer fella I'm going away to save you money from the white man's law."

"We could come with you," she hears herself saying.

"No we!" A little flare of anger in the eyes, but only a little one.

"You want a divorce?"

"Then you have trouble with the house. But you go do what you want at the law office. And make Magnuson pay, that phoney son-of-a-bitch!"

She puts everything down then. "You got a key?"

"No, I put it on the dresser."

She walks by him then and away from him. Raps on the win
dow glass of the taxi where Charlie is crying and the driver is
tap, tapping the steering wheel and muttering to himself. Inside
the taxi she feels a strange elation. They ride around town for
half an hour after she calls Porter. Even in the rattling old taxi
she feels a new security. The white man's law works, she thinks
to herself. But the driver is angry and the cab often lurches
around corners and when it does she feels new fears flying in her
heart. And yet the June sun is on the streets and rooftops and the
child is in her arms.

When she returns to the house, Eddy and Running Deer are
gone and nothing seems to be missing. She puts Charlie in his
crib. Then she sits at the kitchen table and cries for a long time,
her head on her arm. Then she goes outside in the back yard.
The broken twisted bathinette has been tossed against the foun-
dation of the house where the plastic cover flaps in the wind.
Her feet are cold, but she removes her shoes and walks in the
grass and the grass warms her heart again up through her bones.

3

The River

"Where did I come from again?" Charlie asks. His mother Nancy is combing his hair before they go to the God house. There are three houses in Charlie's life—the house with Mother, and the God house and the grey house full of children where his mother takes him every morning when she goes to work.

"I told you many times," Nancy says, stopping to press down a wisp of Charlie's dark hair and to pull the little blue jacket up on the thin high shoulders.

"But tell me again!" Charlie is bargaining because he knows his mother is in a hurry. It's risky though because she might become angry and she will spank. His whole world is still in the face with glasses and dark brown eyes and the mouth that kisses and the round cheeks with scars on the skin.

"You're adopted."

"But where?"

"I couldn't have a child and so when the lady who had you died I took you."

"I was in another lady's stomach?"

"Yes, I told you."

"Where is my father?"

"He died too, a long time ago."

"Where?"

"I told you. He died in an accident."

"But where is he now?"

"He was buried far away."

"With her?"

"Yes, they are buried far away."

"Can I go there someday?"

Nancy doesn't answer. She twirls him around by his shoulders so he faces the mirror and he can feel the anger in her hands. But he doesn't care. He holds his body stiffly inside the jacket and sets his jaw.

"I am your mother. I love you and I take care of you," Nancy says into his ear as she kneels behind him and looks over his shoulder toward the mirror. Their faces are together. His is long, the nose thin and the hair high on the forehead. Hers is round and heavy already with fat under the chin. Her hair is parted high in the middle and is graying a little.

"Who do I look like?" he asks.

"You look like yourself?"

"Did he look like myself?"

"He's dead and belongs to the earth like she does. I am your mother. I love you and care for you and I gave you my own milk when I lost my baby. People who are alive are together."

But, looking into the mirror, Charlie knows that there is someone else looking through his own eyes at him and that person is not himself. Seeing that frightens him. He wants to know, but it frightens him and the eye does too.

"Do I get a hamburger after church?" he asks.

"We aren't going to church. It's a picnic. I've got a salad and some cups to take along."

"I don't want to go there."

"You what?"

"I don't want to."

"You get into the car and stop talking silly. You'll have a good time."

"No, I won't. I don't like them at the church."

"Stop that, now. It's Mr. Porter's church and they've been nice to us. And Mr. Porter has been nice."

He sits in the car watching the white steeple ride up into the windshield out of the soft green spring grass and the iron fence his mother will never let him play on. The steeple presses on his head and he doesn't like it. He feels—remembers in his buttocks the hard oak of the benches inside and he doesn't like it. That is why he sometimes sits on his jacket, even though his mother doesn't want him to. The church people are tall and gray and their noses are sometimes sharp as steeples. They never touch him with their hands, except Tina's father, the minister. Their hands look blue and cold when they hold the books and their faces are blue too in the winter.

He sees the people passing—old slow-moving people with funny smiles winking on their faces when they see him through the window. A blonde boy swings between his mother's hand and his father's, squealing as he kicks his new tennis shoes and twists about.

"I don't want to," he says again, sitting there holding the glass bowl full of macaroni salad.

She doesn't answer him. She takes the bowl away and sets it on the hood of the car. "I'm sweating already. You get going now. You go play now," she says leaning through the open car door.

As he looks at her dress and frowns, she jerks him out of the front seat and he is on his feet by the car. He doesn't look around. He feels like a bird that has landed in a dangerous place—a blackbird among crows or hawks.

But a voice is very soft and friendly. A large, pink full face with bright blue eyes and a yellow flag of hair bends to him. It's the minister and Tina, his daughter, is with him. Tina's mother isn't with them. Sometimes Charlie sees her frowning at him when he touches himself there. He doesn't know why he touches himself there in his crotch sometimes.

Tina is pretty. Tina is very pretty. She has golden hair like the flying girls in the pictures in the vacation Bible school room. Tina is soft and wiggly and good to touch all over. Her father smiles above them and Nancy smiles too, standing there with the great bowl of macaroni salad.

"Come along," Tina says. "We're going for a walk."

They walk away from the card tables and cars and people through the stone place where the people lie dead underneath.

"Can you see what they look like down there?" he asks,

standing on a little sunken place and turning to Tina.

"Oh, it's all ishy, I think." Tina is sitting on a stone. Her knees are pink and chubby.

"My father is down there," Charlie says, after a long silence between them.

She jumps off the stone. And then she laughs. "Oh, you mean down someplace, don't you?"

"Sure," he says. "But I don't know where."

She takes his hand and they are walking away. There is a breath of flowers from her someplace—someplace. The sun is kind and blesses them. The purple lilac hedge bends over as they walk toward it over the green grass.

"It's dark and nice in there," she says. "We can go in there if you want."

"I have my good shoes on," he says. His heart is beating fast and things are strange and tight inside his head.

"Oh, there's a rug in there. It's my secret room."

Tina in the lilac hedge behind the church. The tickly hedge in the soft shadow, the clusters of lilacs purple and sweet above them, a bee whispering somewhere.

"How do you go to the bathroom?" he asks suddenly.

"I'll show you," she says. And she does, squatting.

"You have a winky thing like the top of a rubber piggy bank," he says, squatting beside her, looking.

"You do it," she squeals softly.

But there's a scream from the sky above and the huge faces of Tina's mother and father loom there suddenly. The mother's eyes blaze darkly at them and then Tina is yanked out by one arm, is pulled through her own screaming, her mouth rubbery pink and screaming too. The mother's hands flush and whip on Tina's seat and then the two of them—Tina and Charlie—are pushed out behind the hedge where people can't see all of them.

"He made me! He made me!" Tina screams. She stands behind her mother and sobs, her eyes raised big and wide toward her father and mother.

Tina's father kneels down. His face is softer and the eyes seem to ask a question, but Tina's mother thrusts him aside and puts her face down next to Charlie's. Her mouth is full of big, big teeth and her eyes are blue cold. She shakes his shoulders and a sharp pain breaks into his chest.

"You, you filthy little person!" the mouth says at him.

The father hand tries to touch Charlie through the shaking and the hard words, but Charlie is up and running through the stones and the people and out through the gate. Once he pauses to look back. The steeple rises over the cars and people like a sharp stick. He runs all the way home.

Soon—very soon—his mother comes into the house crying. She rushes at him, pushes him down on the rug. He fights and squirms and wails, "No, Mother, no!" His pants are pulled down and his arm pushed up so far a hot red flash blinks through his eyes. The blows slap, slap his buttocks until he screams for mercy and then begins a long, low wailing.

His mother is wailing too as she pulls him up and sets him on a chair. She kneels between his knees and holds his face in her hands. "You can't do things like that," she cries. "You can't do things like that so they can say things like that. You can't, do you hear me? That is Mr. Porter's church and he is my boss and he has been good to me and that is the minister's daughter and now we can't go back there again."

"But I didn't *do* anything!" he protests. "It was her place and I only watched. She wanted to too."

"But we were the only Indian family in that church and that is the minister's daughter."

"But why do we go there? Why aren't we someplace we aren't the only ones?"

"Because I want something better for you!" She is holding his face up so he would have to look at her. He doesn't know what she means but she looks so sad that he can't say anything. What is *better*? What does that mean? She seems to see the questions in his eyes, though and she keeps talking to him. "I have a dream for you to go to school and to be somebody who is strong and can help people like Mr. Porter does."

"But he's not very big."

She brushes his hair back with her hand. That soothes him. "I don't want you to live in a shack like these others and drink and not have anything."

"But I'm not nice she said."

"An Indian can be a lawyer and anything he wants to be."

"But what is a lawyer?"

"You'll see."

"It wasn't fair at the church."

"So that's why you have to study and work and be someone."

"I don't understand."

"You will. Please believe me."

He is tired of such talk. "Can I go now?" he asks.

"Where are you going?"

"By the station I think." He knows he is going to the river and needs to go.

"Be back by six."

"But the sun goes down later," he says, averting her eyes.

"Be back by six. You take this watch and look at it to make sure. And stay away from the river."

It's a silver pocket watch with black hands and strange numbers but he can tell time on it. "When the hands are here," he says. "Yes," she says, kissing him on top of his head.

Charlie stands barefoot on the sand spur hooking into the current of the big river. He feels happy and sad. The warm wind ripples the sheet of the water. But it isn't completely quiet there. Up river from him the generators whine and howl under the big Oahe Dam. He can see the great mound of the Oahe up around a curve in the river. Buffalo grass grows on it, but it is like grass on a grave, he thinks. Where is my father's grave? he asks himself.

But under the distant howl of the turbines the river has a quiet, patient voice. Inside his head the questions flow too. Who is the sun? Where is the night? Where have I come from and where am I going? Where is the river born? From the sky? Out of the earth? Can I find the place it is born? Is it still being born? Am I? The questions are deep in the shadows of his mind.

Is this place connected with all places? he asks himself. The children in the books at school have very stiff arms and legs and words. They live in another place you go to through the books. Each page in the books has words with the pictures, but the words are not things or pictures. The people's names don't touch anything or tell where they are—except Dick maybe and that's dirty, they say. Good Thunder is a name. "Why don't the people in the book have names that touch the trees or sky and things where they live?" Charlie asks the teacher one day. "They aren't Indian people," the teacher says. "I don't understand," he says. But when the teacher tries to explain, her words run so fast they are like mice when you turn on a light and they run away.

He is standing in it then—has waded into it. The clay pothole is sweet-sour as cow dung and he can hardly stand the smell of it. He washes his feet in the shallow water a few feet away pushing them deeply into the sand. He feels a hardness under his left foot—a long rib of hardness. He digs then with both hands and finds it—an antelope horn immaculate and rare. Why is a dead thing so beautiful and alive? he asks himself. Nothing answers. He goes home early and puts the horn under his bed with the books his mother has bought for him. And he tries to make it one of his secrets.

But the river. It flows and Charlie's mother loves him day and night. She doesn't let him do a lot of things—especially the Indian dances—but her love flows into him through her hands and the low music of her voice and the soft shadows behind her eyes—especially at night when the moon is on the porch and she makes him sit with her. Even when Charlie hurts her she is soft. Once he says to her (When there is no one to play with), "When do I get a brother?" She touches his face and smiles and says, "Something went wrong inside me, so I can't. That's why I wanted you so much." "I'm sorry," Charlie says. He very seldom tells anyone he is sorry.

She is a gentle, strong current in his life. She floats him toward books and places she thinks are good. She gives him questions and lets his answers swirl in the eddies of his own mind until a good one rises to the surface. She expects a lot from him and that is hard because she sometimes says she doesn't know what to expect from herself. "You're going to be awful busy finding out what to do about yourself," she says to him when he tells her one day about the antelope horn and the far-away people in the books at school.

And so the river flows. And Nancy's mother love flows through her fingers and eyes and words. Her heart, her words follow Charlie too—her words in a stenographer's notebook:

Dear Diary,

So like Mr. Porter, says, I'm a loner. I'm not with my people here or the others at his church either and now I'm too embarrassed to go back there either.

Charlie knows hate now. The minister's wife screamed at the children's play. It was like the garden in the Bible. She doesn't know that, I bet.

Charlie, I love you. But your face is different a little they say. I want you to read because to read is power. But will you go away on the words? My Charlie. There is nothing much here anymore except wind and dust. The old ways seem gone now and the people's voices are sad echoes.

Charlie, I write this, but it would embarrass you to see it. This man Mag comes to leave things and to talk to me but I can't tell you who he is. Soon maybe he will say maybe. I can't take a man now. I can't say why. It is going to be hard for me but I will do it someday but not now.

Do you think you have another mother? Are you going to look for her someday? It worries me. Even now I am lonely. I talk to my little book because my heart has a lonely voice.

4

Pictures, Books and Bicycles

He is drenched and chilled from running home through the lashing of April rain but he doesn't go into the house. "Shit!" he mutters. "Shit!" In his frustration he stamps a wet tennis shoe into the mud by the mailbox and laughs in devilish glee as the mud juice spatters both legs of his corduroy pants. He does it again, thinking She can wash them. She can wash them.

The black rain clouds scud low and fast over the river and the lightning zag-flashes down to the buttes along the rims of the high prairie. And Charlie feels infinitely lonely again. The rain whips at his face. "*Good* thunder!" he yells, and his voice breaks and his lank bones chill under the whip of it.

But he doesn't go in. He looks up the street toward the Mobil station where a couple of the other boys might be, but he can't see anything through the gray veils of rain dancing wildly over the cars and pavement. He can't go in because the pick-up truck is parked there behind the house—*behind* the house—on the ragged lawn where it can't be seen from the street. He dances a little splashing dance and aims his eyes at the house and hates them both. "Bitch! Fucking bitch!" he yells into the rain and then, feeling guilty sick inside, he aims his hate eyes at the pick-up, the machine-horse intruder.

Under the storm darkness the lights of the house are on—at least the ones in that room and in the kitchen. What does he have? What does he want? Charlie asks himself. Why is he so big? Why do I hate him? Why do my shoulders narrow and feel weak when I see him? he thinks deep in his head. The mailbox leans forward on a post in a cement tile filled with sand. He kicks the post and then screams with the pain in his foot. He limps around in a little hopping circle, howling and swearing.

When he sees the light in that room blink out, he hops down the driveway toward the kitchen door. He doesn't quite get to knock because the man is already pushing out through the door, pulling on the red and black mackinaw jacket, hunching his big shoulders forward as he does so. They almost collide, but Charlie sidesteps him, catching only the quick flash of the blue eyes in the big round face. The eyes are like blue glass through which something is trying to look or be seen. Charlie looks away as he stands there on the step. He wonders if the man will put his hand on his shoulder so he can shrug it away.

Nothing. Charlie stands in the rain, his eyes blearing with the slap of the water off the roof. He hears the pickup start and roar. And then roar loudly as the rear wheels dig in and cut ruts toward the driveway. Blue smoke floats through the rain toward him and bites his nose. When the pickup jounces up on the gravel driveway, the man gets out, pulls a long-handled shovel from the truck bed and tries to fill in the ruts. He works with short, powerful strokes. Charlie goes inside.

Nancy is standing by the kitchen table under the bulb that hangs over it. He looks at her to see what it is that men do to women and how a woman is changed by being with a man, but he can't see anything, except the little shadow in Nancy's eyes.

"Stay on the rug," she says as she turns and goes to get a towel from a rack by the kitchen sink.

"The track meet was cancelled," he calls after her. He sees that two buttons on the back of her blouse are not fastened. He steps off the rug, dripping.

"Oh, Charlie!" she cries when she comes back with the towel and sees the pools of mud on the floor.

"I'm cold. I got to get into a bath."

"Let me wipe you down a little so you won't drip."

But when she touches him he takes the towel from her roughly and begins pressing it over his face and clothes.

"I wish I had known that. Mr. Porter gave me the afternoon off."

"Did he have the afternoon off?" They can both hear the pickup roaring and grinding backwards down the driveway.

"He came to see if you wanted some work. He wants you to help him with his boats, fixing them up for the fishing season."

"Do I have to?"

"No. We'll talk about it later."

"He cut up the yard with his pickup," Charlie says. He can see the strain on Nancy's mouth, but he goes on as he wipes himself. "He has to park out behind so no one will see him."

"Oh, Charlie, I ask him to."

"Why?"

"It's personal."

"Is he married?"

"No?"

"Are you still married?"

"Oh, please, Charlie! I'm all alone and he's good to us . . ."

"Us what?" He throws the towel and then hates her when she retrieves it and kneels under him and wipes around him in a circle.

When he takes his shirt off he remembers the packet of school pictures they sent home with him and she sees them too.

"Can I see?"

"They're awful. I look like a gopher or something."

"I want a big one."

"You can't get big ones and they look awful."

She is holding the little proofs and wiping them tenderly with a pack of paper napkins. In the pictures, his face is long and his nose is long. His mouth is toothy and open in a silly grin. "They're awful," he says, but he likes the way she kisses them just the same. And yet he asks the cruel questions again. "And there's no pictures of them?" he asks, knowing that inside her the word "them" hurts. In the little silence after the question he can see that her bed is messed up, the blue quilt twisted over one edge and the pillows shoved together.

"Only what you want to draw in your heart," she says, as she has before. When she hands him back the pictures she touches his arm and his hardness softens a little. And yet he sees the bed and the pillows and he hates.

"Maybe I don't need a picture!" he says back over his shoulder when he goes into the bathroom to bathe and perhaps do it as he does before she comes home. In the quiet moments between splashings he can hear her making supper. And he knows, too, that when he comes out again her bed will be made.

Charlie tries to make pictures in his heart or his mind's eye in the days that follow, but nothing quite comes into focus because it is like making up a picture puzzle from broken sets and without a picture from the cover of the box.

One day after school he goes to Buckanaga's Photography Studio where they have some very old photographs leaning backward in the front window. Most of the faces there are too hard and leathery. But not that one—the girl, tall and willowy, her hips swayed to one side in a long, straight black dress without ornament. She is smiling and her right hand rests on the edge of a table on which somebody has put a little vase of flowers and a parasol. Behind her is a piano and behind that a sky that looks as if somebody has rolled it down like a curtain. The photo is black and white, but there is a brown-gold varnish over it. Her eyes are very dark and they look at him with a soft brown radiance that makes him believe that she knows him and that the eyes are alive. She gives him a calmness deep inside and he wishes that she were all alive, except that Nancy would be really hurt then.

He buys the photo. It's a hard thing for a 16-year-old boy to do in a place where everybody knows everybody, but he pushes through the door and says he wants it, standing there by the cash register wadding the three dollar bills in his pocket.

"Say, what you want with an old picture of nobody—maybe not even a nice Indian lady? That is a lady nobody remembers anymore or maybe wanted to forget. It's old. I just forget it there," Mr. Buckanaga says.

"How old?" Charlie asks.

"Maybe 70 years."

"The lady, I mean," Charlie says, his heart beating loudly in his ears now.

"Who knows. Twenty maybe. In a photo nobody gets older, only the photo."

"You going to throw it away sometime? I need it for a project in history." Charlie asks. He has a dollar wadded up into his right hand inside his pocket. Mr. Buckanaga stares at him and wipes his hands off on the sides of his pants. Then he reaches over the little stained brown curtain and takes it out, shaking his head. He looks at it then and hands it to Charlie. It's thick and very stiff. Charlie pushes the dollar into his hand.

"Say, how old are you anyway?" Mr. Buckanaga asks.

"Fourteen." Charlie is trembling and can't look up. He doesn't say anything but starts to walk out, the photo held in both his hands. His heart beats loudly in his ears. He feels like a fool.

"It's nobody anybody remembers!" Mr. Buckanaga calls after him.

There's no one home when Charlie comes into the house after buying the photo. He doesn't like the flowers or the drop-curtain sky in the photo so he cuts them off with a knife and then he is sorry because in cutting the thick varnish paper he makes a mess of it. But the tall woman with the soulful eyes is still there. He hides the picture behind some of the exposed insulation in the unfinished wall of his bedroom. He can reach over and get it out and look at it whenever he wants. After awhile he begins to believe in it because it almost gives him peace.

School. He and the other boys bend their heads down at school. They are surly and resentful and don't really know why. They only know there is a stiffness inside them that gets stiffer and then is a dead thing inside them. The teachers too. They begin the year smiling and asking questions, but nobody ever really reads the assignments—except a few girls maybe. So the teachers begin to scowl in October and by December most are grim when they stand out in the halls and walk into class. "You got a brain. You going to let it die inside you?" Mr. Hanson, the biology teacher asks Blue Elk or one of the others and maybe they say, "I'm thinking about something good" or they might say, "I'm going to live on my looks," and Mr. Hanson shakes his head sadly and calls on one of the girls to fill in the silence with her quiet, nervous voice. That is something at least.

No one is sure where the white teachers have come from or what they have ever done. They are like emissaries from a foreign country reading out of books from a foreign country nobody in the school ever really thought much about visiting except on T.V. if they have it. When the teachers see that even when they find something special for a student to do—like tracing the origin of a name or reading a book, Steinbeck's *The Red Pony* maybe, there is a smile maybe and a shrug of the shoulders and the book stays closed and the geography maps are never filled in. Whatever happens in class ends at the bell unless somebody talks about basketball or football. "You got to sit still until you're 16," Blue Elk says to Charlie once. "Then you can get your ass out of these boxes they put us in."

Charlie tries sometimes. He underlines dozens of subjects once and verbs twice. He looks up words and finds that guppies are named after J. Lechmere Guppie, an Englishman who found them in Trinidad or someplace. To Charlie, most places are paper dots and he wonders if someone made them up. In shop he learns to adjust a jack plane so it won't hack a piece of white pine he paid two dollars for, but then he finds that somebody had gouged it with a knife anway. When the shop instructor, "Crane" Lewis, sees Dick Bissonette deliberately break off a wood vice handle he throws the entire vice across the shop into the wall. Then he goes out into the hall and bawls, slapping the wall with his big, limp hand.

Charlie's American history teacher, Mr. Hale, keeps after him relentlessly. He usually catches Charlie in the hall after school and lays a question on him. "Did you know that great speaking, great oratory, is a big thing in Native American history? The power and the prestige of the chiefs depended on how well they could stand up and tell it right."

"No," Charlie says, "I got to get to baseball practice."

Sometimes Mr. Hale grabs him and pushes a book at him. "Look," he says, "Here is something to look through. You take a look at 'The Surrender Speech of Chief Joseph.'"

"Do I have to?" Charlie asks, but wondering who Chief Joseph was and why he surrendered and what Nez Perce meant. And wondering, too, if the others see him doing it and if he's a coward and not one of them.

"No, but it might help you see that you've got a history too." Mr. Hale is saying. "The book we use in class leaves a lot of people out, don't you see?"

"We should read about Indians surrendering?" It is Dick Bissonettes's voice over Charlie's shoulder.

"I don't know," Hale answers. "Shouldn't he have?"

"If he's dead, can we forget it?" Dick says. That makes Hale angry and he turns to Dick then. "Forget it? You know what amnesia is?"

"I think I seen a guy in a movie have it. Couldn't remember who he was." Dick smirks then. He sees a lot of movies.

"That's it," Hale said. "Unless you've got some idea of your own history and have it up here you've got a kind of amnesia and you can never be sure who you are or where you're coming from."

"I've got to get to practice," Charlie intrudes, trying to head off a quarrel. He keeps the book but he begins to walk away.

"I'm Dick Bissonette," Dick says.

"No you're not. Hell, that's French and you're not French!" Hale's face is sad and earnest, not angry.

"Fuck it!" Dick says as they walk away. Dick socks Charlie on the shoulder. "You got your little book I see. You're going to smother to death one of these days with your big nose up Hale's ass. He's going to cut a corner and you're going to smother to death." When Charlie socks Dick back, the book falls on the floor in the hall. "Leave it!" Dick says.

Still, it bothers Charlie. One night he asks Nancy about Mr. Hale and being a teacher and amnesia while she is doing some bookkeeping on big ledger sheets on the kitchen table. She smiles tiredly at him through her glasses.

"You have a big job," she says. "You have twice as big a job as anybody else, because when you find out what it means to be Oglala Sioux you're only half done. You have to find a new way of life too."

"I'm not trying to find out anything. I don't know what you mean," he says because he is surprised to hear her say that and thinking about all of it makes him tired.

"I don't mean just reading," she says. "I mean that if you go deeply enough into your own soul you will know that the sun is new today and it's a time for change. The old ways are dead."

"I don't know what you mean," he says to her. He wonders why she is so smart and what she knows and how she came to know it. Is it working in the lawyer's office in Pierre? She keeps a good job all the time while the men—the fathers—lose one job after another. Then Charlie begins to worry about all the terrible things there are to know. He also begins to worry about Mr. Hale's history class the next morning because Mr. Hale will have the book with Chief Joseph's speech in it and he will expect Charlie to read it. He thinks about skipping school, but he knows that if he does that he can't go to the baseball game.

"Here you are, Charlie," Hale says the next morning after taking roll. He hands Charlie the book. Charlie begs for time because he is getting a hard on looking at Sue LaFarge's legs again and doesn't want to stand up. Minutes pass. "Charlie?" Hale isn't giving up.

Charlie stands up leaning forward clumsily. He makes no introduction. He reads the title and he stumbles on Nez Perce and then he begins to read without looking up from the pages:

"I am tired of fighting. Our chiefs are killed. Looking Glass is dead. Toolhulhulsote is dead. (Charlie *murders* the vowels in that name, hooting them softly.) The old men are dead . . ."

When he finishes, he looks up and sees the faces of the other students—confused, resentful, stiff-comical. Dick Bissonette is feigning tears and doing back-and-forth rapid scan-the-horizon movements with his head, his right hand cocked over his eyes as if he is saluting. Soft booing. "Nez Perce! Not Sioux!" someone grumbles. Charlie sits down heavily, eyes on the book and then down at his swollen crotch. "You make us read bad stuff," another voice complains. The girl who sits next to him smiles lovingly down at him.

"Thank you, Charlie," Mr. Hale says. "Now we need to ask some questions about all this—how Chief Joseph came to that decision. The date. How all of this affects us or if it does at all. Why we should be upset by this speech."

Nobody says anything. Mr. Hale hands out a sheet of questions. Charlie knows they will have to be answered slowly and carefully by Mr. Hale himself from some mysterious sources of knowledge he has. Nobody will read anything. Mr. Hale explains why they are going to do it, but nobody seems to trust him.

"We don't study no surrender," Blue Elk says. "We are gonna

win at baseball." Cheers. Mr. Hale's face flushes. The girl next to Charlie smiles lovingly at him, glancing down at his crotch. Dick Bissonette glares across two aisles at Charlie. "Quiet!" Mr. Hale yells and some of them put their heads down again on the desk and wait for the bell. Mr. Hale hands out some study questions on Chief Joseph. He has to slide some of them under the hands and faces of students like Blue Elk and Dick Bissonette. Bissonette grabs his sheet angrily and holds it upside down. Then he waves it at Hale's back moving it back and forth like a flag of truce.

The bell rings and they all burst out past Charlie. When Charlie looks back, he can seen Mr. Hale standing by a map of South Dakota. Hale sags against his desk, his eyes full of quiet despair.

As he walks out through the heavy doors at the front of the high school—walks out alone—Charlie knows he is going to have to fight Dick Bissonette. He knows it because the others have walked away from him to avoid having to take sides. And he knows it because there in the middle of the road that rises up toward where he lives, Dick is standing spread-legged and waiting for him.

Charlie knows that he can't walk around Dick. For one thing, there are several younger boys strung out around him and they'll tease mercilessly. For another, he hates Dick and wants to get it over with even though Dick is so coordinated and always has been. Charlie has never had any trouble with the tall ones; it's the quick ones like Dick Bissonette. And Dick boxes with the boxing team from Wahpeton.

As he walks slowly toward Dick, he can hear the jeering echoes of his reading of Chief Joseph's speech back at the high school. The voices are like the calls of magpies and crows. "I am tired of fighting! I am tired of fighting!" they jeer—some of them at least.

Once in the eighth grade a few of the others chased Charlie home from school because he read "The Charge of the Light Brigade" in school and was given a Voit basketball for a prize by Miss Jensen. While he was reading, they all pretended to gallop in their chairs and after school they galloped after him and chased him up a tree. It was terrible. But at least Dick wasn't with them then.

He doesn't say anything. He simply walks up to Dick and fires a looping right hand into the place where the sneer is. He misses and takes a jolting left hook on the jaw. And then the jabs, quick numbing blows to his face until all the bones feel hot and soft and swelling. "Oof!" Charlie grunts when the hooks catch him in the stomach too.

And the words between the murderous bob-and-weave assaults. "Mr. Hale teach you that? Let Old Mag teach you this! (Oof!) You gonna go home and tell you fa-ther?"

But through the words Charlie's left catches Dick on the nose and the blood spurts and the words growl and howl through the rain of blows, the frenzy of blows like a wheel of fists.

"You bastard Good Thunder. Your old lady dead. Your old man down at Rosebud."

Charlie lunges through the whipping circle of the fists and shoulders Dick hard, knocking him to the ground. He grabs Dick's legs and pulls the writhing ankles up under his arms. He menaces Dick's crotch with his foot. "You want me to, you lying bastard? You want me to, you lying bastard?" he hears himself yelling.

But Charlie can't do it and the words rage again and again. He knows he can't hold Dick much longer. It's like catching a fish that's too big. His arms are getting tired and the words have hurt too.

And, finally, when Charlie can't hold any longer, Dick is loose and up again, hammering and hooking, until Charlie goes down numbly and sits there holding his bleeding face in his hands and trying to keep the words from his ears with his hands as Dick squats down to chant into his hearing.

"Your real mother is dead, Big Man. Your one father is down at Rosebud I heard. *You* hear? His name is Eddy White Cloud. He just blew away I heard. You hear? Everybody knows it and everybody knows about the man who comes to your old lady's house which ain't hers either because White Cloud bought it. You hear? You stuck-up shit in school, you hear? You think you smarter than us dumb Indians? You don't even know who it is in your own house, big smart ass!"

The words hammer on Charlie and numb him. He is rested a little and he thinks he might beat Dick if he gets up, but the words hammer him and weaken him.

"You go fishin," Dick calls back as he and the younger boys walk away toward the station where they hang around until the manager kicks them out. He looks at Dick. His ears are ringing from everything. "You go fishin and ask big face, big man!" Dick yells.

Charlie feels a hand on his shoulder. It's Billy Whitefeather. "You tell him to fuck himself," Billy says softly—very softly.

Charlie pushes him away and walks toward the back of the school where the baseball players won't be able to see him. "I am gonna get out of here," he says to himself. "I'm gonna go far away!"

He hurries. The sun is warm on his face and the wind cools his soreness and sweatiness.

The bike isn't locked. It belongs to Kim Pettigrew. He knows it's wrong to take it. He knows she loves it. But he takes it anyway. A couple of boys yell after him as he rides away, but they don't know how far he's going or how crazy he is.

At home he finds the money very quickly because he knows where she keeps it in the drawer under some napkins. He counts out 80 dollars and jams the bills into his pocket. The blanket too—he pulls it off his bed, sliding it out from under the bedspread. Stops. Listens. He sweats again with anxiety. Outside, the bike leans against the back of the house. He swings over on it and pedals over the ruts in the back yard toward the highway.

On the blacktop highway the bike rolls along nicely. The air cools his face and the river rolls southward with him on his left. A few fleecy clouds hang in the western sky. The bike rolls nicely and as he gets farther from town he relaxes and pedals strongly and smoothly toward Rosebud. He has no idea how far it is . . .

5

Rosebud

This time the pickup truck is parked on the front driveway of Nancy's house, its motor idling as she leans in toward Magnuson's face and talks quietly but earnestly. In the dim yellow dashlight Mag's face is taut and worried about many things. He taps the steering wheel and looks around and then over to his right into the rear view mirror.

"I don't care if it is dangerous," Nancy is saying as she too lets her eyes glance quickly up and down the street.

"Damn dangerous, I said."

"You want him arrested?"

"What the devil did he do it for?"

"I don't know, but I can guess. Do you want to guess?"

"No, I don't want to guess. It was some wild tail maybe. He's sixteen and you said he's playin' man games." He doesn't look at her, saying it.

"Is that all? Is that all there is?"

"I'm not sayin' that, but it doesn't make any sense and that means a woman usually."

"It's not a girl. I know it's not. It's something else, bad maybe. They saw him going south."

"Big grassland out there. It's spring. They go out there."

"No, he's out looking for something and I'm worried and he took my money."

"You want to go with me and look? We can drive south."

"We have to pay for the bike first or the Pettigrews will call the sheriff. Pettigrew is not a tribe man. He works for the post office."

"You mean I got to pay, don't you?" Mag is already fumbling for the money. "How much?" he asks, looking at her finally, seeing the big tired eyes.

"Thirty dollars. I haven't got it now."

"Some goddamn bike. What has it got on it anyway?"

"It's got a boy on it now and he's riding it down south toward the White River and Rosebud. He could get hit too."

"He's supposed to come out and help paint boats and now I got to lose a night's sleep too chasin' him."

"You wouldn't have to," she says abruptly and yet gently. "He wouldn't be going there if he hadn't found out something."

"He's a wild one."

"No he's really not. He's like you. He can't make up his mind either. Something is driving him."

"Well, you give those expensive folks their money but tell 'em I ain't buying him a bike. If it comes back all right I want twenty of that back at least.'

"Are you going? I'm worried."

"I'll see. I told you I can't run around all night after a wild kid."

"You afraid you'll find yourself?"

Mag is backing the truck away slowly and Nancy backs away. "I want to know what's happened and don't come back if you don't go out there!" she cries. He keeps backing and waves her away, but as she stands there shivering in the cooling night air she can see the pickup bounce across a little field of grass and then climb up on the highway running south.

Charlie pedals the bike along the edge of the asphalt road and sometimes, as he goes, he cries little bleats of sorrow and tiredness. When the trucks go by with a flash of light and a great whoof of air the bike staggers a little and then the darkness swallows him again.

The road is black shiny ahead of him. He swings and follows the white band in the center of it while no cars are coming.

Ahead of him the road is a long triangle converging vaguely
somewhere ahead at a closed place and he feels a tightness in his
chest seeing it. The road makes the pedaling easy and yet it's a
hard thing, a thing that gives no peace or rest. It's like a long
black whip laid down and it drives him. Clotted broken husks of
rabbits mat on its surface here and there and once, down over a
little hill, he sees the scudded flat carcass of a deer pounded into
a stain the rain will wash away.

The grass. It waves in soft ripplings and whisperings under the
night wind. The old grass is still there too, brown and stiffer and
wind rasped. The new grass breathes its moist earth breath in
long, long cool earth ribs. The spaces of grass around him are infinite and comforting and at the last reaches of it the little stars
glow softly in the grass and in the sky too. The high stars are
bright and sharp as silver bird cries. Each pond is a sky with
stars. Bitterns and herons stand in water and stars, priesting
them. Distances are near.

Charlie cries out a little mad cry, exordium. Nothing cries
back. Hunger is a steel spoon in his belly. He kicks off the bicycle and pushes it down the highway embankment toward the
grass. Eats a candy bar. Folds the wrapper and buries it. His
knees feel weak but he walks slowly and unsteadily into the sky
of grass. He feels taller then and he pushes farther and farther
until he has no awareness of the road and the trucks are far
away.

There is a place in the grass that is warm as if something had
been there. The musk trace rises into his nose and he takes it,
breathing it in deeply like invisible smoke. There are a few
small red cottonwoods in a little draw nearby. They bend toward
the earth, wind humble and crowned with small birds roosting
for the night.

He realizes then that he has left the bicycle behind him
someplace and that he has only the blanket. He tries to retrace
his steps, but it's no use. The grass bends over everything.

He's too tired to cry about it. Tomorrow, he says down in his
lazy heart—tomorrow because he doesn't care either and he
wants the night and loves the grass and wants to nest in it like a
mouse or a bird.

The musk smell is still strong but he lies down. The whole wide reach of stars is around him. Is he dizzy? They seem to turn around him in a great wide circle. The hard things—the square and triangular things of the road—the tar mat and the yellow signs and the great roaring boxes of the trucks—recede. The nest is round. A rush of quick birds titters and whirs over his head from a small cottonwood at his neck. They come back and their eyes are shiny and they aren't afraid. The stars blur in his eyes and are soft blossoms in the fields of sky.

The musk smell enters his head and hooves pound softly far off. He throws the blanket off and listens.

From the west, thunder, muffled and quick as hooves. A tall neck of clouds riding on a wind with lightning blazing.

He watches, doing nothing and feeling that there is nothing to do. He lies on his back, his belly up and his arms spread palms up. Licks his mouth trying to find moisture from within himself.

The cloud rides out of the west, blazing lightning from its head and rains a soft green rain, scant, but bright as it falls under the stars. The hooves of thunder are gentle as the touch of birds voices and tongues of leaves and the little rain blesses him. And then because he feels tall and strong, he stands up and begins to run after the little head of clouds with its black back and shoulders and its veiled hooves in the grass, running like a man who would catch and mount a horse. He runs crazy, runs losing shoes and the blanket. Then he falls to his knees and, kneeling there, watches the clouds ride away on the grass toward Rosebud.

He has run toward the highway and he can hear the rumblings of trucks again. And something else closer and more insistent and hard and sharp—a horn, a horn that blares the stars into stiff cold ranges of icy stars—the horn of a pickup truck.

He can see it—the two headlight beams leaning off the shoulder of the road into the grass soft dark and dimming as the horn is pressed—and he knows who it is. He thinks about running back, but he can't. The road is plain and open to him and the man has eyes even though he never really says anything. And what can he do? The bike is lost for sure.

He walks toward the road, limping on the shoeless foot. The

rain wet grass recedes away from the swell and thrust of the shoulder of road and the road is hard under his feet. He shivers and waits.

The lights of the pickup catch him and then the horn honks again. He waits, shivering. There's no warmth in the light.

Or in the voice either, a voice heavy and muscular.

"Where's that damn bike?" it asks first.

"I lost it," he says without turning to look at Mag, who has pushed open the passenger side door of the pickup.

"Well, for God's sake, how the hell did you lose it?"

"I lost it walking in the grass."

"Walking in the grass. Walking in the grass. What the hell is the matter with you?"

"Nothing." He shrugs it as he says it and wishes he had his other shoe because he knows he'll have to answer for that too.

"Well, get in here so I can get you back, damn it."

"I'm not going back. I got to get to Rosebud."

"What the hell for? I paid for the bike. What kind of trouble is it anyway?"

A truck roars by, its exhaust chortling from the deep iron belly of its diesel engine and its lights flashing once in passing.

"It's no trouble." He can feel the door against him as Mag lets the pickup idle slowly into him. He shrugs his shoulders against it but he can feel the warmth from the heater inside and that chills him.

"You better get in. Your mother's worried sick."

"Is my father worried sick?"

The engine idles. Stops. Mag is out and around the front of the pickup. Charlie still doesn't look at him but he looks closely at Charlie's face. Charlie can see his pointed western boots but he really doesn't want to see the rest of him.

"So, who worked over your face? Let me guess. It was one of the tribe at school. And you made him mad and he said something."

The night breathes, waiting.

"He said Eddy White Cloud is Nancy's husband and Nancy took his house and sent him off to Rosebud," Charlie says.

"Bullshit!"

"He said everybody knew it and he said some other things too."

"I'll bet!"

Charlie can feel the hardness of this man through the dark. It's like he is punching him and there's no reaction, no pain, no nothing. "He said I should go fishing with you too."

"Oh, you will, if you think you won't lose the boat and the anchor and your ass. Now what? You coming home? The bike is paid for and your mother is worried and I've got a lot of work to do."

He starts to take Charlie's arm but Charlie shakes it off. "Son-of-a-bitch!" he exclaims.

"What? You callin' me a son-of-a-bitch?" A hard fist at Charlie's shoulder, a challenge. The question comes again. "My mother cooked in a cafe over in Winner and my father never came back from World War I. Now are you callin' her a bitch?" Another jolt to the shoulder. He staggers a little step to the left and thinks about hitting but he doesn't.

"No," he says, finally.

"Well, get your ass in the pickup. I'll put a kerchief on that sign over there so you can look for that bike when you come out again."

"I'm not going."

"Fine, you want to see Eddy White Cloud? Well, I'll tell you what. Mr. White Cloud is now a resident of Minneapolis, so I'll tell you what. Your mother may kill me, but maybe you should go there and see for yourself. And maybe you should see for yourself how good your mother has done and how she's tryin' to make something for you. I don't agree with a lot of things she's doing, but she's tryin'."

"Maybe," Charlie says.

"You come along and I'll drive you up to Minneapolis. I got relatives all over Minneapolis and I heard Mr. White Cloud lives right near downtown and hangs out there all the time."

"How far is it?" Charlie asks, getting in finally.

"Well, it's about 450 miles so we should start early," Mag says, but he hasn't started the truck yet. "Thing is," he continues, ". . . your mother won't like it, but you won't clear your mind, I can see, until it's done, but it's goin' to cost me. I can tell already."

Mag starts the pickup, turns it around and heads back to Ft. Pierre. Mag has fallen back into his thick man silence. He drives steadily and looks out at the road rumbling under the wheels. Charlie knows he's being taken home and yet he feels as if he's being taken away from something.

"What was it you were lookin' for out there?" Mag asks as the truck rattles into town.

"Nothing I guess."

"Bullshit!" Mag says. "And you saw something too. You had a wild hair look standing in the light."

They stop before going to the house. Mag stops to get a six-pack of beer. But he comes back to the truck without it after spinning around on his heels a few feet from the truck.

"What's the matter?" Charlie asks. He can see the Rex's Bar neon sign above over the building has been turned off. Its letters are twisted and white cold as ice. "Closed!" Mag says.

At the house Nancy stands in the doorway. When she sees Charlie, she comes toward the pickup and takes his arm when he dismounts. He limps with her. "Charlie! Charlie! What happened to you?"

"I'm going to Minneapolis!" he says.

She sags against him. "What? What?"

"I'm going to Minneapolis to see Eddy White Cloud. Mag's going to take me."

She whirls away from him. He has seldom seen Nancy so close to anger. She groans her words at Mag, her hands raised like claws around her head as if she might clasp it to keep it from bursting. "Are you crazy?" she groans. "Are you crazy to do that?" She runs toward him and he waits for her to let her scream it all out.

When she has stopped and stands there whimpering softly and desperately, Mag says, "Well, there's no keeping him from it. He'll run away again like today. At least I can keep an eye on him."

She turns toward him with her last burst of force. "Oh, dear

God, Charlie; why do you have to do all this? Why can't we be together here and be happy?"

"You said he was dead!" Charlie says.

"Oh, he's gone away so far and in so many ways he's dead. You'll see. He couldn't come back from the war. He never could leave the war. He couldn't just work and be at peace. He had to be in a battle somewhere and drinking. I couldn't keep him here."

"I don't know if I can believe you much," he says.

"Well, you better believe that I'm your mother and I love you and take care of you."

"Maybe he'll see that if he goes," Mag says over her shoulders. "The rest he can see local."

"Don't come back here after you come back," Nancy says. "Don't try to ever come back in the house."

"I said it would cost me," Mag says. "But I'll be here at seven!" he yells over the noise as he backs out.

"You go in and take a bath and go to bed," Nancy tells Charlie.

After he has gone in Nancy stands watching Mag's pickup jounce along the road leading northward to his boat docks and fishing camp. "Men! You men!" she cries after him. ". . . now when the hard baby raising part is over and you see you have another man like yourself you don't care; you just . . .!" She begins to cry again and the hollow place deep inside aches the old ache of barrenness again. Around her under the roads and houses and new spring grass the earth turns slowly in its sleep. It is full of new green roots and all of the fullness and beauty of it makes her sad.

6

The Tower and the Shadow

When Mag hammers on the kitchen door in the morning, Charlie struggles up out of sleep and kicks his legs out of bed. Nancy has gone to work, but he can see his clothes—tan jeans and a blue shirt with white buttons—hanging neatly pressed on the door of his bedroom. He hurries because he knows Mag won't come in and because his heart is tight with new excitement. When he pulls the jeans on he feels the paper in the front pocket and knows it's a note and some money.

It is:

Charlie,
Here's some of the money back so you can stay by yourself if you want. But don't stay long—I think if you go there you'll understand what I did and why. If you don't, you'll have to see how I love you some other way because I do. In your heart you know that.
Hurry back.
Mother.

He doesn't care just now. He hurries a comb through his hair and drinks a long gulp of milk from a carton in the refrigerator and pulls on a jacket. He hurries back to the bathroom and urinates, reaching for his toothpaste and a deodorant stick and a toothbrush, squirting on the floor as he reaches. But he doesn't care about the floor. He feels the call of distances in his heart and the magnet of a great new place pulling at his loins.

The two of them hardly talk on the long drive. Mag says, "Got to fill up now" or "Got to empty out now" and Charlie says, "Sure," even though he's not sure of anything. Charlie knows that Mag has a reputation as the best hunting and fishing guide on the river but he also knows that people who go with him complain a lot about his silence. "He don't say much. He just puts them blue eyes at the sky or down into the water and gets us birds or fish," he heard one old man from Sioux Falls say once while the old man waited for Mag at the boat dock.

Charlie sleeps a lot on the way. The jiggling of the pickup makes him get a hard on. When he wakes up he tries to cover it with his jacket but nothing can cover Mag's laughter. And still it's not a laugh that makes fun; it's a sharing laugh, a laugh at some shared old man secret. But Charlie keeps the jacket over himself just the same.

The land turns green and fills with trees in the river bottom land and the groves along the farm houses as they drive into Minnesota. The open vistas of the prairie close in and the plowed soil is black loam, rich and dense. He wonders what the girls are like and sometimes he wonders why he's going at all because he doesn't quite know what he wants to see.

"Another hundred miles," Mag announces just before the engine trouble. Then Mag curses the pickup slowly into Mankato. They find a Standard Oil station along the river that divides the big town. They've been lucky because the pickup has rolled, sputtering and steaming, nearly two miles down into the Minnesota River Valley.

It's nothing serious—a radiator hose squirting steaming piss-green coolant. The station operator is husky and affable with a great belly and bushy white eyebrows and an incredible ability to talk while he works.

"What's your name?" he asks Mag as he hunches over the hot engine.

"Magnuson."

"You from South Dakota?"

"Yah."

"Well, from what I saw west of the river you can give it back to the Indians."

"Maybe so."

Charlie has wandered into the room where the cash register is. He dives into a pocket for change, pulls a can of Coke out of a machine and gulps the cold liquid.

"Gonna find a beer!" Mag announces to Charlie. "Back in ten minutes!" he calls back as he walks out past the pumps.

The station attendant has to take payment for gas. After he closes the cash register, he smiles at Charlie. "Only be a little while," he says affably.

"Mr. Magnuson will be glad. We thought we might not make it into town," Charlie says.

"Mr. Magnuson. What's your name?"

"Charlie—Charlie Good Thunder. We're goin' to Minneapolis to see someone."

"You want to come out in the shop and watch me?" the man asks. Charlie can see a change in his face, but he doesn't know what it means. "Sure," he says.

But when Charlie goes after another coke and stands at the big plate glass window watching the cars cross over the river and the wind blowing the dresses of girls walking across on the ramped sidewalk, the man comes back again. Charlie looks at him. His face is strained and severe. "I got a policy that no one is in here by the register when I'm not." "Sure," Charlie says. "I'd like to walk a little anyway."

He walks north along the river behind the station. There isn't a tree for miles, only slopes of huge concrete ramps and dikes. But he walks along because the sun is warm and good on his back. He walks along wondering if the river is a dead river in a dead city because it stinks like a dead thing.

And sees the plaque—thick and formidable in some kind of tan stone. He reads it and yet doesn't quite read it because it is like reading death in the presence of death in a place of stones.

When he goes back, Mag is there with a bottle of beer, paying out the money. Charlie sees $26.12 ring up on the cards at the top of the cash register and he hears Mag say, "Christ, what did you all do to it anyhow?" He lets Mag back the pickup out before he gets in. "I said it was goin' to cost me, but that man is a son-of-a-bitch!" Mag says.

"It's not a nice town," Charlie says as they drive out and head back to Highway 14.

"There's something else?" Mag asks.

"The stone out there says they hung 38 Indians by the river."

"That was a long time ago."

"When the river was alive?"

"Yes, when it was alive." Mag says. "And you ain't seen nothin' yet. You are goin' to be damn glad to get back to Ft. Pierre maybe."

Charlie doesn't answer. He has many deep thoughts that he can't reckon with. Below him the river purls in its concrete troughs, brown and thick as coffee with cream in it and moving very slowly. He leans over into the door and presses his jacket over his lap and sleeps because it is easier than thinking so much. And yet he thinks a great deal.

It's the noise that wakens him again—a scuffing of tires and howling of engines going by. And Mag cursing. "The son-of-a-bitch!" Mag growls. "The son-of-a-bitch! Look at the bastards in their big cars. You watch now. There's a little space in front of this old horse and one of those slick bastards in gray suits and a Cadillac has got to shove into it. This whole place has a hard on."

Charlie opens his eyes wide. A shiny big Olds sweeps by close and fills the opening in the lane in front of them, then brakes and zags around a small green foreign car.

"We're here?" he asks Mag.

"We're here. The whole place is full of sooners humpin' space."

"What is that?" Charlie asks. It's really two questions because he doesn't know what a sooner is and there is something else. But Mag doesn't answer.

Ahead of them at the place where the freeway seems to converge in the shadows among a few tall buildings a great glass-plated steel tower looms in the fleecy clouds and afternoon sun, serene and blue, fluted in the vertical glass sections, rising and thrusting.

"Even the sky," Mag says. "They take a piece of sky even."

Although the mirror glass of tower seems to take on the movement and coloration of the clouds, still it holds steadily among them, a tall imperial presence. Its dark blue baronial head of six capping stories with flashing lights and antennae commands the skyline. It rises so tall that Charlie wonders if the sun, too, has to ride around it.

"The sun too!" Mag says. "Sticks right in the eye of the sun!"

"How tall is it?"

"Taller than a whale if you put one up on end—the tallest building from Chicago to San Francisco. It's got a spine of steel up the middle and ribs like a fish and skin and some Eastern son-of-a-bitch done it for some other Eastern son-of-a-bitch. It don't belong out here on the prairie. The prairie is the long haul of rivers and buttes and (Mag takes both hands off the steering wheel) room to stretch. That son-of-a-bitch Tower an Easterner put here like a New York building and they sit up in that and count their money and look down on the river and all and think they own it."

He has never heard Mag talk so much or seen him suddenly look so tired.

"Do you know where I should go?" he asked.

"First we get a motel cheap and then you can go over to that tower where they are supposed to hang out they tell me." Mag pauses then. "I'm not hangin' around more than tonight and tomorrow morning. If I stay longer and people find out, they'll steal me blind out there."

"Who?"

"All those guys building the dam and sitting around in motels when they're not diggin' up everything so they can finish the last of it."

They check into a motel. Charlie senses that Mag has been there before because he knows how to get the cheapest room—the $12.48 one for truck drivers. "I got my rig over getting fixed and this is the boy who helps me load," Mag says. Charlie sees that the clerk—a rat-faced, olive-skinned man—doesn't believe it, but he also sees Mag's big red fist on the counter and the money carefully counted out next to it.

The room is grimey, the bedspreads orange and ragged and thin from wear. It all smells of stale sweat and restless nights of man sleep. The toilet runs all the time and the faucets drip, drip in spite of Mag's twisting at the handles. But Mag has a six-pack and the color TV works. Charlie can see that Mag is tired and is going to flop down awhile.

"Here's your key," he says, tossing it to Charlie. He walks outside and Charlie follows. Even in the motel courtyard they can see the tower clearly up over the roof, even though the tower is a mile or so away.

"Listen," Mag says, "people have told me things. There is a street down there called Hennepin where he used to hang out with his old army buddy. It's not a good place and you can't be there at night at all. When you go there you talk only to Indian people—say an old man or an old woman. Don't smile back at anyone and don't go with anybody into an alley or anything."

"Sure," Charlie says.

"Sure. Sure." Mag goes back into the room and lies down. He's taken his shoes off and has propped the gray pillows under his head. He watches Charlie standing there in front of the big mirror over the little chipped sink and Charlie wonders what he wants, so he turns and looks at him.

"You take that telephone number off that phone and keep it in your pocket and call me if you need me. When you start nosin' around the world because you want to know about everything you can bet you're in for a few surprises and not all good ones."

"Are you going to visit your relatives?" Charlie asks.

"Why, no, I'm going to lay on my ass and rest up before I have to start chippin and paintin' boats and haulin' fat ass money men from Des Moines and such up and down the river. And in a way, you could say I'm visiting my relatives."

"How's that?"

"Why this whole town is full of Swedes and Norwegians and Finns and what have you. It's hard to be in town without visiting relatives."

"I don't know what you mean?" he says to Mag as he starts to go out.

Mag stops him. "Get that number off that phone and get back

here soon's you can. I'm going back at checkout time in the mornin'. That's ten. And you got to be back here by midnight or they'll arrest you on the streets."

"Sure," Charlie says, writing the number on the tail of his blue shirt.

"Sure!" Mag says. "You're not sure of anything except that you have to run around and fish in a lot of corners. And your mother's worrying sick to death back there and trying to figure out how to lie to the school people."

"It'll be all right," Charlie says.

"You call or get back here, damn it. This trip is goin' to cost me!" Mag yells as Charlie steps out into the motel courtyard.

What is it? Charlie wonders—what is it that pulls me like a magnet to the bottom of that place? The cars swarm roaring and swarm toward the red and green lights. And the people, expressionless and driven by some vague force inside them or at the signs, press onward past him both ways.

He finds himself walking southwest toward the tower and the avenues beyond it. A blind man surprises him as he turns away from a store window full of mannequins in bright green and red and yellow summer clothes. The white cane swings at Charlie's feet. He skips over it and hurries down the street.

He's surprised that the people hardly notice him—except one young man with a blonde beard and a pink face and a soft, fluttery greeting of "Hi!" And he's surprised when he finds himself walking up or down the shadow of the tower as it leans away from the late afternoon sun. There are no shadows like this on the grasslands, except maybe the thunderheads, but those are not shadows because the sun takes its turn, usually, and then the rain takes its or they share an emerald green glow over the land.

Once he passes the end of a long corridor and sees the elevators open on both sides of it. When the doors open, the people stare across at one another for an instance like mannequins staring from one store window across into another. He sees boxes in boxes, rooms in rooms and the women's clothes are sometimes square at the shoulders over their breasts. Everywhere he sees a great geometry of squares and rectangles and only a few circles out in the plazas and then, of course, in the strangeness of people's eyes.

Then, suddenly, he's in the great interior of the ground floor of the tower and he gawks, slack-jawed, at the wonder of the high, arcing crystalline openness of it blazing with light. He gawks and pushes against someone but they don't turn around. It's like pushing against a coat or dress in a store. There's a procession in the place up into the second level on an escalator—hundreds of people in a processional.

But then, on the hard white cubes, below, on the hard geometric white cubes on the sunken great square slabs of stone he sees the old men—the Indians and the bums and the others not moving in the processional. A security guard stands near them, watching and listening. Sometimes he folds his arms and walks around them; sometimes he hurries up the escalator and talks in low, earnest tones to the young black men leaning over the railing above. When he walks fast, the long black nightstick at his belt clubs the back of his knee with little bouncing motions. And the little black radio on his belt squawks names and numbers and words about door alarms high in the tower.

He approaches the oldest of the Indians very slowly trying to read his eyes. Although it's a warm day the old man is wearing a tattered sheepskin jacket—over a soiled undershirt. There are holes in his tennis shoes and his striped gray pants are grease blotted and baggy at the knees. He approaches slowly because the old man is chanting something hardly audible and because his eyes are so coal black that they are like the eyes of a crow or a starling.

But he asks—two or three times, lying as he does it, but not really lying either—"I am looking for my uncle from South Dakota, Eddy White Cloud."

Nothing.

He repeats it and still nothing—only the eyes of black stone. The security guard hovers nearby, a nervous little blonde man with pale blue eyes and a crew cut he scratches from time to time.

And then one of the three gets up, rising heavily from the white cube he has been sitting on, and moves his thick body and blue-brown puffed face toward Charlie.

"He don't hear. He's gone from here—out in the wind or someplace he likes." It is a voice from a cave, a voice from dulled flesh. It comes hoarsely from out someplace under the wheezing noise of his breathing.

"I am looking for my uncle, Eddy White Cloud. He used to be at Rosebud and Ft. Pierre."

"A lot was. What's he look like?"

"I don't know. He came here with his friend in the army."

"What's his tribe?"

"Oglala."

"You ain't."

"Ain't what?"

"Oglala. You got no eyes for it."

"What is it?" Another voice intrudes. It's the security officer, his eyes angry and suspicious. One of the other old men laughs a deep, guttural laugh.

"I'm trying to find my uncle Eddy White Cloud."

"Well, they don't know. These old winos don't know who *they* are."

"Mogen David," one of the old men says.

"I just got to find him. They said I should go to Hennepin."

"Oh, boy. You hold it and let me ask. You wait here."

The guard walks away and begins to talk into the little black radio and then he goes to a phone in the information booth and calls someone. The three old men are all sitting down again watching. The guard watches Charlie carefully as he calls. Swarms of people swarm around Charlie like water around an island in the river.

The guard comes back, shaking his head and laughing. "They know about him at the Native American Center on Franklin because they tried to get him inside someplace last winter. You have to go to the canoe place on Minnehaha Creek and then you have to go down on the river, that's all I know."

"Where's that?" Charlie asks, worrying and sick in his stomach.

"You know your way around town?"

"No."

"You get on a bus there," the guard says, pointing out at the roaring of buses on the street at the west base of the tower. "You get on a bus down to Cedar Lake and you'll see the canoe place. You ask them there."

"Thanks."

"Are you staying someplace? You can't sleep on the ground or down here or anything."

"I'm staying at a motel with another uncle."

"Stay out of trouble and that means stay off Hennepin. It's not like South Dakota any more than this is."

"Sure," Charlie says.

"As he walks toward the big stainless steel exit doors Charlie looks at the three old men. They sit like old wide-nosed badgers sniffing for mice or sun but not finding anything. They seem to have a dignity but it's only the dignity of wooden things. Their bodies are heavy on the white cubes but their eyes are black as the eyes of crows and their souls seem to be in another place.

7

The Island of Ash

He looks anxiously behind him as he paddles the canoe along the east shore of the lake and toward the mouth of Minnehaha Creek. The drum of traffic is insistent and heavy along the boulevard that winds under the grand houses on the brow of the hill on his right. As the canoe glides under a stone bridge, cars rattle and pound over him and dip and glide toward thick streams of traffic on the north side of the lake.

And he sweats with the strangeness of the place—the wild ducks swimming tamely and unfrightened a few yards ahead of him, the long-legged girls in white shorts and green knee socks twirr! twirring! on roller skates and screaming something at nobody, the manicured lawns rising through nests of shrubbery to vast white open porches and gardens with gray statues reaching over a profusion of yellow and red and blue flowers. Nervous dogs, tugging at black tight leashes, sniff and squirt at trees. A man stumbles weak-kneed against a lamp post, turns and slides down to sit there. And ahead of Charlie over the crowns of elms the imperial presence of the tower, tall and serene and confident as it flashes in the sun. And he sweats because he's afraid and he's afraid because the eyes of the bearded young man at the canoe rental looked sad and squinted with worry when he gave Charlie directions and told him he had to be back by nine.

When he turns the canoe into the creek he enters another world. Through his knees, as he paddles the canoe, he can still feel the vibrations of cars and buses somewhere above him. But in the creek on the iron-brown water under dark cedar fences and stone abutments and the yellow-green draping of willow boughs he finds a world of bitterns and herons and secret places where minnows poise and dart and current carries him with gentle, urgent force.

A blue heron, startled, flaps up over a red tile roof, cranking the sticks of his legs. Sails back toward the lake.

He passes a little family in another canoe—a white couple, both wearing steel-rimmed glasses, and between them a black child smiling and pointing and crying shrieking wonder at the redwing blackbirds and the high clouds running across the sky through the trees above them.

And Charlie is lonely—deep, sick, empty lonely. He could almost cry out and he feels lonely from himself and a little crazy in a spooky way.

The canoe breaks into an opening and the voices of children shriek at him. It's a park. The creek widens and opens for a little island. He back paddles and holds the canoe against a concrete slab. Above him a bronze statue of two Indians rises over a plaque that says, "Hiawatha and Minnehaha."

"You have to be kidding!" he says, breaking his own long silence. The two of them are terrible in their dark, stained frozen immobility. The man is holding the woman, one hand high on her waist, the other over her left thigh as he pulls her toward him. Her moccasined feet dangle and her legs are supple and smooth. Her arm rests on his shoulder and she is smiling. Together, they seem eternal and invincible. He shoves away from them.

The island, he figures, should be about half a mile farther down the creek, but he knows that he can't take the canoe much farther. A few yards ahead of him a fish trap bridge stretches over the water and there are signs saying, "No Boats or Canoes Beyond This Point."

He beaches the canoe, pulling it up a concrete ramp and hiding it in the vines and brush. He cuts his right hand on a broken bottle as he slides the canoe along. Yelps and sucks the index finger of the hand. The island, as it's called, should be visible from the top of the ramp. He climbs, sucking the hand and hearing the thump of his own heart.

There below him and to his right the island lies under the river side levee at the foot of a railroad yard. It lies there with its gray-black flank out of the water like a beached, great fish covered with dead custaceans.

He can see what the man at the canoe rental meant when he said it would be dangerous and that he recognized it was really serious for Charlie. There are black-lettered "No Trespassing" signs on the high steel fence that runs along the yard and the yard itself is an open tracework of rusting rails and creosote-black railroad ties. And he can see what the man meant when he said, "It's not really an island or he couldn't really get there." It's really a peninsula of cinders and ash where a few straggly willows and weeds have somehow managed to take root. It was once probably part of the yard itself when steam locomotives came to dump the cold remains of their coal fires.

He walks along the edge of the fence until he finds a torn hole. Then he slides through and, keeping close to the sumac and other brush, hurries down to the levee. When he climbs up on the concrete levee he knows he can be seen, but he also knows he has to see. He scrambles up the riverward edge and sprawls on his belly to watch.

Below him the man sits on a piece of driftwood in the center of a fan of debris—bottles, wrappers, tin cans and vague, rotting things. He's alone, but he seems to be talking to someone or something, his voice a deep chant the wind carries away. His long gray hair has been twisted over the shoulders of his green jacket and he moves his neck and head like a limb rocking slowly in a current.

Suddenly he stands up and turns toward the railroad yard, his fist raised up toward Charlie. Charlie winces and freezes there.

The man begins to totter toward him. He's not a big man. But he's thick in the legs and body. But his face is wide and purple as a piece of liver.

When he lifts the bottle to his mouth, his nose is so purple wide he looks like a shark or a turtle someone is feeding.

"Hey you!"

He's tottering closer and Charlie is looking at the face so intently that he doesn't see him throw the bottle until it flashes in a whistling wobbly arc and crashes in front of him.

He panics and stands up. The man is close, tottering toward him, a great dark stain in the crotch of baggy khaki pants and his tennis shoes spottled with pink-tan vomit. He makes the notion of throwing again and again, pulling at something in his left hand, then aiming with his left arm and throwing with his right.

His eyes are fiercely bright and seeing but they are disconnected from his mind.

"What you want? You got a bottle?"

"I came here from South Dakota," Charlie says.

"Whatya want? You got a bottle?"

"They said you would be down here."

"Whatya want? You got a bottle?"

"Are you Eddy?"

"Eddy be damned. Whatya want? You got a bottle?"

"I'm Charlie Good Thunder."

"Whatya want . . . "

He shuffles closer, his eyes dark and bright as a crow's. He chants it again and again. "Whatya want? You got a bottle?"

Charlie sees that it's like talking into a telephone when a recording comes on and you want to say something but can't because the voice in the phone keeps saying the same thing over and over. He begins to back down the slope of the ramp and into the railroad yard. The voice follows him.

When he has backed down into the railroad yard he stands there a moment. The voice has stopped. The wind whipples his shirt gently. Off in the yard a crow flaps its black bright wings and caws. Beneath his feet the railroad ties are still warm from the sun. The smell of creosote bites his mind. The crow caws.

"Yes!" Charlie exclaims. "Yes, I heard you!"

He should have heard the yard security officer's footsteps too because he's there behind him as he turns—a burly, cool, gray, tough, old man wheezing softly from the walk.

"I saw you from the yard office," he says.

Charlie doesn't know what to say.

"I said I saw you from the yard office. Can't you read? How'd you get here?"

"Canoe," Charlie says.

The man glances toward the creek, but never really takes his
eyes off Charlie.

"Are you getting smart with me?"

Charlie let his face go loose and tries to look at the man with
his best slack innocent expression.

"No," he says, "I came from South Dakota to look for someone and they said at the canoe rental he was down here."

"But he don't know you," the officer says, picking up Charlie's train of thought. "At least he don't know you unless you
got a bottle of Mogen David or something."

"No," Charlie says—to something. "He doesn't hear anything."

"Just the river maybe—and some old sounds down inside
him."

"You can't talk to him anytime?"

"I never try. I should kick him out but he was with the
Wolfhound Regiment I was in in Korea. And there's not much to
kick out anyway."

"Wolfhound?" Charlie is curious again.

"The 25th Division. His hand is half gone from a grenade—
two or three fingers. That was a little before your time. I didn't
know him but there was maybe a dozen Indians in that outfit
and they were good and now he's good for nothin'. He just lies
around hearing somethin' far off down inside his foggy head."

"Where does he sleep?"

"Where does he sleep. I'll show you and then you get the hell
out of here. He's been robbed a dozen times and somebody tried
to kill him—some psycho beat the hell out of him and put a
note on a pin through his cheek, sayin, " 'Get rid of this filth!' "

The officer is walking away and Charlie follows through the
ancient, rusting freight cars on the rail sidings. From the river he
can hear terns mew and, as he looks back, he sees them circle
and dive on the slow water eddying on the up-river side of the island.

"Sometime I'll find him, I just know," the officer says.

"What?"

"I figure some morning I'll come out and see him lying down
there on his back and those damn birds perched on him feeding."

"He doesn't sleep down there when it's cold?"

"No, he sleeps up ahead over there."

They are walking faster, stepping over the rails and dodging among the ponderous broken carriages of freight cars and the red wreckage of an old caboose.

"Here!" the officer says.

It's an abandoned semitruck trailer. Its tires are flat and it leans toward the yard on a broken spring. The mud flaps with *Fruehauf* in white letters on them are still intact and tall white letters announce "Cargill" on both sides of the trailer.

"In here!" The officer points at a small door at the bottom left of the tall, locked steel rear doors of the trailer. Then he backs away. "In there," he says. "The whole thing is full of newspapers. Uses them for insulation. I bet he bought two or three here every day for 10 years."

When Charlie opens the little door and peers into the darkness, he knows why the man held back. From the ragged opening of a tunnel made by a cardboard box there comes an odor rank and vile as the stink of dead animals long in the sun. He recoils, bitten in the nose and nauseated. He coughs and does a little dance of disgust and anger. "Jesus!" he cries.

"Smells dead, don't it?" the officer says, not smiling but serious, his eyes wrinkled with age and something else.

"You say you're related to him?"

"My mother is."

"You want to leave something so someone can call you someday?"

"I don't know."

"The city will take care of it otherwise. Of course, I might not be here and you sure can't count on me. He don't see anything of course, but I got a notebook here and you could write it and hang it on a rail inside." He is taking out the notebook and an orange pen, as he says it, his face softening into kindness.

"How am I going to get it in there?"

"Suit yourself. You can leave it with me, but I might not be here after this summer."

Charlie takes the notebook and writes "In case of trouble. Call Charlie Good Thunder, Ft. Pierre, S.D." He takes a deep breath, thrusts himself through the little door, and finding a nail just over the door opening, hangs the note there. Then he kicks back out into the fresh air outside, his lungs bursting and even his skin cringing from the vile stink. Outside he coughs and dances and waves his hands as if he is brushing swarms of small, vile insects away from his face.

"You better get goin' now. It'll be dark and another yard officer is comin' on. You won't like him. At night here nobody likes anybody and he doesn't fool around."

They walk slowly along toward the place where Charlie has hidden the canoe. Their shadows stretch out ahead of them as they walk.

"Where's the hole in the fence?"

"I'll show you," Charlie says. "It's down in here," he says stepping in through the brush.

"You hurry now. This is no place for you. It's like the end of the world. If you ever come back except because of your note, I'll have your ass thrown in jail for trespassing," the officer says, not smiling or frowning, and saying it softly like he feels he has to.

"Thanks," Charlie says as he scrambles down through the hole in the wire.

"It might not ever do any good—except for you. Go back and find your people. This is no place for an Indian if you're an Indian."

"Thanks," Charlie says again. He bends to slide the canoe out. When he looks up, the old face and the uniform are gone.

Paddling back is hard work. The current is gentle but insistent and Charlie is weak from hunger. A bittern, mottle brown, stands next to the brown-tan ranks of thick reeds. He straightens his neck, pointing his scissor bill at the sky. When Charlie looks again the bittern has merged his plumage with the reeds. And yet the diamond of his eye blinks in fear or knowing.

And Charlie is spooked by his own reflection in the green-black mirror of the water. He dabs his paddle through it and hurries under the lever of falling darkness. He's alone on the creek. Starlings hang their sleek, black pelts on the leaning willows. The heron flashes his startled wings and rises in stiff pumping strokes through the poplars and elms. He hurries under the statue of the two of them in the water below at the park, not looking up to them. He's relieved when the canoe darts out into the open lake. Behind him, the mouth of the creek closes in an obscurity of darkness and leaning trees.

The bearded young man at the canoe rental waits on him, checking in the paddle and the canoe and the orange life preserver Charlie hasn't worn.

"I'll only charge you for three hours," he says finally. "I have an idea the canoe sat most of the time."

"I hid it in the brush by the fish trap," Charlie says, "but it was all right, I guess."

"You find him?"

"Yes."

"Here's your deposit—$20 dollars—and your change, 85 cents."

"Can I get something to eat here?"

"You've got about six minutes."

"Thanks."

"Are you from the Native American Center on Franklin?"

"No, I'm from South Dakota."

"If you have any serious trouble you should go there."

"Why?"

"Because they can look after you there."

"I'm here with my uncle."

"Fine. Better grab your hot dog."

He wolfs the hotdogs down fiercely, nearly choking on them in his hunger. The coke is so cold it gives him a dull ache high in the middle of his head. When the wooden doors and shutters of the concession pavilion clatter shut behind him, he thrusts the hot dog wrappers through the jammed opening of a garbage can and begins the climb up to Nicollet Avenue.

A long gray car resplendent with chrome and rolling on huge tires with fat sidewalls glides by and poises at the crosswalk, its engine tick-ticking under the long hood. Through the windshield Charlie can see the little pink smile of the blonde girl sitting upright on the wide seat near but not next to the black man, who smiles too and then smiles at Charlie—smiles and then rolls the great heavy car down the incline into darkening, mysterious regions of the city when the light changes.

The bus doors rattle open at the bus stop across the intersection and swallow up little congregations of people. He runs crazily through screeching tires and horns honking and voices swearing as they fade away.

He catches the bus, though—a 16-A—and feels better because he has. He tries to give the driver a dollar.

"I don't give change," the driver says, as he reaches over to pull the doors closed behind Charlie. When he fumbles in his pocket for .35 cents he drops two quarters on the floor. They roll under a seat, but the two women in the seat sit upright and disregard them. When, after dropping his change into the little glass box, he kneels to look for the quarters, the two women get up, brush by him and sit three seats farther back on the bus.

When he gets off the bus, he thinks about going back into the great court at the base of the tower, but decides against it. He thinks about going home right away if Mag isn't too tired. He thinks about getting out of there and forgetting all of it, but he knows he can't. And while he feels the tall presence of the tower above his head and hates it he is drawn to it too. He's gawking again, looking up at it. In the cooling darkness it is silver sleek and swims through the first stars. On its head blue-silver lights flash, flash like the arcing of a giant welding torch. The tower seems to belong to no place and no people and yet it seems to beckon him to enter it, to climb up inside it, to live in its great blue cold head.

He hurries toward the motel. As he lopes into the motel courtyard, filled now with cars and some music, his heart catches and cries out because the pickup is gone. He works the key frantically and pushes into the man smell of the room. Mag's bed is a crumpled heap of pillows and sheets and a nobby orange bedspread. Charlie cries out wearily, pisses noisily and sags into the other bed with his clothes on.

Morning light, Mag shaving there in front of the wide mirror. Mag doing his tremendous, got-to-get-the-bowels-going morning farting like the firing of a big outboard engine tilled out and then back into the water. Mag pulling the wrinkling sections of his long face down flatter for the razor. The face familiar to Charlie as he rises out of sleep.

Mag sees him watching and turns. "Well, you still alive? When I come back at midnight or so you were lyin' there with your mouth open cough–snoring and moanin' like you were goin' to die."

"I don't remember anything," he says, meaning the sleep.

"That bad, huh?"

"I don't snore like you do. You stop breathing when you snore. I woke up and couldn't go back to sleep because it would be five minutes between breathing and a snore, like you had died, maybe."

"You find out anything?"

"Nothing much. I saw the place and I saw a man out there but he didn't know anything or anybody."

"That bad huh? Well, we got to get back and we got to get scrapin' boats and paintin' and we have got to make some runs on the river to see how the currents have changed over the winter. So get your stuff together. The river is rolling and it's time."

"I do have my stuff together."

"You didn't buy anything?"

"Only a bus ticket and such."

"Well, let's go. I got enough city stink in me to last five years. I should hang my clothes on barbed wire in the river when I get back."

Outside as they leave Charlie leans into the old pickup affectionately and swings himself up into the cab. He sleeps most of the way home—except when they stop to eat. Through the narrow slits of his sleepy eyes Charlie sees the prairie flowing eastward on the right and left of the truck and his soul widens back into it.

8

Prairie Spring

"She home?" Mag asks as they sit there in the pickup and look toward the darkened house.

"I think so," Charlie says. "The Plymouth's here."

"Sure," Mag says, "but I got a feelin' about empty houses so you better check and see if you can get in so you got a place to sleep. You look like I feel."

"She's home," Charlie says because he's not sure she's home at all and tries to help by wishing it.

He stands at the door and knocks and shivers. A cool breeze flutters in under his jacket and when he knocks, the noise of it is small and empty inside the house. He knocks again and then turns toward the pickup, shaking his head. Knocks again and rattles the door handle.

When Mag idles the pickup farther up the driveway, Charlie walks over to the driver's side. Mag's face is white and drawn with fatigue and his eyes droop as he leans over the steering wheel.

"I figured it would cost me," he says.

"She might be sick."

"No, she's not sick or mad either. She doesn't get mad; she just does things. I don't know if I did the right thing, but that doesn't matter for you. Get in. You'll have to sleep out there and I'll bring you in tomorrow."

"I can get in," Charlie says. "I push the screens in hard and the hooks pop."

"Well, get in then so I can go."

The pickup grinds into reverse but doesn't move. Sits there, its engine nuk-nukking from the hard driving. What? Charlie wonders. What is it that he doesn't say and I don't say and she doesn't say?

"You're sure welcome," Mag says.

"What?"

"You get out there Saturday morning early so we can get some boats in the water. This trip cost me two days."

"Sure."

"Well?"

"Thank you," Charlie says, finally thinking on the "you're welcome."

"You've seen the big town now. It wasn't any good time, but it never ends up that way anyway. You drive into a city feeling like you could jump right over all the buildings and you drive out feeling like they all jumped over you."

"But a couple of people were nice."

"Sure."

"But I'm glad to be back here."

"Well, we're back here anyway."

Mag backs the pickup down the little slope of the driveway, pulls the lights on and jounces down along a little crossroad that twists up to the road that leads to the marina where he has had the boat landing for years. Charlie watches him numbly, his eyes glazing with fatigue and a small sorrow that has no cause he can touch in his mind.

He gets into the house easily through the rear window of his own bedroom and stands inside listening. There are only wind whispers—no human breath. When he turns on the light he sees that everything is neat and clean. He checks for the picture behind the insulation in the wall. It's there, but he sees that it has been moved and that angers him. In the kitchen there are no notes, but there is milk and there are cupcakes—four or five chocolate ones. He eats them all, washing them down with the milk as he swigs it right from the carton.

He is sleeping or he is thinking he is sleeping when the rattle of something wakes him up. He can hear that a car with its big, noisy V-8 engine idling tung, tung, tung, tung, is sitting in the driveway. When the house door opens, the car revs up, backs out and roars away.

She is standing over him. She hasn't turned any lights on but in the soft glow of light from somewhere outside his window her face is sad, the large eyes mournful. He knows she doesn't smoke, but she smells of smoke and places he didn't think she ever went to with Mag or anyone. He wonders why older people are so often sad when you catch their faces when they don't know you're watching. He wonders if he did it all himself and if you always have to do it this way and hurt and get hurt a lot. And he wonders, his eyes cunningly kept nearly closed, if she was hurt by the picture. And then, down inside him, he begins to hate a little too because it's better than all the other feelings squeezing him.

She stands there, breathing softly and smelling of old and bitter cigarette smoke. Then she cries it out softly, "Oh, little boy, I love you!"

He strangles in his own throat and pinches his legs mercilessly under the covers. He fights it, keeping his eyes closed and then he's relieved when he hears her in the other room crying softly as she prepares for bed.

"I won't go! I won't go to her!" he cries to himself, his upper teeth pressed over his tower mouth and chin, the tears welling out of his closed eyes and running down the sides of his head.

He lies there a long time, staring at nothing at all while his inner eyes search into things—the man at the gas station, the dead hump of the ash island, the bicycle lost in the grassland and what to do about Dick Bissonette in school the next day. Late, very late, sleep cools him down.

Nancy has already gone to work when he wakes up. He hurries to get to school on time and wonders what to say when he gets there and faces the principal, Mr. Larson. It would be easier to face Mr. Larson if he just got angry and raged, but he never does. He just sits asking question after question and putting it back on the student so he carries away a lot of little nagging things that are hard to shake out.

But, between gulps of milk and spoon shoveling the Cheerios into his mouth he sees the note and the note about the note. The note is on a big piece of yellow paper with blue lines on it—the kind lawyers use and Nancy always brings home from the office:

Dear Mr. Larson,

Because of a family emergency Charlie had to go to Minneapolis. I hope you'll excuse him.

Signed: *Mrs. N. White Cloud*

Under it is another note in a little blue envelope. He tears the envelope open so he can get it over with. "Come on!" he yells when he drops it on the floor. It's short:

Charlie,

I don't think I lied in the note, do you? Make up all your work and be a good boy.

Love,
Mother

He throws her note back on the table and hurries out, stuffing the other note into his pocket.

At school he feels strange, nodding and saying hi to the others as he negotiates the worn stairway to the principal's office. Principal, he thinks. Remember how to spell principal as in *pal*. Smirks to himself and gets ready for the questions. When he walks into the principal's office and leans over the counter with his note he's surprised to see that he's alone and it makes him nervous—more nervous.

"Charlie?" It's Mrs. Whiteheels, the secretary. Her eyes are sharp and perceptive because she knows everything. Her body is thick and her great stomach hangs over her desk when she reaches over to get an admit slip, but her hands and mind are quick and nobody talks smart to her. Once Billy Whitefeather muttered "Mrs. Shitheels" as he passed her in the hall after she had put him on detention for a week because Larson was gone and because Billy had skipped. Before Billy could quite manage a smirk she had him by the ear wincing and dancing down to the office.

"Do I have to see Mr. Larson?" he asks.

"No, You don't have to see Mr. Larson. But you have to get all your makeup sheets done and signed by the end of the day or you'll see him."

He's incredulous. "I don't have to see Mr. Larson?"

She looks him over then. "If your mother wrote it, it's true. If it's true, you don't have to see Mr. Larson. Do you *need* to see Mr. Larson?"

"No," he says, pulling the assignment makeup sheets off the counter and turning to go.

"Say, are we going to have another fraticidal war after school?"

"What?"

"Fratricidal as in brotherly."

"Him?"

"Him. You'll have to figure him out and work it out. Maybe on all this schoolwork you'll have to work on it *inside* yourself and make it like your own private room nobody can get into."

He doesn't answer her with his voice, but he looks at her and she nods at him saying yes, yes with her head.

Assembly—a great barn of a room with a little partitioned-off library at the rear of it. Assembly—a great barn of a room compressing life in little wood and cast iron desks in long bolted-down rows. A window light high overhead buzzing with prairie wind. Faces, dark and knowing and dark and unknowing. Runty boys coughing. Feet, legs, glasses, kids. Discipline. Mr. Hanson keeps iron discipline. Mr. Hanson once caught John Steel sticking a girl with a pin on a ruler. John smarted off. Suddenly his arm is locked up behind him and he is jump dancing down the row crying, "God! God!" And behind him, Mr. Hanson, chanting in a bull voice, "That's what I am in here and don't forget it!" Who cares! Charlie thinks.

They look younger when Charlie comes in. They look like kids, most of them, and Charlie is amazed to realize that he has grown older being away. His seat is four down in the junior class section. When he sits down, he sweeps the varnished surface of the seat with the side of his hand. A tack pips off. Smiles. Tittering. Hanson converging short armed and burly to stand near him, his arms folded.

Dick Bissonette sits to his right, or rather leans back straightlegged and smirking and nodding off left to the sophomore girls.

Girls. What does that look mean? Charlie has grown up in school with them but he has lived apart with his mother and he doesn't know them. He's on fire inside thinking about their legs, their legs, but he doesn't know them or really how to talk to them. Their legs converging at the top.

The day goes well. He keeps things inside of him. The makeup assignments are a joke—an exercise or two or "Keep reading chapter six" or "prepare for unit exam on Wednesday," but he listens carefully, pretending to be bored and cynical, when Miss Drew reads about the Huck Finn and his father, even though Charlie won't read the book because the others aren't reading it either. He finds a calmness inside listening to Mr. Hale explain why the frontier was officially closed in 1890 and how the frontier was so important in American democracy according to a Mr. Jackson or Turner or somebody.

It's Friday and the day goes well. But he has a feeling that there is something else. The bike, of course, but the girl disregards him all day. He has forgotten about the bike lying out there in the grass. As he walks out of the school building he passes Dick Bissonette sitting on the brownstone ramp along the edge of the concrete steps. He tries to disregard him.

"You come back already!" the voice exclaims, following him. A little chorus of laughter from three others, leaning and standing against the outside of the steps. Two of them are smoking. One walks around in a little circle and taps his cigarette when Charlie turns around.

"Sure," Charlie says.

"You run off real quick. You hiding or something?"

"No," Charlie says, "Is there something to hide from?"

Dick slides off the stone ramp and puts his cigarettes back into his shirt pocket.

"You didn't get enough, I see."

"No, I didn't get enough. I'm just getting started."

"Where'd you go?"

"A couple of places."

"You stole a bike, I heard."

"Who said that? Where does it say that? Who called the police?"

"But he covered your half ass didn't he?"

"Who?"

"The big mister your mother used to have over before she got herself a big construction worker."

The right hand catches Dick flush on the jaw with a "clock!" Dick rises and sets his hands to punch but he's wobbly and his eyes are glazed. His punches slat on Charlie's arms, but they're weak and Charlie hooks into and under the left-right, left-right movement of Dick's hands and connects. Dick stumbles off sideways, bent over in gut-sick pain.

"Don't Charlie! Don't!" The voices call into the wild blur of his anger and slow him. He looks at Dick, bent like a wiry gnome over an outside white drinking fountain and he's sorry because Dick is coughing and trying to not bawl and mostly because Dick is beaten. He turns into himself again then and walks through an opening in the crowd of students who have gathered there—most in silence and maybe in relief. He hears nervous laughter and a cheer or two, but he doesn't like the feel of it.

A hand grabs his—Billy Whitefeather's. "You got him good!" Billy cries. He's wheeling around Charlie in an ecstasy of congratulation.

"Sure," Charlie says, "and now what's he got except to maybe try and kill me?"

"What's the matter with you? Where'd you go anyway? What's the matter with you? That bastard had it coming for about three years."

"What'd you say?" He thinks about punching Billy too.

"What? Well, go to hell, big man!" Billy walks off, a little stiff in the knees and hurt somehow.

"I'll tell you Monday!" he yells after Billy.

"Fuck it!" Billy yells.

There was something else then, Charlie says to himself walking home. I'd like to go someplace he says to himself again and again. But where? he wonders.

"Hi!" The voice is sweet and it's close at his ear because Kim Pettigrew is riding a man's bicycle—a new blue bicycle. Her eyes are brown bright with excitement or something as she tries to keep the wobbling bike going and then jumps down with both legs straddled over the seat bar.

He looks at her. She has combed her black hair back, parting it in the middle. Her mouth is fine and small and purses seriously as she leans over to bend the chain guard away from the bike chain.

"It's new," she continues. And then she laughs, a long laugh with a little squeak or shriek at the end of it. "It's nice," she says, "and I'm glad there wasn't any trouble over the other one."

"Thanks," he says, wishing she would go away and that she wouldn't go away. She straightens her legs out stiffly and balances up on the black seat of the bike. Her legs are olive bronze, fine and smooth under and out of the dress. "It's O.K." he says, trying to shove those thoughts out of his head because he doesn't know what to do with them.

"He has been mean to a lot of kids," she says.

"Who?"

Quick laughter. "Dick," she says. ". . . he pushes girls around too but different."

"I didn't want to hit him. I wasn't so lucky last Tuesday."

"Are you going home?" She looks around when she asks it and he wonders, "Around at what?"

"I guess so. I have to try to get out and look for the bike. There's a marker. It's out south of here."

"In the grassland? "You were out there? Alone?"

"Yes." He looks at her to see what she wants or if there is something else she is asking, but she turns away and looks out toward the road to Rosebud.

"I would like to see it again if we could find it. It's not as nice as this but it's special. Have you got a car?"

"Yes," he lies, "but it's being fixed."

"Do you want to buck me out there?"

"It's about four miles."

The sun is still high in the afternoon sky as they start out. She rides on his folded jacket on the carrier behind the seat and manages somehow to hold onto the seat under him. He pedals fast and the wind is easy. A few cars roar by and the two of them disregard the whistles and obscenities. The grass on both sides of the road ripples in smooth shiny patches and darker undulations. Her breath is in his ear, her mouth wet touching the back of his neck sometimes as she tries to see or loses—catches her balance. They both talk loudly about silly things and the lost bike and how nice it is.

He sees the kerchief Mag has tied on a section post about a quarter of a mile just ahead of them. "It's off to the right!" he yells over his shoulder and she leans over close with sweet mouth and breath that ripples him inside like the grass in the wind.

They get off the bike and walk down into the ditch. Out ahead of them a mile or so Charlie can see the little thicket of red cottonwoods where he must have sat under the thunder storm.

"What were you doing out here?" she asks.

"I just walked out to look around," he says.

"Alone?"

"For a little while, but then I wasn't."

"You're a funny guy. Some of the girls say you're deep—or something." Laughter again, the lovely shriek at the end of it, like robins before rain. Oh, spring rain!

They range through the grass, poking, criss-crossing and calling to each other. He watches her and when he does she turns and waves sometimes. She walks with smooth easy steps and moves as quickly as he does.

In the grass ahead of him he sees the bike and yells at her. When she runs toward him she is tall and lithe and strong and high in the hips and her hair swings in dark beats over her shoulders.

"It's o.k.," he says. "I put it down here and walked over there."

"What were you going to do?"

"I don't know."

He knows he ought to go back, but he pushes the bike toward the red cottonwood thicket, his heart hammering down into his hands at the bike handles. She takes the other handle, fondling it, her mouth pursed again in a little girl's studious delight. Oh, my God, what is this? he asks himself.

"Is this the place?"

"Yes." Heart hammering.

When they sit down—she on his jacket, her knees moss dappled and bronze-pink—they are in a separate world out of sight of everything except the sky."

Heart hammering.

"This is sweet grass," she says, holding a little tuft of it up. "My uncle says that it is a sign of peace and good feeling to throw pieces of it down."

"They make small baskets out of it too," he says, feeling like an ass saying it.

"What did you see here?"

"I don't know."

"A vision?"

"I don't know."

"They say that a vision comes to you in a crazy time or a sick time. I never had one. My father says vision is looking ahead to get a good job. He wants me to go to pharmacy college at Brookings. That's his idea of a vision. My uncle says my father is no longer Indian."

"What do you want?"

"Now I don't want anything."

He stands up, restless, angry, and yanks the bike up out of the grass.

"You could hold me," she says, her voice frightened and a little hoarse.

He kneels down to her and kisses her. He would, he would, he would. She holds him from entering her, but he presses down, sun springs bursting in his loins, a red turtle of fire sliding down the inside of his back, pressing pressing toward the dark soft earth place, the willows singing the smooth ripple of flesh. She shudders softly, under her dress, a stirring of earth. Tallow smoke. Loin dank.

"I haven't," she cries. "I don't want to be mean, but I haven't. I will someday, but I haven't."

She kisses him, holding his head up from the side of her neck. He kisses her fiercely again, then puts his temple next to hers and kisses her softly on the neck and then tasting her tongue, he holds her to him again, and holds her tongue inside of him for a little while.

He rolls over, softened and warmed but not done because he has not touched her deeply. And yet there's no anger, no urgency to leave as with the others. There is something else. He looks at her, breathes her breath into his, presses his lips on her eyebrows. Loves. She will be new every time he sees her. He studies her face, kisses at her breasts under the blouse, kneels to kiss the swell of her under the belt of the dress. She pulls his head up. Love smile.

She coughs—a little series of quick, dry coughs.

"Are you cold?" he asks.

"No, I'm happy. Was I mean to you?"

"It's all right. I mean it's all right."

"I watched you a lot of times this year and last."

"I saw you too."

She laughs and sits up. "You saw me the first time today."

"Since first grade I've seen you everyday probably."

"But we stopped talking or anything for a long time."

They begin to walk back toward the road. He touches her back and seat and the smoothness smooths him out inside and even his face feels it. "You better brush off," he says, brushing at the high curve of her seat. She runs and he chases, pushing the bike. They kiss again and again, their mouths cool and sweet in the wind.

"Are you going to keep my bike?" she asks. "It would be nice thinking you have it."

"It depends on Mag," he says, "but anyway I will have a car. I'm too old to have a bike as my main means, et cetera."

She coughs again and swallows hard as they mount up on the bikes. "No racing of any kind," she says very softly. " I think I'm a little allergic or something."

"I could stay here. I don't want to go back."

"We'll come back. I just know we'll come back," she says.

They pedal slowly back to town. He bumps her, touches her across the little quickening intervals of spring night. Above them in the cold streamers of high clouds still washed by sun, the vapors of jet aircraft spred their silver tracery across the western sky and converge in distance. Oh time, oh love!

"Oh, Charlie, it's so nice!" she cries, looking up with him as the lights of the town blink on and the first stars shine.

9

The Man Fish

He dreads going into the house. And he realizes, through his blind, thick feelings that Kim had been terribly worried and that she had suddenly turned away from him, her face a little feverish and strange, to pedal her bike toward the new house where she lives along a line of other neat houses at the south edge of town. It worries him to think about her face because he wonders if she's angry or something.

And now his mother. The tan Plymouth he has been begging her to let him drive is in the driveway, its rattly sheet metal hulk leaning over slightly toward the house. She won't wash it becauses it costs and he won't wash it because she won't let him drive it. A red-tan layer of clay spreads over most of it and even the taillights are splattered with it.

He pedals up along the driveway on the right side of the car and stops to check his pants. They have dried somewhat with the ride into town and the wet doesn't show, but he knows he'll have to wash them out when she's gone.

When he leans over on the car to balance himself he sees it. At first he thinks it is only streaking where someone has brushed against the car—maybe at a gas station—but then he sees the letters, clear and unmistakable: OATS F_S N.W.

Cold anger slides off his shoulders. He rubs the letters out with his hand. Oats? Oats? The big car that backed away from the house that night—is that it?

Inside the kitchen Nancy is stirring at some food she has put into the frying pan—pork chops and some potatoes.

"Hi," she says. She is wearing a mint green summer dress and she looks younger, but not exactly young. Her hair is combed back too and she is wearing a perfume that exhales sharply through the smell of cooking.

"Hi," he says, keeping sideways to her and devouring the food with his eyes.

"You hungry?"

"Sure."

"You found the bike?"

"Yah, we—I found it by the marker Mag put out."

"That's all?" She turns holding the spatula in her left hand over the dinner plate.

"Yah," he answers, moving sideways.

"They came over."

"Who."

"Kim's parents. He's a postman. They were worried. It was nearly seven then and pretty dark."

"She's all right," he says, but thinking Why don't they leave us alone? And you're going to take it away from us or never let us have it maybe.

"So it's begun," she says, turning back to the stove and filling the plate.

"I don't know what you mean."

"Sit down so you can eat," she says, turning with the plate full and a glass of milk. She stands over him when he sits down and puts her hands on his shoulders. He begins eating. "There is an old song," she continues, ". . . there is an old song that the heart hunts alone and that chasing love is like chasing a green ghost or a brown one in the wind grass."

"I don't know it," he mumbles through his food.

"There are two now, aren't there?"

"Two?"

"The picture."

He stops eating. "The picture?"

"The girl of a dream."

"You had no right . . ." he begins.

"No, I didn't," she says, interrupting him. "But is it a girl friend or a mother?"

"I bought it when I was 12," he lies. "I don't know why I bought it, but you had no right."

"No, I didn't," she says, moving away and standing there at the stove again watching him. He eats, but he knows she's not through. "I've got to stay out of your room and let you have it. I'll give you bedclothes and I'll clean it, but I won't go in unless there's something to fix or something. You have to have a room now." She pauses. "But, Charlie, don't hurry anything with a girl, will you? I hope you'll do something someday and maybe get away from here. There are a lot of dreams, not just one."

"I won't," he says.

"You won't. You won't. You're lucky you're a man, Charlie. In this place where men have so much trouble doing something worthwhile women have to stay even lower. Do you understand that? And if you get a girl pregnant she has no time for herself at all and even her own bones don't have time to fill out if she's too young."

"But you've got a good job," he says trying to shift the conversation.

"But I have it alone. I work as an Indian woman alone and Indian men don't like me and I'm getting old and we aren't really with anyone now. I haven't got any women friends anymore except Ann Whiteheels at school and what is it we could do together?"

"I guess we have to make up our mind," he says between sayings at the pork chops.

"Yes? I mean—oh, never mind."

"Did you like Minneapolis?"

"No. But this tower was huge . . ."

"I've seen it. It's tall and lonely and it looks like it's not quite connected. It has the signs of the sky but not of the earth. It's a man building."

She's looking at her watch then. "I have to go. Will you clean up? He wants you out at the mailbox and ready to go at six."

"At the mailbox?"

"Yes. Why?"

"Nothin'."

She pulls off the apron and hangs it at the side of the refrigerator. When she comes back from her bedroom and the bathroom she's wearing a tan spring coat. He sees that in her eyes is a shadow and that, somehow, she doesn't quite want to go or want to go wherever she's going. Her face is rouged slightly and she wears a rose lipstick and that surprises him.

"Where you going?" he asks.

"To my room," she says, ". . . to my other room."

"Maybe tomorrow I can get off early."

"That's it—maybe tomorrow, Charlie."

He can hear her start the car and then sit out there a long time doing something. He does the dishes and cleans up the kitchen. When he finishes, he pulls his jeans off, hand washes the crotch, hangs them up and dries them with a hair dryer.

As he lies in bed thinking he looks up through his window and knows that every star is lonely. And yet he feels remembers Kim and the grass and the earth and the lovely quick shriek at the end of her laughter.

When he awakes he can hear the truck idling out in front of the house. He hurries, tugging his slacks on and stomping into his big shoes and splashing water into his face. The door to Nancy's room is closed, but he can hear her rattle snore in deep sleep. He hurries.

That day begins to pass in sweating rituals of boat hauling and scraping paint and firing outboard motors in the barrels of water Mag has set up along the boat shed. Charlie sees that Mag is his fierce, hard-driving self again. Mag's long face is set in a long rigidity of determination. He doesn't work; he fights things. "The son-of-a-bitch!" he cries at a carburetor stuck tight with hard varnish from the gas and oil mixtures they use in outboards. A boat is a "piss-ant" when, after scraping and sanding it, Mag finds that the gunwales are too rotten to hold screws.

He also seems to have some terrible quarrel with an unnamed He who causes inexplicable things. When the wind blows a can of used oil down on two of the boats so they have to be scrubbed with gasoline and laundry soap, Mag cries out, "You had to do that, didn't you. You found that necessary to do, didn't you. You got it in my ass, haven't you? I start out trying to do what's right, but you have to do that, don't you?"

Some people, Charlie knows, think Mag is crazy, but Charlie sees the hard work and the loneliness in Mag's life and he too sometimes feels like saying, "You had to do that, didn't you?"— and does. And he sees that Mag never turns physical anger on him—never. Mag can be right in the middle of one of his mad litanies and when Charlie asks him where something is, he'll turn suddenly and say, clear-eyed and sane, "Right under the carburetor cleaner pail" or "Look behind the seat in the pick up."

Once, when lightning struck the little flag pole by the fish cleaning shed and both of them rolled under the orange blur blast and ball that spun out of the strike and thunder, Mag lay on his belly a few feet from Charlie and said very quietly, "The Father must love us yet, the old son." That made no sense and yet it did make sense too.

Dinner comes unannounced because when it's time Mag washes his hands, more or less, and disappears into the log hut he has built into the riverside—in the brow of a sandhill thrusting up out of flood level. He washes his hands (more or less), pumps some water for coffee into an old blackened aluminum coffee pot he has left sitting on the well, and disappears through the rough sawn wooden door to do the cooking.

The cooking is always the same. "If it don't fry, I don't buy," Mag says. There at the big burner of the gas stove is a big, thick-sided iron skillet full of home-canned beef and sliced potatoes and sauerkraut.

The eating is always the same. "Set your self down," Mag says, standing there behind an old greasy flour sack stuck in his belt for an apron. There are no place mats and the card table is filthy. "You want to turn the page?" Mag asks. Charlie looks down at the newspaper spread in front of him, reaches out, and pulls over a clean sheet. When he puts his plate down, Mag dumps a steaming mountain of food on it. Then he sits down, bows his head (Charlie looking at the top of it and seeing the hair thinning), and then eats slowly and steadily.

"You know the season?" Mag asks.

"Well, there's no season on the river," Charlie says, puzzled because Mag has never asked much more than, "You got pepper? You in love? You eat before you came here?"

"No, I mean God's seasons, not the ones on the river."

"Oh," says Charlie.

"I shall make you fishers of men," Mag says.

"Oh?"

"Jesus said that to the whole bunch of them. Fishing is a divine occupation, by God. It's right in the Bible."

"You go to church?" Charlie asks.

"Funerals and such. I used to. I used to play Annie—hi—over the Lutheran Church if the pastor wasn't in it. We would yell 'Anni-hi-over!' and throw a ball up over the shingles and she would try to catch it. And the doves used to rattle and flap out of the belfry and fly around. Sometimes we could play until dark and then it was like throwing at the stars and was like prayin'."

"Yeah?" Charlie says.

"You done?" Mag says, but seeing Charlie isn't done at all. "I got to nap now," Mag says.

The nap ritual is always the same. Mag stands up, emits a grand belch and then, stepping sideways, falls on his cot and is sleeping in seconds. Charlie goes on eating and wondering. In the warmth of the dugout he becomes drowsy. He sits back in his chair and dozes off too.

"What the hell? You gonna do nothin' but eat and sleep!" Mag yells into his dozing off.

Outside, the day seems newer after the naps. There's no end to the work and sometimes Charlie protests the scraping especially.

This day Mag stops the work at five o'clock, hauls Charlie into a drive-in restaurant for a commercial hot beef and a beer, and then, to Charlie's surprise, leads back toward the boat docks again.

"What're we gonna do?" Charlie asks. He is thinking about Kim and getting back to town and things. His blood is thinking too.

"I know you need to get back," Mag says, "but tonight we

have to try out the river. It's the night to try out the river. I have felt it all afternoon."

"Isn't it early?" Charlie asks, thinking Where is she? What is she doing? Remembering how quickly she turned her face away and rode like a frightened stranger down the street. Feeling he needs to see her smile to make it all real again.

"It's time before they all come out and we have to haul them up and down and help fat ladies into the boats. It's our night to fish and try out the river."

"Sure," Charlie says, realizing that there's no turning him back anyway and that he's going to give him the bike for the day's work and seeing that his eyes are zealous and excited as he's never seen them before.

And so he doesn't argue, but fills the minnow bucket with big sucker minnows and smaller ones for the jigs while Mag hurries as he never does for an impatient businessman from Omaha or Des Moines.

They push off into the clear, quick water that flows out of the turbine spills under the dam. Mag has always hated the dam for "stalling" the river, but it holds the huge widening lake above it and the engineers control the water flow so that, except for a couple of days after a heavy wind or rain, the water is bright and clear.

The whistle of a steam locomotive—the Dakota Special—blasts their ears as it pounds the tall steel bridge above them. In the long shadows of the evening its boiler fire flares orange fire when the fireman stokes it. Hooting stanzas of steam and the clank, clanking of the great pitman shaft push-pulling the black steel wheels. Sparks. Sparks! The bridge picks up the rhythm of the engine and clank-clatters on its caissons.

"That's another thing gone soon!" Mag yells over the noise.

"Has a heart!" he yells. "Has a heart, hear!"

The boat drifts away and the locomotive follows its headlight over into the rolling buttes on the west side of the river. Charlie dips his hand into the cold, smooth flow of the current and lets the water caress his hand. He bends his shoulders together and listens for the wind through the cottonwoods to his right on the bank. Over the wide sand stretches of the river behind them a hawk, fierce bright with lingering sun, gliders up the thermal currents and cries into the dark below it.

"That is some lonely hunter, that one!" Mag says.

Then Mag starts the big Johnson motor and threads the boat through the deepest part of a shallows.

"Watch it now!" He throttles the motor down and turns around and into the current. It's an 18-foot wooden boat, a varnished ancient one, rare on the river anytime. Mag likes it because it's steadier and quieter than the aluminum and plastic ones. He stands up, holding the steering arm down behind him and looking, hawk-eyed, down into the rocks and boulders, there in dim outline under the electric lantern.

"Jigs and minnows!" he calls out. The boat surges ahead. Then the motor stops. "Plunk!" goes the anchor. Mag stands up in the boat again, looking up and down the current. He blows his nose, honking like a goose. Swiks a great gob of snot down into the water.

They use weighted yellow jigs with hair skirts and minnows hooked behind through the head. They work them carefully, casting just far enough and retrieving fast enough to keep the lines tight, jigging them a little down in the rocks, but not letting them get snagged.

Nothing hits. The walleyes are fasting in the cold water. Charlie can't see them clearly in the dark water, but he knows what they look like, the females especially—heavy with eggs and riding deeper, their eyes blank white pebbles in the current.

"Well, shit!" Mag says. "They are temperamental as usual. They are not in season tonight."

The gun metal gray gloaming over the buttes on the western side of the river darkens into deep purple.

"You see him?" Mag asks.

Charlie shakes his head. Mag's eyes are silver blue behind the hooked nose. What is it that he has seen.

"Could've felt him go under even," Mag says. "You thinkin' somethin' else? You hungry already. That wasn't much back there." He is handing Charlie a sandwich, but looking downstream.

Charlie takes the sandwich—thick sausage and mustard on

thick bread. He is hungry all the time. There are no lunches at school. He usually eats a candy bar and an apple and the sandwiches Nancy sends but it is never enough.

Mag is looking at him, his fishing gear out of the water. "Here," he says, pushing the bottle of wine at him. It's sweet and full and he finishes his sandwich with it, not drinking much, but sipping it. He hands it back and Mag finishes it. Then he does something he never does. He drops it down into the water.

"Now what?" Charlie asks.

"Treble hooks—big ones. I think he went to town. I think we are going to follow him to where he lays under a shoal right in town learing at the lights or whatever he does. And we are going to hook him by God!"

"Paddlefish?" Charlie asks.

"Sure."

But it tires Charlie just to think about it—nap or no nap. Walleyes or northerns are one thing. They could whip and rapple under the boat and even tangle an anchor line. They had minds: they fed or they didn't and that was it. They had eyes, but they never looked at you when you got them into the boat and a club on the head would end it. A dead walleye's eyes weren't so different from a live one's. They never closed really—like they had never been that alive anyway.

But paddlefish in the night currents under the concrete river retaining walls in Pierre were something else. They didn't take a lure. It was more hunting than fishing and when you hooked one, it was more like roping a horse or alligator maybe.

Darkfall on the water the current tug, tugging. Mag yells at Charlie to tug the anchor up. He runs the boat slowly through the wide surges of the river. Charlie eats another sandwich, yanks open a can of beer and begins to feel a little silly dizzy happy from it. Mag only lets him have two and then its pop or nothing.

Moon rising pale and white and close. Up river from them the great shoulders of the dam hold the lake, the lake still widening and deepening as it quietly floods the cottonwood trees and the buffalo grass along Cottonwood and Cheyenne Creek. They

thread logs and skags and moon-ribbed sandbars, lean as skele-
tons. The turbines under the dam howl like tight-throated
wolves. Charlie feels a great presence like the tower—a man
made thing, dark-shouldered and burly-wide and ominous. He
lets the water stroke his hand. Lifts his face to the moon. Thinks
on Kim and soft earth blessed by sky. But the moon is cold and
Mag's face a Swedish crescent.

Then someone throws a switch and the lights along the road
on top of the dam flash on—long strings of them running
through the night over the whale-deep black water on the north
and the cliff drop to the clear, moon-silver water ribboned over
boulders and sand shoals toward Pierre. Under the lights—the
crystal glories strung like beads—the buffalo grass is humble on
the earth bank of the dam, is humble as grass on a grave.

"The son-of-a-bitch!" Mag says. And Charlie knows what he
means. In the April night under the moon they ride toward Pierre where the river is an alley, a backstreet nobody ever knows.

They pass through corridors and walls and thick abutments
with signs on them the moon illuminates brightly: Stohrs Beer,
Hodapp's Men's Clothiers, Western Wear, A and P. Mag stands
up. He pushes past Charlie and pushes Charlie back to the motor. He stands up tall in the prow of the boat and pisses inso-
lently under the moon. Can anyone see us? Charlie wonders. Is
anyone wise to us? Above them the electric signs wink neon
words: Empress, Casey Tibbs', Rex's Bar. Mag is turned away
from Charlie. He shakes himself, pulls back far and zips. Turns.
Farts enormously. Charlie laughs, then wrestles with the steering lever and throttle as the river slaps on rock shallows.

Then, below the parking lot where the car lights sometimes
swing over and lay blinding beams of light on them Mag tells
Charlie to turn the boat into the current and to hold it steady in
the current.

"Big treble now, Charles," he says, snapping the big treble
hooks into the cable leader. "Big treble, big rod!" he exclaims.

Charlie gives him the fishing rod he always uses—a long,
thick shanked outfit with a reel big as small truck wrench. He
holds the boat steady as the river runs under them.

"He's in town tonight, lying down there learin' and wishin' he

could climb up out of the water and raise hell and dance on his
tail right up into the mornin' sun, by God he is! Would drive a
pickup if he could, by God!"

Mag casts. "Whoot!"—out goes the line and treble hook, the
reel squee–squee–squeeing. "It's sand!" Mag yells. He hooks
many things—barbed wire that whips dangerously around the
boat, a sheet of construction plastic that veils the moon when he
holds it over Charlie. "He's got a moon in his eye!" he yells. "He
is crazy for light, the old fool!"

Then as he pulls back, Mag snags something that cranks back
in great wide tugs like a steer in slow motion at the end of a fine
rope. The boat dips on one side, splashing water in. Mag bends
and keeps his balance. "Charles, my boy, we have caught him
at it, by God! The old sinner is hooked by the ass!" The line
flashes, whips in a wide circle toward the north with them in
the center of it. "Turn with him! Turn with him!" Mag yells.

They ride upstream, the reel snarling and Mag laughing while
he cranks and bends and recovers his balance. The fish is hooked
high in the back so it has enormous leverage in the water and
there is no way Mag can pull it straight in. They move in dangerous circles of combat and the circles move upstream. Charlie
knows they have to close the circles and that he'll be at the deep
center of one and it scares him.

"See 'em, Lord God!" the voice yells above them and at them.
A chorus of men—half a dozen or so—stands on the bank of the
river above them in front of a little frame church. They are wearing dark suits and ties. A bell clank, clanks somewhere behind
them. "See 'em, Lord God!" they cry again. Their faces turn
away from him as he turns the boat around with the running of
the fish. Then they come back again as he turns the boat around
with the run of the fish. Then the boat runs with the fish under
the bank where they're standing, gaunt elders of some church—
transfixed Men of God on the shore. The bell clanks in Charlie's
head—clanks like it is stuck in sand.

The circle of the fish closes around the boat and the pulses of
its tugging slow. The reel hums hot and fills with line.

It surfaces, planing clumsily against the line. Mag cranks
steadily and the fish is close. As it swings its paddle snout up,
Charlie can see the deep, sad eyes—repentant with pain or fear—

behind the paddle snout. When he sees the hooks barbed through its sleek-skinned back, he wonders why it doesn't cry out or squeak or something.

It rises with slow, fin-quivered resignation alongside the boat. It is nearly half as long as the boat itself and rides silver green in the light of the moon. "Jesus!" Charlie cries, fascinated by the eyes, the power and bigness of it.

Mag doesn't gaff it. He leans over and, nearly tipping the boat, pulls it over the gunwale and stands on it, deftly cutting the two barbs of the table hook with a plier and pushing the barbs out so there is barely a mark where the hooks have been. "Old sinner! Old sinner!" he chants. The fish is strangely quiet while Mag cuts off the hooks.

Swat! the tail slaps Charlie's face like a great wet hand and he nearly cries out from the pain and blear of it.

"Sinner!" Mag yells. He is out of his shirt and bent over the fish. Then the two of them—man and fish—are up in the boat as fish begins to thresh around again. Mag is wrestling the fish, the two of them kicking and flap dancing, the snout wagging at the moon until the two of them fall in and disappear into the dark flow of the current.

Charlie cuts the motor and lets the boat drift. Then he worries that he has gone back too far. He tugs the starter rope and eases the boat upstream, worrying. The moon lights the path of the water, but the path of the water is wide and empty. He feels like bawling, but can't. "Who is he?" he keeps asking himself. ". . . Who is he?"

He knew that he *would* see him and he sees him standing in the river on concrete steps cut up through a thick abutment and leading to the buildings above it. He is mink slick with wetness. He hugs himself and laughs crazily. Charlie turns the boat toward him and brings it up close to the bottom steps.

"You see?" Mag cries, dancing there in the cold moonlight. "You see the old sinner, Charles? You see what I told you, Charles, my boy?"

"Where'd he go?" Charlie cries.

"He's out there feelin' sorry for himself, but he liked it, the old sinner. He'd come out of the water and walk down the streets right up to the sun in the mornin' if he could. But he can't! He can't. This is close as he gets, the old sinner. This is as close as we get, Charles, don't you see? Everything is tryin' to get better, but sometimes all it gets is a few minutes of it, do you know?"

"Should I run it in? I can use an oar."

"No, you throw me that roll of clothes I got in that bag."

"Aren't you coming?"

"Throw me the *clothes*! I'll get a ride back!"

Charlie lofts the bundle of clothes up on the steps with one hand, pushing them like a shot putter pushes his shot. He feels a deep anguish, a terror at seeing something so life deep and creation deep that there are no words, no questions even. Where is everybody? Charlie wonders. Where have the people gone? Why isn't anyone seeing this except me?

"Now take her back!" Mag yells, waving Charlie up river with one hand as he pulls the clothes on.

"I can't!" Charlie cries, thinking about the fish deep in the current and about shearing a propellor pin and loneliness—especially loneliness.

"You get your ass back there! You take it back where it belongs!" Mag yells.

Charlie is startled to see that there are other men ranged on the steps above Mag—tall, confident men, a dozen or so. They are all smiling. At what? Charlie wonders. How long have they been there? From behind them and shrieking through them comes the laughter of women, knowing laughter, nearly as deep as the laughter of men. The town, too, suddenly begins an orchestration of lights and noises, a honking of horns and the thump of the beat of music in the heart of a bar someplace.

"Hurry up!" Mag yells. "I'm not standing here all night!"

Laughter. Charlie torn between fear and pride. Mag climbs up the steps and through the rank of smiling men and into another region of muted men's and women's voices above.

He wants to cry because everything is so out of place like in a bad dream. He wants to cry because the men above him on the steps are like mannequins. They don't seem to belong there. Nothing seems to belong except the fish. The river rapples and flashes on the lower steps in the moonlight; the motor chortles and begins to shake from too much low throttle.

He throttles out into the stream and heads the boat north into the widening of the river just out of Pierre. He whimpers a little but the boat is heavy and steady in the current and he begins to remember the river as it flows toward him in the silver-yellow moonlight. He begins to feel better, but he worries about the fish. He wonders if it might be following him, not to hurt him but to lift his squinting sad eyes up into the light and arch his wounds into Charlie's sight. But Charlie figures he sulks somewhere, heaving his gills and healing his marks and remembering or forgetting.

The boat comforts him because it's steady in the current. He passes no one. It's too early for that. Shoals gleam and flash; the boat runs through the deep water next to them. Charlie's steering arm is strong but detached.

The shack there ahead of him beyond the hulls and husks of Mag's boats. The chickens, the wild chickens, have come back to roost in the little cottonwood trees. They are silver white ghost blotches in the moonlight. Charlie hates them and wishes the minks and raccoons would finish them off.

Up on the shore he leans the outboard motor against the side of the doorway into the dugout. Up river, the dam looms like a great shadow but in the span of bright moonlight its lights have dimmed and, except for the howl of the turbines, it seems asleep. The moon sees everything and touches everything, but it touches the earth softly. Only people are crazy under it.

He goes inside into the blackness and man smells and cooking smells. None of it bothers him because the light outside is silver clean and has washed him and because he is not afraid of the river and never should've been. He stumbles against the hard edge of his army cot, falls and drifts into sleep. Somewhere there are coyotes barking, close and invisible. He's afraid he may dream about the fish, but the fish is downstream and he remembers the steadiness of the big wooden boat. The river flows and Charlie knows he will never have another day like this one. He touches his cheek with his hand, thinking of her, and is comforted.

Breath and a Shadow with Popcorn

K.P., K.P., K.P.—he writes the initials secretly inside the cover of his notebook while he sits in class, always keeping something over them. It's an evocation, a little prayer, a desire he has to mark out somehow and someplace. Kim Pettigrew sits behind him in all three of the classes they're both in and he wishes she were up front so he could look at her without turning. If he turns, his eyes will have to swing by Dick Bissonette's dark, steady hatred and the others will know why he's turning and will begin to tease and might hold up obscene signs behind their notebooks. He looks for photos of her, but the best he can find is a silly little one from a ragged old yearbook in the library. He hates that one because her face is pinched into a toothy smile and the face is like the face of a boy—mischievous and sexless.

He relives the moments in the tall grass a thousand times, thinking about it. It. What if? Why didn't he push her down and thrust his hand down under her belt. Why hadn't he? He should've. Could he have? Only a few clothes, a thin cover of clothes. Oh, dark moist electric fur! If only . . . He thinks about it a thousand times and pulls himself out of it a thousand times. So close! So lovely. It tires him.

And she—looking always the same, as if nothing had ever happened, turning once only to smile briefly and shyly. She doesn't linger after class even and always walks in a covey of girls. He can't call her on the telephone. He can't. Don't ask him why he can't. That means that he won't be able to talk to her and that means it will go on and on.

He begins to believe that maybe something terrible is wrong. He begins to believe that, among other things—dark, sinister things—he is ugly. His nose—he pushes it into plastic contortions as he leers into a mirror. His mouth he regards as a piece of rubber that no girl would ever . . . His feet seem monstrous and sometimes they smell. His hair he combs with angry strokes of a big-toothed white comb, but it's no use really. His mother insists on haircuts and he wears his hair shorter than many of the others, but it always hangs off to one side in a stiff, bent brush. And he hates it.

He tries other things. He makes loud noises in the hall when Kim walks past. And once he jumps up to slap-touch a transom window over a classroom door. It cracks and he's sent to the principal's office. Why did he do it? Showing off his tip-off jump? He guessed so. Does he understand it's school property and his mother and all the others have to pay for it and now he'll have to pay? Yes, he says, although it sounds like it'll be paid for twice.

There's a poem the 11th Grade English teacher hands out. It's called "Constantly Risking Absurdity." It's about a poet trying all kinds of things on a high wire and risking making a fool of himself. Miss Drew, Old Iron Hair as they call her, asks Charlie to tell everybody what it means. "Is it only about a poet? Is it about what it means to be a human being generally?" she asks very earnestly.

"I don't know. It don't make sense," Charlie says, knowing the "don't" is stupid, but doing it anyway for the others.

"It don't make sense?"

"Not to me."

"Do you take risks?" Tittering in the room, like a rising of small birds.

"I guess so."

"Don't you usually take them when you're trying—really trying something?" More tittering.

"And isn't it then that—say on offense in basketball—a hard lay-up—that you can either look terrific or terrible?"

"Beats me," he says, and then, grabbing at the opportunity, adds, "I never try that hard." Laughter, even a wry smile on Dick Bissonette's face.

"I don't believe you, Charlie," she says, removing her shell-rimmed plastic glasses and staring at him with eyes deep with reading and correcting papers. She doesn't let it drop though. She leans toward Charlie over the music stand she keeps her notes on and says, again, "I don't believe you."

"Oh, he's a little fibber," Dick Bissonette says.

"What? What? You may be a classic case of arrested development, Richard," she says, her words hard and quick blows at Dick Bissonette.

That's bad. She spoils hours of good feeling and at least some tolerance of what she's trying to do by suddenly striking out with things like that. Nobody quite understands the words, but everybody gets the insult.

"But, of course, nobody's perfect," she adds—too late. A coolness pervades the room. She takes the glasses off again. We must look far away, Charlie thinks—and we are now. You can lose people easily, he thinks to himself.

They file out after class very slowly and Dick glares back over toward her standing there looking a little bewildered. But she takes her glasses off and, Charlie thinks, watching her, that she has gone away for a little while.

"Could I see you for just a second, Charlie?" Her voice is kind, not apologetic. He turns, distracted for only a second by Kim's passing on the other side of the room and by the others' staring at him and asking with their eyes and faces, "Why do you talk to her? Why do you give her friendship by even talking to her?"

Charlie waits and lets her walk over to him. The others are gone. They're alone in the room with something.

"Oh, it was terrible, I know," she says, "but I sometimes lose patience with the games we all play. I play like I'm teaching and I give grades for attendance and in the fond hope that the miracle of my voice has left indelible lines of poems inside their heads. And you play I don't care and I don't read and I'm indifferent and I'm kind of one of them, but you're not."

"I got baseball practice." He's watching the door nervously.

"Sounds harmless enough—the great American game but it's an official American game. Pretending you're not aware of anything is the unofficial game you're playing."

"I don't . . ." he begins. He wants to get the hell out of there. Somebody is tearing at his cover, is getting close.

"Ah, but you do. Are you trying to be a Native American? But then, what is one? If you're trying very hard are you getting *at* anything? You could be growing up absurd. In fact I think you are."

"Listen, I don't mean to be rude, but that's crap!" he says. He's getting angry and he knows he doesn't have much time to get to baseball practice.

"You think I insulted you, but growing up absurd means there is a terrible contrast between what you want deep inside you and what's happening or what you're really doing. Don't you know that you've got to get the two together?"

"I don't understand poetry like you do."

"Oh crap poetry. It's your life too."

"You *said* it."

"You are going to have to take some risks. If you want to act ignorant with everyone then do it, but *know* you're doing it and if you don't like the ignorance part of it just read and listen quietly. There's a voice inside you. It's called your destiny. It's what you've got to do to be happy."

"I'm sorry, but I've got to go."

She looks weary then, as weary as Mr. Hale so often looks in American history. And yet down in her eyes there's a toughness, a something that hasn't given up.

"Did you read any of Ferlinghetti's other poems?"

"No."

"Here!" She thrusts a mimeographed sheet at him. The violet print on it is barely readable. "Here! Find out what happened to America. Find out what it means to understand the West. Hide it and read it. Just read it."

He takes it and hurries into the late afternoon hallway. When he pauses to look at the poem before throwing it he reads a couple of lines. It's a poem called "Starting From San Francisco." It's too long. He has no time for long poems. He reads about the locomotive and the death faces and he thinks about the locomotive that ran over the bridge behind Mag and him—only for a second he can hardly acknowledge. When he turns around after crumpling the poem and tossing it he sees Miss Drew. Her face is iron and her voice seems to come from an iron place.

"Absurd! Charlie! Absurd!" she calls at him as he hurries out into the May sunshine and fire-green grass.

It is that night after practice that he sees Kim again with her parents. Her father's new gray Chevrolet is parked at the end of the walk that leads up to the front door of the high school. The three of them—her parents and she—are standing for just a moment on the sidewalk, almost as if they are posing for a photograph. They do not look like the other families. Her father's hair is short and trimmed neatly and he wears horn-rimmed glasses. He's tall and leans slightly over the other two, his hands in the pockets of a gray suit. His eyes are hard but not strong, his legs are so lanky they seem to bend backward at the knees.

Her mother's face is loose over the bones, her mouth grim, the eyes blurred with something. Her hair is shoved up into a dark mass on one side. Her stomach bulges in the blue dress and her legs are thin. She leans to one side away from the man who leans over her. The mound of hair seems like the only strength there as if all her vitality had grown into it.

Kim, oh lovely reed-slim girl in a tan coat, her legs dark, dark brown, knees supple, her eyes soft dark brown. He remembers. The mouth is worlds away; the curve of her belly in the grass under him is a haunting thing inside his own belly and loins.

For a moment he catches her eyes. They are strangely bright and open, seeing him. They remember with him and are shyly glad and wistful as she looks out of the photo of her family standing there together.

She coughs, and, standing there with his rolled-up sweaty jeans and the flat supple pitchers glove, he looks into the father's eyes.

Hate. No. Contempt? No. He drops his own eyes, averting the look. What is that look? It says, Stay out of this picture. It says, Go away. It says, I don't like you and I saw it and stay away. It says, This is why she doesn't talk to you.

When he turns to look at them again they're walking up the thick sandstone steps into the school building, the father's arm over Kim's shoulders, the mother a little behind the two of them. They pause at the door. Her father steps back, opening it and allowing her mother to go in. Then—just then—her father's eyes find him again with their cold stare. He feels something is terribly wrong. With what?

He stands alone. The other young men have wandered in a noisy, bustling little army toward the pop machines and candy bars at the Mobil station. Even pitching—and he's good at it—he feels circled by young men who don't quite like him or trust him. He catches it in a lot of ways. "You bat like you're going to take a crap," Blue Elk says to him, not smiling but smirking and then looking at the others. If he's not quite on with his curve and walks a few, he knows they won't say anything smart. But they won't try to pick him up either the way they do with Blue Elk, coming up to him and saying, "You got it going now. Pour it on" and things like that. Sometimes his stomach hurts and he feels tired as hell. And sometimes he feels like somebody dropped him down from the sky right into the middle of a strange land.

East over the river and south a hawk hangs on fire in the red sun through the western storm clouds. It is feathering the thermal drifts over the buffalo grass and water and earth. When it pivots on wing, its underside is brown as autumn grass, but in the blood light of the late sun it burns as red as the horse on the sign at the Mobil station. Am I strange? Am I queer? he asks himself. Why do I think about hawks and horses? What is wrong with me? And what does the hawk think in the narrow bones of his head? And am I thinking or is something thinking in me and him and all things?

It tires him and he walks home. When he gets there he showers and lies on his bed. He thinks about the photo there in the wall but he doesn't touch it because Nancy has found it and he wonders if she checks the exact position of it to find out if he's been looking at it . . .

Nancy wakes him up. He turns over abruptly to hide the great hardon bulging in his jeans.

What is it? he asks into his pillow. He wonders, Does she see it?

"Did you have a good practice?"

"It was o.k."

"Do you see Kim at school?"

"Sure."

"But not otherwise?"

He wants to turn and see what's in her face, but he can't just yet. Why, why do they do this? he asks himself, resisting an impulse to slam his fist down on the bed.

"But not outside school." She answers her own question and then she sits on the edge of the bed very slowly and carefully. He wiggles over toward the wall.

"Kim is very sick," she says.

"What do you mean? Why are you telling me?"

"I wondered if you knew, that's all?"

"How would I know. She acts funny or something, that's all I know."

"I'm sorry, Charlie. She acts funny because her parents got after her."

"Because of me? I saw them today and he looked at me like I was poison or an evil spirit or something."

"Her father wants her to get someplace. He probably thinks we're not good enough or that you're like the others—not going anyplace. He's ambitious—I understand that."

He turns over then and sees her face. It's kind and soft but not pitying. "The others think I think I'm going someplace—wherever that is—and they don't really like me I don't think," he says.

"That comes and goes," she says. "Give it a little time. When you're young every thing that happens is like it is happening only to you and is terrible, but give it a little time. Kim will be back again and she'll be well."

"What's wrong with her?" he asks finally.

"It's T.B. They thought it was allergies and let it go and let it go. It wasn't a good doctor and it was too late."

"She coughed a little," he says. Saying it tugs at his heart because he remembers her mouth too.

"She liked you," Nancy says.

"She never said anything after we got the bike."

"That was two things. One I told you. The other is that she probably didn't want you to get it."

Chill. Get it? Do I have it? he asks himself.

She touches his foot very gently. "Her father didn't let her take the tests with the other Indian kids—probably because he thought their new house and kitchen and things wasn't going to let it happen."

"I took it and it turned red," he says, "The test for it, I mean."

"Most do. We have a lot of it among people here. It's one of the things we want to get away from."

"When is she going?"

"Tomorrow."

"Where does she go?"

"South someplace, I think." She pauses then, perhaps to let him have his moment before she goes on. "Charlie, you should go for a chest x-ray I think."

"Why?"

"It'd be a good idea, that's all. It's free and I'll take you in tomorrow. I'm sure it'll be all right."

"I can go myself."

"All right." Another pause and interval of silence as she gets up and goes out into the kitchen.

Bittersweet. He catches himself at a bittersweet game. She didn't want me to get it, he thinks, but he also thinks, There is something wrong with me that people don't like.

He gets up.

"I want to take the car," he says to Nancy.

"Not tonight, but tomorrow you can take it."

"Shit. I can take it to get a fucking x-ray!"

"Oh, Charlie, don't! I just have to get someplace tonight. You can have it tomorrow night. Come and eat now. Aren't you hungry?"

"Fuck tomorrow!" He says it directly at her face and then, grabbing his shoes, slams out the door, limping first into one shoe and then another as he cries into and out of himself, "Who gives a fuck! Who gives a fuck!"

He walks toward downtown Ft. Pierre.

"Hey, Charlie!" Billy Whitefeather yells to him, driving up alongside and sitting there in the old Buick Roadmaster like a squirrel on a tan sofa.

"What'a you want?" he says, but getting into the car right away anyway because there is practically no place to go anyway.

"Old Squaw Bird that got Blue Elk arrested for not paying for a little shit batch of popcorn, we are going to do something for him in his popcorn wagon as soon as it's dark," Billy says.

"Why not?" Charlie says.

The hydraulic lifters in the old Buick clatter like hail on tin but the big car moves out, Billy cranking the wheel with great swings of both hands because there's so much play in the steering wheel.

"Blue Elk will hook a rope over the tongue of it and onto the bumper of old Swenson's cop car he always parks right in front of it so he can eat free popcorn."

"I don't know," Charlie says, thinking, Is that all there is? Is that all there is to do, for Christ's sake?

"There will be popcorn all over town."

"There is already on Friday night."

"That old shit is going to be surprised," Billy says, cranking at the wheel and wiggling his bony thin monkey body as he talks.

"He's not so bad as all that."

"He's an old fart who got Blue Elk arrested and cost him $100 and his father hit him a lot of times. Now we're going to take a look."

"Scout it, huh?"

Billy reaches under the seat and pulls out a squashed black felt man's hat. He punches it out and puts it on with one hand as he aims the Buick down the road, squinting into the chrome hood ornament. "Indian mafia!" he says.

"Indian idiot asshole!" Charlie says, getting into the spirit of things and not giving a damn.

The popcorn wagon, a hulking wooden vehicle which resembles a small stagecoach painted white and windowed in with tall auto safety glass, sits on rubber tires behind the white Dodge city police car. Black lettering proclaims tall bags of "DELISHUS

POPKORN" at 20 SENTS or 30 SENTS" or "BUTERED 40¢." Inside, a squat man with black eyes and a nose like a magpie's bill bends at his work. When he empties the hot popper, yellow-white cascades of popcorn pile against one window like white clover. He salts the pile with quick shakes of a big tin salt shaker.

"Boy, is that old bird in for a ride," Billy says.

"That could be dangerous," Charlie says.

"I seen it in a movie, something like this," Billy says. "American Pie, it was."

"This ain't no movie."

"What you want to do anyway? That old man screwed Blue Elk. What else you want to do anyway?"

Charlie slumps into the greasy, tattered mohair of the front seat. "Nothin!" he says. "There's nothin".

The engine idles, clattering. Billy adjusts his hat, eats a candy bar, pulls at a pint of vodka and pushes it at Charlie. "Go ahead," he says. "There's no smell on your breath at all, but that's my last candy bar."

The vodka makes Charlie light-headed and the cares of the day float away somewhere after a few more minutes.

A car roars by and flashes its lights.

"That's the signal! It's on!" Billy squeals.

Billy wheels the old Buick through an alley and parks it where they can see the police car and the popcorn wagon up to their right about half a block just at the intersection of Main and Brule Avenue.

The policeman, Archie Swenson, dozes in the front seat of the car, his left elbow resting on the window sill. From time to time he plucks a kernel of popcorn out of a white sack with the tip of his tongue. His face is florid white and amorphous in the car under the streetlight.

"The two of them are goin' to get it," Billy says. "And there's nobody around hardly on the street."

Two small Indian children stand at the window of the popcorn wagon, thrust coins up at Squaw Bird and receive bags of corn. They smile and walk away happily.

The car roars out of an alley toward Billy and Charlie. It's honking and the driver is flashing its lights up and down as it squeals and careens down the middle of the street.

"Holy shit!" Billy squeals. "It's the decoy car!"

Through the noise and flashing headlights the two of them can see Archie Swenson throw his popcorn out the window, reach down to start the car, and then reach up to turn on the pursuit lights just as the car roars by Billy and Charlie.

"Now for sure!" Billy screams.

The police car lurches out a few feet, tilts when the rope snaps tight and jump-hounces out into the Main Street, the popcorn wagon trailing it in a wriggling trail of pulled out wires and spilling popcorn.

In the quick lurch and swing of the popcorn wagon at the end of the rope behind the car Charlie sees the look of terror on the face inside. It is stricken with heat and motion and stings of flying popcorn.

"Holy shit!" Billy cries. "It's comin' our way!"

The rope has snapped and the wagon, after jouncing its two right wheels up on the curb, is running on a wobbly but unerring course directly toward them.

In a second it's on them in a crash and shriek of sheet metal as it climbs up the wide black expanse of the hood of the Buick and, shattering the windshield, hangs itself up on the top of the car, it's rubber tires spinning rapidly as it rocks creaking on the top of the car.

And there it sits. Inside, crouching under the dash and bawling laughing-crying-screaming, Billy and Charlie hug each other and wait for the police because the doors of the car are jammed and they're both drunk.

Nancy is there at the police station to post bail and to bring him home in the morning.

"I wasn't going to do anything that dumb," Charlie says to her, ". . . and I'll have to pay you back."

"I was afraid of tonight," she says. "It wasn't a good night for me either. But Mr. Porter down at the law office will help you. He won't get you off, but he can help you."

"It was stupid," Charlie says, trying to get some of the smaller glass particles out of his pants cuffs. Then he begins to laugh hysterically. And she stops the car and they both sit there and laugh hysterically until they are both a little sad and very tired.

"Never broke but one window and he only got a little burn on one hand from grabbing at the hot popper," Charlie says. "He must've fallen into his popcorn. The guy at the police station says to me, 'what the hell you Indians think this is—a stagecoach raid or something?' But it could've been bad."

They both laugh a little then and Nancy drives home in silence, her eyes sad with something else deeper—some worry that Charlie sees is getting worse and worse and doesn't have to do with him or Mag either because Mag doesn't see her any more.

Their fines are heavy in spite of Mr. Porter's quiet consultation with Judge Breamer.

"You could have killed or very seriously injured an old man who sells a little popcorn for a little money to children," he tells them all gravely and slowly.

Mr. Porter and Charlie agree that they will tell the judge that after school is out—a couple of weeks away—Charlie will be working all day all week out of Ft. Pierre and out of mischief for the summer. "Why not?" Charlie says, "There's nothin' here now anyway this summer." The plea, as Mr. Porter calls it, helps a little—there's no probation, only some damages to pay. It helps in a way but the others resent Charlie's getting off a little easier."You see," Nancy says afterward". . . you see that knowin the law and being educated can do things for people."

What about Billy and Blue Elk and Standing Cloud?"

"Why, he kept them out of jail or detention."

"I don't understand it," Charlie says.

"You will someday."

"I mean I don't understand how just words change something. It was a mean thing to do."

"Yes it was, but if you're lucky the mean things you do when you're young don't hurt permanently. Older people do things sometimes that hurt permanently."

"Funny thing is . . ." Charlie begins.

"Funny?"

"I mean that Squaw Bird kind of seemed to like it and talks about it like it was great and funny or something."

"We were lucky this time," she says, as they pull up into the driveway.

There's a letter on his bed—in a little square blue envelope. He picks it up, knowing what it is and wondering why there's no return address on it. He pushes his door shut, sits on his bed and holds it a little while before he opens it:

Dear Charlie,

I have to go away for a while because I'm sick. I hope you're alright. I'll remember.

Kim

He reads it over and over again and then over and over again. And yet, he wonders what it says and why it's so terribly short when there is so much to know.

11

Summer on the River

"Don't you watch now!" Her voice ripples behind him with throaty laughter into the soft wind coming over the sand bar. He has anchored the fishing boat on the big lake above the dam.

He holds the beach towel behind him—a big terrycloth double one, green and blue and store fresh. He holds it behind him as he stands, spread-armed with the corners of the towel tucked into the bottom of his hands and the middle of it over his shoulders and the back of his head.

"Is there anyone anywhere near?" the voice behind him asks again, this time a little breathlessly.

He adjusts his feet in the bottom of the boat, holding it steady as she moves her thick, fleshy feet and drops the slacks and then, even more softly, the other things, the other things.

He feels like an ass. Ahead of him the great expanse of water is virtually motionless, blue gold in the morning sun and edged with great sand fingers and the dead tops of drowned cottonwood trees. There are slim traceries of boats trolling and speeding far north of them, but there is nobody near them either in the water or on the long rolling rise of the eastern shore. Standing there makes him a little dizzy. His arms begin to ache and his mind drifts on the slow pilings of deep water.

"Is there?" she asks again, pushing her words into his reverie.

"No. The boats are too far away too," he says.

"Do you mind?"

"I guess not." His arms are aching now.

He can feel the sway of her upright body behind him and then he can feel her turn, a slow rotation of rubbery full flesh—thick and deep, but not fat.

"I'm going in. I've always wanted to. It's a kind of thing Dr. Schussler said I need to do."

He doesn't understand. Is she sick? Is it another kind of exercise? Dr. Schussler.

"You don't understand, do you? You don't know what kind of doctor, do you? Lucky boy!"

"No," he says, gritting his teeth now and getting angry. He rocks a little with weariness, his leather boots thumping and squeaking against the aluminum. And he hates aluminum boats even though he doesn't have to paint them.

"Oh, I'm sorry!" She touches the towel and then, a breast touches his back and his loins hollow out and pulse back. The core of him is touched, the dark core of muscle and root.

"Oh, God, I've let you stand like a slave and hold that towel for hours. I'm an indecisive person. I just *do* things like that."

He expects her to say more, but she doesn't. The boat tilts dangerously as she steps alongside the motor in the prow and jumps in. Even as she jumps the weight of her flesh sounds in the water.

He waits, his heart beating hard.

"You can put the blanket down, but don't turn yet," the voice yells at him. "When I come back toward the boat please stand like you are until I'm back in, please!" she yells through the splashing and girl giggling.

She swims behind him in little weak circles made with sprints of slow crawl strokes. He thinks. Charlie Goodthunder, ass and Indian guide, 20 dollars per day. Opens beers, puts stuff in the boat, baits hooks, smiles when fat-assed old guys from Milwaukee fart in the boat or stand up and pee in beer cans or the water or the bottom of the boat. Charlie Good Thunder, ass and Indian guide. Gets 15 dollars a day less than Mag, which is all right.

He's in a bad mood. Seven days a week of hauling boats, of saying "Yes, I think I can find some walleyes" when the vice president of Remis Bag asks, "Say, guy, you *are* going to get us some fish, aren't you?" Of saying, "We can't always hit. Wall-eyes are like some women: some days they will; some days they can't and some days they won't. Ha! Ha! And then there's, "Do we have to pay if we don't get anything?" But mostly what gets him is something else. They do things in front of him as if he's not there: dress, undress, fart, pick, scratch—even the big tube of Preparation H—what a hog bottom that was!

Charlie Good Thunder—nigger Indian or Injun or something
. . .

"I can feel the bottom!" she is squealing. "I should walk up on the sand. Don't look!"

But he does—a glance furtive as the ones at the magazine stands when the man next to him turns a page. She is splashing up out, her breasts swinging heavily purple-tipped, her back rippling with long smooth muscles, the white at the small of the back. And the loaves, he thinks, the loaves of her ass. The legs heavy, vein mottled, but bronze curved too. And the loaves of his own hunger. It all makes him sick with wonder and anger. Why do they do it? Or, why do *they* do it—the older ones so ripe and rich fleshed they do not understand a boy can't start with them or thinks he can't. If she turns, he thinks . . . if she turns, I will really hate her, but I wish she would, but I will hate her.

Glance two—furtive glance. She, like a beached fish, curved in little arcs—splashes in shallow water, her legs floating. He hears her splashing and knows that she is in deeper water and that he has been spared and yet tormented. Her husband, he thinks and then does not allow himself to think about her husband as he thinks about her husband and everything.

The lake soothes him as he looks north out on its flat, blue-gold expanse. The long peninsular sand fingers run out into it and across it, to the west, Cheyenne Creek flows into it. Not entering it like man and woman, but flowing softly, not entering, but joining, flowing without pain.

"I'm coming in!" she cries behind him. "Please put up the towel for me!"

He stands up wearily and hefts the towel up, letting it fill out a little as the breeze picks up. The splashing comes closer and then the boat leans under her hand.

When she tries to climb in, the boat tilts and Charlie staggers, but then, suddenly she's in and wiping and putting clothes on. The smell of the water in her hair is old, leaf rich and old.

"Oh, thanks!" she says finally.

When he turns around he sees her hair is stringy wet and gray-streaked dark. But her face is rosy and scrubbed and happily calm.

"You think I'm crazy, don't you—and insensitive for doing this, but I can't go out alone; I'm afraid."

He doesn't reply. She slips by him so he can run the motor and he avoids her eyes because they are examining his face as she moves by.

"You saw, didn't you? Oh, well, how could you not see? The boy next door when I sunbathe—oh, well.—It's not so much. I'm 43—43. I don't even like to go to the beach, but here the sky and the sun—it's all right. They don't say anything. They're like you and I like you. You're not angry, are you? Oh, God, I remember how crazy it was. When will I ever . . .? Now I tan to cover the little veins. Oh, well, do you want to go somewhere else? I don't know where to go."

"Do you want to try for some fish," he says finally. He has heard her voice falling slowly as she has spoken and he sees her eyes have taken on edges of weariness.

"I don't care," she says. "Drive on and on. At least today I know my husband is really playing golf." She laughs then, opens the cooler sitting between them, opens a can of beer and hands it toward him. Then she opens some wine.

"You don't even know what I mean, do you? You don't even know how a city can swallow up not just all your dreams but all your suspicions and all your certainties and then push them all back up like black corks on top of the water. It's not like out here where you can see who's watching and who's where and who's not where. People get away from you in the city."

She has finished the small bottle of wine already he sees and has spilled some on the knee of her tan slacks. He starts the motor and, reaching past her again, pulls the anchor rope up. As his face passes by hers he can smell the rank fruit smell of the wine in her mouth.

"I've been to Minneapolis," he announces over the motor as he steers southward. "I saw the IDS tower."

She laughs, but not unkindly. "You saw him? You saw him all right. They call it the Empress of the North, but it's him." She seems to shift suddenly, then, her voice lowering again. "Did you have a good time?"

"No, I didn't like it. Mag didn't either."

"Mag, the man at the marina?"

"He owns it and all."

"Is he your boss?"

Charlie feels the sun hot on his neck. "Sure," he says.

She laughs again. "You know," she says, "you're not much older than my tennis coach in Minneapolis. He's twenty or twenty-two, a student at the University."

"I'm not that old," Charlie says, thinking, How old do I look? Is that it? Is that it?

"No, you're not!" Laughter. A slap on Charlie's knee and she is suddenly man strong and bone heavy to him.

And yet she looks at him as he guides the boat in and out of the little bays receding among the sand peninsulas. She looks sadly at him and he turns away.

"You want to try some fishing?" he says.

"No." She sits with her hands draped between her legs as she answers.

"Wide and empty is the sea." Her words seem to come from another place. She sighs. "You know," she says. "I know older women always embarrass young men."

"It's o.k.," he says.

She looks at him again, half-staring and yet dull in the eyes. "I know I'm sad when I look at you because you're young and fine. Someday you'll understand that and please forgive me."

"It's o.k.," he says.

"I'd like to go back," she says, not looking at anything at all.

"I can find some fishing if you want."

"No, you're nice, Charlie, but I'm done now."

He doesn't hurry. He thinks about losing half a day's pay.

"I'll pay you for the whole day."

"No, I can take out somebody else."

"I'll bet you can. Now I won't ask any more stupid things. Except, are you going to stay out here the rest of your life?"

"I don't know. I might go to school."

"College, you mean?"

"I'm not sure."

"But you can always come back if you want to. Except winter must be awful. I hate winter, winter in the box. One day you wake up in Minneapolis and it's there."

"I got basketball," he says.

She looks up and closely at his face, the big beach towel over her knees. Her face is settled and tired and her eyes steady. "It wasn't very nice of me today, but I needed to. Did you see the movie *The Graduate*?"

"No," he lies, remembering.

"Thank God or you'd think even worse of me. I feel like I'm on the edge of something and I can't get away from it. The wine makes me dizzy."

"You swim o.k." he says because she is crying softly into the towel. Her hair is thin as she bends toward him and her shoulders quiver. He circles the boat out into the lake again to buy some time. She lifts her face into the cooling air, sniffs, pats his hand at the side of the boat. The boat makes great white slow circles.

"One day," she says, calmly, "you swim out far before you come back. Do you hate boxes?"

"I come out here or by the river below. I like the river below better, but I walk out—I just walk out and there's a big circle around." He is trying to make her feel better but he's sounding silly. "Should I go in?" he asks, seeing that she has stopped crying.

"Yes."

On the western shore above the dam he beaches the boat and cranks it up on the boat trailer with the windlass so he can haul it down to Mag's boat dock, which is on the river a mile and a half south. When he opens the pickup door on her side, she grabs his ears, kisses him roughly on top of his head and gets in.

"You can't win them all," she says, as they rattle into the fishing camp past the tents and vans.

"I could've found some fishing maybe."

She laughs then as she dismounts from the pickup. She lingers, holding the door and holding the balled-up towel tightly against her stomach. "I'll bet you could," she says.

Sitting there he sees the two ten-dollar bills lying on the seat. And through the windshield he sees, too, above the white golf shirt the face of her husband. It is tanned and round and smooth. The hard eyes glint with bemused contempt. Charlies drives past him, trying to not look at the face and guessing why the eyes are hard and what the glint of binoculars on top of the dam was all about.

He finds out. Because in the rear view mirror he can see Mr. Allen following with a steady and military step in the tan slacks. And Mag is waiting ahead, looking at both of them, his long face set hard too as it is when customers pull something or try to.

Mag waits, his hands on his hips. He and Allen have been talking about something, Charlie thinks. But what?

Mr. Allen, the husband, is there—so close that Charlie can almost step down on him from the pickup and, when he stands down on the ground, Charlie is close—too close to the eyes.

Mag waits.

Allen stands a little taller than Charlie. He seems to be raising himself like a bird about to strike at another as birds fight in the spring. Charlie looks down, resenting it.

"I'd like to go fishing," Allen says.

Charlie looks up and then at Mag. No help there yet. "You got half a day coming," he says. "Mrs. paid me for a whole day."

Glint. Overbearing. "I'll bet. Do you think she got her money's worth?"

"No," Charlie says. "She didn't fish at all."

"Well, I'd like to go out," Allen says, glancing toward Mag.

"On the river or what?"

"I'd like to go on the river."

"O.k."

Allen stands there. "It's a funny thing," he says. "You do this so well. You see, I'd like to go fishing but I can't find my tackle box—the one I paid a hundred dollars for at the Chicago Sportsman show. That's not counting the tackle."

"We got reels and stuff. You don't need much."

"Oh, but I do. I need my missing tackle. I like it."

The eyes try to pierce, but Charlie, sensing something, turns on Allen.

"I'll go get the boat ready if you want to look for it," Charlie says.

"Oh, but I have looked for it."

Charlie begins to walk away.

"Just a minute." He turns to Mag. "Before I get the sheriff out here do you want to look in his tent? Or should I?"

Charlie turns. Thinks how the soft paunch over the belt will take a punch.

"No," Mag says. "You aren't going to call the sheriff and you aren't going to pry in his tent . . ."

"Nothing?" Allen says. "This Indian kid gets to haul my wife up the lake for skinny dip stuff and . . ."

"He's no kid and he's honest. I don't need to look anywhere."

"Where'd he come from?" Allen asks, turning to Mag, his face flushing with anger.

"Good people," Mag says.

"I have no choice then? We have legal counsel in Aberdeen. You're not getting by with this." Allen is turning. "Are you going to look?"

"No."

And then she is there with the box, a huge tan plastic thing. Allen takes it, opens it. Layers of glinting metal spoons and multi-colored lures flash in the light. Truth, you son-of-a-bitch Charlie thinks.

"Oh, it's all there," she says. "Nothing of yours was taken today. It was under your bunk." She turns toward Charlie. "Boxes!" she exclaims. "Boxes! Boxes! Boxes!"

"You can just knock it off!" Allen says to her.

"Oh, I will."

As she walks away, Allen walks down toward the boat dock. "Which one is it?" he asks over his shoulder.

"Drown the bastard!" Mag whispers, standing next to Charlie. "You can drown the bastard. The tackle box is a floater." Then Mag yells, "Take number seven!"

Charlie sets up everything as Allen watches, standing on the dock. A wind is picking up and the boat clunks against the dock.

He holds the boat for Allen, but Allen doesn't step down in; he steps on the gunwale next to Charlie's hand. "Ow!" Charlie cries, faking it. With a yell and a splash Allen dunks in the shallow water, then rages up, wedged between boat and dock and swearing and then free. He climbs up on the dock.

"You little bastard, you did it on purpose!" he cries.

Mag is there then, one hand on Allen's shoulder; the other shoving the tackle box into the man's wet belly. Luckily the other boats and people are out on the water. Allen looks around, sees that he's alone.

"Now take your goddam bus and box and big shot mouth and get the hell out of here!" Mag says. "You are lucky after what you accused that you are walkin' and talkin'."

They stand together watching Allen do a mad wet dance up to the big van. Allen appears at the back window, a big towel over his face, his mouth working in terrible anger. What about her? Charlie wonders.

The van starts up, kills, backs up. As it grinds and roars past them Charlie sees her face framed in glass and despair in the back window.

"You didn't." Mag isn't smiling saying it.

"What?"

"No, you didn't. I shouldn't've asked. You don't have to take that from anybody. I had to wait a little. I was afraid of my own anger."

"Did you see her face?"

"Sure, but don't think too much about what you can't do anything about. There's some people comin' out that called from town—nice family people from Nebraska. If nothin' is biting you can take them up to the Hanes' stock dam for bullheads and bass."

"What time are they coming?"

"About an hour."

"I'm goin' to lie down awhile," Charlie says.

"Sure, but think about something else."

He does. There has only been one letter from the sanitarium.

He takes it out of the little packet of money and junk, but he doesn't read it. He tries to not think about her about how she would look that way in the water.

He drifts off and thinks about Kim. They are on a green lake, calm and deep and warm. Goldwing blackbirds cry and the diamond sand flashes on the water. Fluted green reeds whisper and bend over them. She smiles a lovely, blurred and unchanging smile as she swims. Her arms and legs seem thin as wings of a dragonfly caught on the water, but when she walks out far up the beach her legs are full and strong. She turns to look at him—turns the upper part of her body only. Her face is fragile, skeletal, her eyes deep and bright. Her breasts are high and the nipples tight purple buttons. She turns and he feels the deep, involuntary seepings start in his loins and fights it . . . She smiles and pulls back. He fights it and loses, loses it into his shorts.

When he wakes up he changes his shorts, stuffing the tallow wet ones under his cot. Outside, he sees Mag standing by the group of people—a family of parents and two young boys, all holding fishing rods and looking out at the water and then toward his tent. He knows Mag has been at the tent and left. He guesses he has seen something, but he knows nothing will be said and that the tent was given to him partly because he had seen such things before.

As he looks toward Mag, the old question comes back through his yawning and the stupor he feels after the nap. "Who are you?" he asks toward the man standing out there. Nobody I've met so far this summer among all these strangers has helped me know anything much—except what I don't want to happen to me. Is gettin' older meaning things happen to you you don't want to happen?

"You ready to show these people the river?" Mag yells.

"Sure!" Charlie yells back.

They are all smiling as he walks toward them—wide, hopeful smiles. Charlie looks at the two small boys. "Gee, it's a young guy that guides!" the younger one exclaims.

Charlie walks tall in their admiration and he hopes to hell this one will be just bullshit and fishing. And, still, he wonders, Who am I going to meet this summer and what is he going to tell me?

12

The Errand

The summer passes in jerks and starts and subtle broad changes in the riverscape. June is bright green-blue, with flowers nodding their heads in the buffalo and sweet grass on the hills and buttes. July is blue-gold and silver green, the great irrigation pipes throbbing and squirting in the rows of corn high along the east side of the lake.

August blazes him, burns him on the water, turns his face a deeper bronze. He is often sleepy with wind and heat and the slap, slapping of water. His muscles tune sinewy tight with rowing and with hauling anchors. Time is a beat of light and a flow of water. The water is clear, usually, and steady—except for the days of the high winds and howling storms.

He sits in the boats with them—dozens of them: bored wives nodding under wide straw hats, their flesh sweat cooking in the sun; men lean and tight at their rods and gleeful mad at the tug of the fish; children—some blond as angels—burning their faces; old men who bow and accept the end of a day or a season, smoking their pipes and quietly rejoicing; women querulous with discomfort and wishing they were not so far from clean kitchens and swimming pools and all the other things not found in a fishing camp. And young girls, flirting and flirting between silly questions: "Are you a Sioux or an Iroquois?" "What do you do in the *winter* out here?" or "Don't you love the Bee Gees?" Their shorts pull up tightly and he looks at them from behind his dark glasses. And some notice. Then they quiet down and seem afraid. And most seem silly and vain as the little dolls with frozen pink smiles their sisters keep in the back of station wagons and vans. They are like yellow birds tilting on tree branches and ready to fly somewhere else to tilt on tree branches. Because Kim is still steady in his mind, her face smiling up from the earth and grass. Brown eyes and dark hair for the sun. Not golden like the sun, but dark brown for the sun. He sometimes thinks on her wearily and suppresses little bleaps of pain.

"You watch those people from Iowa!" Mag says to him as Charlie stands on the dock above the boats.

"They takin' their own boat?"

"Sure, but you tell them that they can't even leave here without safety vests on. There are eight of them and they are goin' in one boat and won't rent another one."

The wind is strong and steady out of the northwest. It tires him. It makes him quiet. He doesn't answer Mag. Mag and he don't talk much. There is something wrong, but not between them. It's something in town and it's something that is going to happen and not just stay there unspoken.

He sees the family—a stand of coveralls and a couple of little dresses flapping in the wind. They hold their fishing rods like they're shovels or hoes. They also have thick cane poles. The father is lean and lanky tall, the mother cross-eyed and pink-faced plump.

"They look like they are goin' out to hoe burdocks," Mag says at Charlie's ear.

"Or have been doin' it."

"You watch 'em like you're just fishin' yourself."

"Can't you?"

"No."

"I'd like to go to town."

"I *got* to go to town."

"Well, shit!" Charlie says. "I get to sit out in the water and get nothing for nothing."

"I'm not explaining anything more to you. You just get out and watch them."

"What if I don't? That's not my job."

Mag turns at him then, his thumbs tucked into his belt and his blue eyes asking, "What's this? What's the matter with you?"

"You *do* it so I can get to town."

"Sonofabitch!"

The hard heel of the quick right hand on Charlie's shoulder. He staggers a little step forward and thinks of hitting back at Mag's angry face.

"Who, me?"

"You can't make me do this shit. It's not my job!"

Charlie catches sight of the big family still waiting there on the shore as if they are still posing for a picture and are afraid to lose their places and spoil it. Quiet people Charlie thinks. He can't look at Mag because he isn't mad at Mag. He doesn't know what he's mad at.

Mag sees it and his voice softens. "I haven't had much chance to talk to you. You remember the time you started shooting mudhens on the water because you missed all the mallards and bluebills? You were pissed at one thing and hurt another."

"What's that got to do?" Charlie asks, knowing that it *does* have to do with him.

"I'll pay you," Mag says. "Those cheap people don't have to pay but I'll pay you for watching. It worries me. We don't need a drowning out here now."

"I got money."

"But I haven't got time. There is a lawyer son-of-a-bitch—a *real* son-of-a-bitch—that is trying to get hold of this shore, the whole shore. He wants to make a recreation area out of it—a golf course and all that. I got to get in and go to a hearing. I know what you got on your mind—I got that on my mind too, but I got to get in. And if I have to stand here explaining any more I'm going to beat the shit out of you, by God!"

Charlie doesn't look at him or say anything. He looks out on the water and hears Mag's boots clat away behind him on the dock.

They are all up on the dock then, stepping into their boat. When they are all seated, the plastic gunwale is barely above the surface of the water at the back of the boat. They push off and the motor howls, thrusting the boat downriver toward the deep area he has told them to go to.

He follows a couple of hundred yards behind them and then anchors where he can see them.

They sit stiffly and seriously at work. They are farming, Charlie thinks. They are taking anything that gets hooked. They are farming the river like they are digging potatoes or something. They keep anything that comes in the boat.

The wind out of the northwest suddenly whips Charlie's boat at its anchor and then, under the scudding clouds, it begins to brass the water with steady howling power. Dust blows in biting, face-whipping clouds off the shore.

He stands up and yells at them, motioning them back. Their faces are strained with fear and they hurry to pull in their lines. The river current darkens, muscular with wind force. Somehow they get the anchor up. The boat bobs, water splashing in, and then turns northward up river howling under full throttle.

Following them, Charlie sees that the torque of the big motor at the back of the boat is tunneling so deeply in the water that the people's heads are level with the top. Squeaks of screaming children catch at his ears. If their motor stops they will capsize. And they are barely making progress. He tracks them, riding deeply in their churning green-white wake. They all seem suspended on the huge muscle of wind and current.

They make it. They tuck in under the little ring of cottonwoods around the fishing camp where the wind is weaker. The father is out of the boat, his face fierce with fear and anger as he swings the anchor rope over his shoulder and pulls the boat in. Charlie pulls his own boat in alongside.

The children shriek and bawl together as they jump out of the farmer's boat and then swarm around their mother. She bends over them, comforting with her hands and words as she sweeps them toward the panel truck. One of the little girls holds the dark wet crotch of her overall and sucks her thumb. "We could've drowned!" the other little girl shrieks.

Charlie helps the father haul his boat up on the trailer and winch it in. "This is a terrible place!" the father says over and over again. His overalls are wet up over the knees and his mouth tight with anger. "This is a mean place!" he says. "It damn near killed us all, by God! You ought to tell people about that god-dam river. We are goin' back and fish bullheads in Minnesota on a lake that don't go crazy. You people ought to tell people about this, by God. It ain't human!"

The mother sweeps around the side of the panel truck under a chorus of bawling faces at the windows above her. She wheels toward Charlie, a child under one arm, a rubber thing in its mouth. "This is no place for farm people," she says at Charlie. "We aren't coming out here again. And it's all empty out there, grass, grass, grass and wind, wind all the time. You Indian people can have it. We aren't going to be scared to death again."

And yet, though they seem to be on the verge of scolding him, they don't. They are scolding something else like it was mean to them and it seems silly to Charlie. These people who should know wind and rain and the forces of the sky are scolding the wind and the river and it seems stupid. They got no sense. They think they can sit on the river like they are sitting in the plow-ing in a grain wagon.

"You can tell your father or whoever it is that we are going to complain at the tourist center when we get in," the mother says.

"Come on, now. He come out to look after us, I think. We shouldn't've come out on it." The father pushes her toward the front of the panel truck. "He told us we had too many in the boat," he says to Charlie, nodding back toward sometime when Mag must've talked to him.

As the people leave, Charlie sees other boats coming up the river toward the camp. Suddenly, abruptly, the wind drops and the sky clears over the calming water. The boats pause and turn back to circle and then drop anchor again.

He walks through the camp and up on the brush-shaggy brow of the butte above the camp. The sun is yellow bright in the blue sky again and a brown hawk circles, circles over the river. The grass ripples in soft brown joyful runnings behind him. What is the source of my body in all this? he wonders.

It is not empty. He is not lonely. The rustling of leaves, the soothing of the shade, the ripple and flash of the water make him a little sleepy but not lonely. The sun is calm and bright. I am ashamed sometimes, but I don't know what I'm ashamed of. I am ashamed before the sun, but I don't know why. These things have no words but there is still somewhere behind all of them a word. These things are true and beautiful. There is something inside of me that I am ashamed of too because I'm not true to it.

These thoughts frighten him. He cries out one little weird cry but not a word. Then he listens and watches from inside himself but not so deeply inside himself. People scream and they complain; they talk and talk at you, but there's no strength in it. They think there's nothing to see, and nothing to hear, but there is the wind and something under the wind—a secret you listen for and never tell.

These thoughts frighten him because the voice that thinks them is his and not his. It is much older than he is or will ever be. He breathes up the solitude and feels stronger. I am learning something his voice says to him. And I don't know what it is or who is teaching me, it says to him. You are still at a window of glass, it says to him. There is something more, it says.

The car horn honks into his reverie and reaches out to him to call him back. At first he guesses it's another fishing party, but as he walks slowly toward the camp he's surprised to see that it's Nancy's. She honks again, holding the palm of her hand on the horn button because she doesn't see him walk up toward her on her right.

When he stands next to her on the driver's side he sees she is wearing a dark blue dress and he can smell the perfume she wears at the office. She jumps when she turns and sees him, jostling her glasses crooked. "Oh!" she exclaims. "Where did you come from? You scared me!"

He smiles at her, but he waits without speaking. He wonders what she's come for. And he feels a distance from her that he needs a little time to cross. He smiles as she bends to pick up some papers on the seat next to her.

"Mag is in town," he says finally.

She looks at him, examining his face carefully as she has so many times when she wonders what he's thinking. Her face is different, though—harder even if it is heavier than it was.

"I know that. That's why I'm here."

"There's something going on. He was upset when he left."

"Charlie?" A question. Something is coming I didn't expect he thinks. I've never seen her like this—her eyes bright with something big and new and maybe too big for her.

"It's Mr. Porter," she says.

"Mr. Porter?"

"Mr. Porter has plans to do something, to make something good out of all this. Look!" She is shaking. She has laid a wide sketch in black ink over the door sill. "He wants to make this whole part of the river into a recreation area—the biggest in this part of the country." Watching him again.

He sees "Golf Course" and "Missouri Luxury Motel" and "Marina of the West." He knows the river; he can see the place where the marina has been drawn over where the fishing camp is now.

"He doesn't want it, Mag doesn't."

"But, Charlie. Look. There's nothing here except a lot of old boats and a rickety dock and some tents flapping in the wind. It's nothing. There's nothing here."

"He doesn't want it."

"Oh, but he would if he could only see how beautiful it can be. And jobs for people."

"Mr. Porter wants it, but Mag doesn't."

She doesn't get out of the car. She's not that strong he thinks. What else does she want? he wonders.

"I want something for you and me besides an unfinished shack and an old car and people like the Pettigrew's looking down on us—not Kim, of course."

"Where are they looking down from?"

"That's not the point. When this is built I could be a manager and you can go to school and come back here and make something of your life. Can't you see out here how fabulous it would be? Not just dust and grass and empty space, but a big place on the river and people coming out here and fun and everything."

"Why does Mr. Porter need it? He's got stuff enough already. This is Mag's life. It's not just a place."

"Mag? There's a lot you don't know, do you? He's not a

responsible person. He doesn't really take *care* of things. He doesn't really *do* anything at all and he *can't* do anything for you except give you a summer job."

"It's not so bad."

"He's a big *boy*, Charlie. He runs a fishing camp and he never is going to do anything else."

"Why are you so mad at him? What is it he did except take me to Minneapolis when I would've gone anyway so he figured it was safer to take me. And he lets me keep good money . . ."

"If you just knew!" she says.

"I know a lot," he hears himself saying. He goes on: "I know you got mad and there is another man and now you're with Mr. Porter who gave you a job and is doing something to get a whole side of the river."

"He helped both of us when you were a baby. He helped us both when we were in trouble."

"Trouble? What kind of trouble?" He leans toward her, but she is looking away through the windshield. He can see that she has been acting a part she has to act and that she's already tired out straining at it. He doesn't press the question, but he can guess what the trouble was. Except that he doesn't know what his own part in the trouble was exactly.

"Oh, Charlie!" she exclaims. "We've got nothing. You see what has happened to so many people. What have we got? What's here? If we get something good here you can do something with your life and not have to move. You can stay here but it'll be so much better."

"What was I supposed to do?" he asks. He's looking up the road to see if Mag is coming.

"*Was* supposed to do? I guess talk to Mag. Maybe if he saw you weren't interested in this whole thing and you said something he might not fight the project."

"I won't," Charlie says.

"Well, there may be no stopping it. It's an area natural resources council thing and they can box him in or make tough regulations for him. Nobody benefits."

"You talk different," Charlie says.

"It's not to hurt Mag," she says. "He can get a lot of money for his land and he could run the whole boat part of the resort."

"But he won't. And how can anything be good for someone if he doesn't want it and can't do it?"

He can look down into the front seat of the car next to her. The papers she has gotten from Porter are there and the books she uses at the commercial college. And a little packet of white tablets in cellophane for her stomach.

"You're not mad at me, are you? I get so tired sometimes. I'm trying to do some things and I have to do them alone all the time. I don't want to fight you. I know you like it out here, but you can't stay here the rest of your life."

She looks into her rear view mirror and back up the road into the camp. "I suppose I'll have to go," she says.

"Why? He won't say anything."

She laughs. "He will now. By now he's been at the hearing and has found out how they can control road access and everything. He'll come roaring down the road in that old pickup and then he'll get drunk or something."

"Then it's not good for all of us?"

"Oh, Charlie, it's going on. People out here don't change; they don't even know how to. I'm not very good at saying things but it's going on and some people just fall back. See." She points up at the vapor trail of a jet. The trail arcs, thickens and disappears behind the invisible plane. "It's true, isn't it?"

"I don't know," he says, thinking she talks different. The plane isn't going anywhere I want to go. The truth is a serious thing.

Then, suddenly, the old high-rumped green pickup truck is rolling slowly down toward them, its worn shocks clonk-clonking as Mag winds the steering wheel and aims the truck toward a little copse of trees where he always parks it out of sight and where birds methodically splatter it with white zag-splotches.

She sees it. "Oh!" she exclaims, twisting to push the maps and papers under and into the briefcase. "Come and see your mother once in awhile!" she cries as she bends, frowning, over the steering wheel and tries to start the old Plymouth. He re-presses an ironic smile as he watches her. He doesn't quite like the way he feels and the way he studies the back of her head and doesn't quite like her anymore but feels something else new and not pleasant. "Oh! Oh!" she exclaims.

The car doesn't start and when she begins pumping the accelerator Charlie can smell the gas and he knows that she's flooded it and can't get away. That makes him feel good and bad.

"You flooded it," Mag says, standing there. Charlie expects to see him smiling, but his face is serious and earnest and sad. "You could open the hood so we could take a look," he says. "But you don't have to. Only you crank it a few more times and you'll have a dead battery too."

She stops and sits, her hands at her side—sits looking forward at nothing at all as if she could look away from what she herself is doing or was doing at least. Charlie reaches in through the open window and pulls the hood release, saying, "It's all right" to her as he does it.

"Turn it once!" Mag says. His head and shoulders are down into the engine compartment. She turns the key and the engine cranks once or twice. "You got no spark. I got to open up your points a little."

Charlie touches her shoulder when he sees the tremors of her fear. He thinks You are acting a part that is no good for you— You are doing something that will give you no peace even when it's done. He thinks, looking at Mag, This could have been good with her, but not anymore. You look at the pictures on the paper and think they're good, but they aren't and when all that is built out here it will be dead all outside and you will be inside someplace half dead.

"Have her try it," Mag says.

The engine cranks slowly, sputters and fires, rattles and then steadies into smooth running. Mag slams the hood down.

"Oh!" she cries, still looking ahead.

Mag comes around to where Charlie is and stands there again, his hand on Charlie's arm.

"Thank you," she says, looking toward them and down.

"You tell Mr. Porter that he ought to send you out with a decent car at least—like maybe that gray Cadillac that sits alongside his office."

She is crying then—fear crying—as she bends into her handkerchief.

"Well," Mag says. "I could cry too when I think of what that son-of-a-bitch is going to do out here."

"Please!"

"They are going to put a big Dari-queen over there and a little golf course with plastic carpeting over there and a motel that can hold a thousand people from Chicago eating and shittin' and watchin' TV and throwin' gum wrappers in the water."

"That's not true!"

"That's true to me," Mag says. "They are going to have a parkin' lot so big that all you'll be able to hear out here is horns. Nobody'll ever hear the wind again clear and free."

"That's not true," she says. "I wish I never came out here. There's no use is there?"

"Why *did* you come out here anyway?"

"She . . ." Charlie began.

"No, Charlie!" she says. She has turned to look at Mag, not angrily, but with the desperate courage of a trapped creature. "I came out here because it's going to happen anyway like all the other things that happened and none of our people could do anything about. This is a chance for Charlie and me to do something. Mr. Porter doesn't need me for this. I asked to do it. It's going to happen and this time it's going to be something for us. He can't just go fishing and playing Huck Finn all his life. I don't want to see things happen to him like they happened to the others."

"Where do you get the 'us' thing?" Mag asks. "You and I aren't *us* anything and Charlie isn't either. But at least I belong out here and I live with things the way they are and try to let them alone. Takin' a boat across the river doesn't leave a mark and in the winter you can hardly tell I'm out here. But that lawyer bastard is going to make this *his*. He's got to have it and cover it."

"That's not true," she says again, still dabbing at the tears.

"It's true to me," he says.

"It's no use! I wish I hadn't come out. I only wanted Charlie to see what it would look like."

They both look at Charlie. "He'll make up his own mind," Mag says.

Charlie looks away. His heart is bitter with the sadness of

their quarreling. Yet the wind is cool and free and the round world open and alive with grass and water and trees as he turns. They are talking about me and not to me again, he thinks. And that means that their truth isn't mine now and might not ever be, he thinks.

"You come in!" she cries at his back. "I miss you."

The wind is sweet warm in his face, warmer than her words.

"I won't talk about this at all and there's some good news about somebody."

"I'll see," he says.

"You can come out here," Mag says, "but get those damn points fixed. I won't bother you."

"Nobody is going to bother anyone," Charlie says over his shoulder toward both of them. "It's going to be a truce from now on and nobody can do anything about anything." He doesn't turn even when he hears her start to drive away.

"There's nothing to say," Mag says behind him. "You are already think-saying so much in your head you wouldn't hear it anyway. But there is one thing: you got something to find out. I don't understand it because I only half begin to understand you. But you're not trapped. Something good can happen. You have to find out what it is . . ." He pauses. "Oh, shit!" he says. " I have to get drunk. Will you take care of the boats?"

"Sure," Charlie says, thinking, there's a lot happening I never thought would happen and I wish somebody would touch me so I didn't feel so alone.

13

Golden Girl

He has escaped again—from school, from the house and from the haunting sad eyes of Nancy. He sits quietly in the boat as it tugs gently at the anchor rope. It's mid-September but the air is warm and birds practice summer songs in the fired leaves of the cottonwoods along the creek. The sun is lower in the noon sky than it has been, but it beams a warm blue-gold blessing on the water of the lake above the dam.

He's still-fishing for walleyes, letting the wobbling live shiner minnows down, then reeling up and jigging six to 12 inches above the bottom. Silver-green flare and tug! A good fish! The spinning rod arcs tightly, rap-rapping on the edge of the boat as the fish runs, spiraling up. He plays it in—a fine walleye, yaw-yawing its mouth on the hook and minnow as it flap-clanks in the bottom of the boat.

He wets his hand, pushes the hook barb out, and pitches the fish back in. The wind picks up, creasing the grass on the hills, swaling it in darker air ripplings.

"Jesus Christ I'm lonely!" he exclaims. "I'm so lonely I feel cold as a fish." He thinks, there has never been another letter from where she is for four months. Thinks, it never happened at all and I can't think it back again ever. It was something that opened me up all down the middle to have her fill me out, but not it's just me opened up and not closed again. Thinks, Why do I go fishing when it makes me lonely and even the water seems flat and hard? And thinks, too, But if I lean over and listen to the wind and the summer cry of the birds in the thickets and if I let the sun touch my shoulder with its hand, I will not be lonely. The sun leans down toward the earth as water comes; things nest to sleep and dream. South of him up on the roadway of the dam a few cars drone across, but the lake is quiet and only a few local boats drone across its surface or lean their sails like gulls lifting one stiff wing up into the wind.

When he hears it—over and under the wind—he thinks dog, but not dog barking. Dog yelp—screaming like they do when they step into a trap sometimes. He pulls the anchor up and rows up the creek, wondering, Will I have to kill this one too like the little one with the broken back?

He sees the girl first—tall, summer bronzed, her eyes blazed bright blue in the tan of her face, her hair a golden flow down her back, her legs long in the thighs and ripple lean. He sees her first and stares slack-jawed with wonder because he has never . . .

"It's Jock!" she screams, pointing at the half-drowned top of a cottonwood that has finally tilt-toppled into the water because its roots have been washed out. She stands on the bank above him pacing back and forth on a wide ledge of grass, her arms folded under her breasts and jiggling in exasperation and then pointing again.

"I can't see him!" he says, hoarsely, because he hasn't looked and hasn't wanted to.

"Oh, he's in the tree and he's caught! He's going to drown! I threw a stick in . . ."

Charlie sees him—a tan cocker spaniel twisting spasmodically under the upper branches, its brown eyes pathetic with fear. Charlie also sees that he can't get the boat in close and that the cocker's fur is caught in some wire.

"I can't get the boat in there!" he yells as he lets the boat drift in against the limbs and the yelp-whining of the dog.

"Oh, please! Oh, please! I'll pay you or anything, but don't let him drown."

He looks at her again. Her legs, he thinks. The stupid fucking dog! he thinks. Barbed wire in my balls! he thinks. Her legs! he thinks.

He turns the boat up into the current and heaves the anchor as far as he can to hold the boat where it is. He peels his T-shirt first, then decides he can't stay wet afterward. The clothes can't all be wet.

"Hey!" he yells.

"What?"—an impatient what.

"I have to get my clothes off to get him. You can turn around awhile."

"God, that's dumb! But hurry up!"

He peels his blue jeans and, keeping his shorts on, slides into the water with a knife from the tackle box.

He's shocked at the chill of it, the stupid chill of it and the tug of the current and the slime slickness of the surfaces of the limbs of the tree. He hangs by the upper limbs and lets his body drift downstream. The dog yelps feebly, waiting. He's near it and can see the rusty curve of the barbed wire tangled in the coat. The dog bob-floats in slow pulsings.

He's surprised at the fury of the animal as he tries to pull it loose. It growls and snarls and snaps at him dangerously. He almost loses the knife. In the wash of the current through the limbs he begins to numb a little and it frightens him. Through the noise of it all he can hear her pleading and bossing above him.

He strikes the dog with his right fist, hitting it flush on the forehead. It yelps feebly and floats dazed. He cuts the hair and shoves the wire back and, tugging the animal by the wet fur at its neck, begins the slippery acrobatics of getting back into the boat.

She's in the boat—in the boat, standing wet and beautiful and angry above him as he lifts the dog up at her and hangs in the water to keep himself covered and to see the fine legs in the wet blue shorts.

She begins to shake. "Did you have to?" she screams. "Did you have to hurt him to get him out?"

"He was caught in barbed wire and biting the hell out of me

and I am freezing and getting numb," Charlie says, getting number in the cold water flowing over his belly and legs. And getting mad hot in the head.

"I'll bet!" she cries, bending over and drying the dog with Charlie's pants as the animal lies there looking up pitifully at her and reproachfully at Charlie.

"I'm coming in, damn it!" he says, hating the dog for being a fool and not liking the way she stands or talks or shivers either for that matter. He heaves up into the boat and stands there in angry insolence.

She looks at him and he remembers or remembers to remember that his white shorts wet are nearly none at all. She looks long, taking only a little, quick surprised breath as she does.

"Your pants!" she says, shoving them, wadded and dog stinking, at him. He turns and pulls them on, shivering, angry.

"You're welcome!" he says, hating her and the dog too because now there is something else that might not be real and because he thinks women have something you need and want and you have got to hate them for making you do things because you need and want it. "You're welcome!" he declares again.

"All right! All right! You're thank you'd!"

When he turns around, he knows he knows her—that deep in the tanned, freckled face is *that* girl, that girl from that other time under the church steeple and the lilacs and the scream of her mother's face when she catches them playing there.

"You could get us back on shore," she says. "I'm frozen to death and filthy and Jock has to get to a doctor."

"You're welcome," he says, rowing violently on a straight course up to the shore and looking furtively to where the long, tanned legs level down from the knees to the dog at her lap. The cocker's eyes are friendlier and it wheezes tiredly.

"You could turn the car heater way up if you've got a car."

"I've got to get going and get him to a doctor."

"Suit yourself."

When the boat nudges the shore, she jumps out with the dog under one arm and turns to him. "Where do you live? I don't have any money, but I want to pay you something." He pulls the boat up without answering. She backs away. When he stands in

the grass near her he is taller than she is. Over her shoulders he
can see the gray metallic gleam of a car top.

"I've got money," he says, his eyes leveling on hers finally.

"I know, but where do you live?"

"Where do I live?" He hears himself repeating it.

"All right, then, for God's sake. What's your name and then
where do you live?"

"Charlie Good Thunder and I live out at Magnuson's boat
landing weekends."

"Thank you."

"Your name is Tina," he says. The dog is shivering on her
arm.

"How do you know that?" Hostile, suspicious blue eyes regard
him.

"That's a long time ago," he says.

"I'll bet. But I hate that name."

"Well, don't bet and don't pay," he says, turning to the boat
and shoving it out on the water as he jumps in. Was it then that
he saw the man by the car—an older man, full of face over the
collar and tie?

The boat drifts down the creek mouth and into the lake. He
rows and keeps rowing angrily. Why do I want what I don't like?
he thinks. And then, why do I hate what I want? She's like the
sun—too bright and even man strong, he thinks. And then, the
tall grasses lean into his memory and he thinks. Kim and Kim
and Kim in the leaning grass on the soft dark earth in the evening. He rows fiercely toward the tall boulder-faced front of the
dam. But then, when he sees the waves slap-dash on the stones,
he rows back toward the western shore and drifts suspended on
the water, watching the gulls pivot and swing in mewing circles
above him.

The days drift, too. The classes at school are the same, the
teachers the same, the faces the same. But Charlie thinks, I'm
not the same, I'm walking around with all these people and talking a little to them and eating with them and shooting baskets
out on the schoolgrounds, but I'm not with them. There is
something inside my head like a hard shell so I'm not with
them. And I stay in a house with a woman who is now a

stranger who works for a stranger and goes to eat and sleep and whatever with another stranger. So, on and on it goes.

The September days drift to Saturday and Charlie goes out to the boat landing to see Mag who has become as brooding and queer as the Hamlet the English teacher makes them read about, or tries to.

"Charles, my boy!" Mag exclaims with the one bright smile he will manage for the day.

"What do you want me to do?" he asks.

"You know what to do. Wash out the boats and stack 'em under the canvas. Hell, we might use them only once more. It is Ragnarok coming."

"Who's that?" he asks.

"Ragnarok is the day of the wolf in the old Norse world—the day when even the gods couldn't do anything because the great wolf catches the sun and the serpent comes out of the deep and brings the flood and blows poison all over the world."

"Whew!" Charlie says, "—gloomy stuff like *Hamlet* in school."

"You know the poison is really not from the snake; it comes from man. The flood and the fire and the poison are all bull shit. Those old people weren't crazy. They knew that someday we would be destroyed by what we do with fire and to the water and the air."

Mag's face is strange as he speaks, his eyes far, far away and deep in his face. "But the great tree of life, they say, won't go down. The earth, they say, will rise up again from the water clean and sweet again, green and fair as it was in the first time."

"Where did you learn that?" Charlie asks softly, very softly as if he were interrupting a prayer.

"I don't know," Mag says. "I know I had great uncles that were poets in Iceland."

"It's strange," Charlie says.

"The last battle, they say, will be on a great plain by a river. But you know, I can't get at anything. You can't get at anything to fight it. You can't fight a piece of paper and you can't start a fight with men sitting smiling at you. They would have me put in prison and then I'm no good to do anything."

"We could get people together," Charlie says.

"How? You don't belong to any people and me—I'm a coyote or a wolf myself sitting out here howling and growling all day and night."

"We could still fight when they come out here."

"It'll be too late then. That's the day of the serpent. That's the day the serpent lays its eggs and the poison comes."

He pauses. "You ever see this Porter?" he asks Charlie.

"No."

"He's getting fat now. He sits there with your mother writing down everything and he gets fat. And she doesn't see it's Wasichu."

"White man?"

"No, not just white man. It means taker of fat—maybe swallower of fat. He's not mean looking. He looks like he wouldn't hurt anything or anybody and he talks to her with nice soft words high in his throat. He's smooth with fat that Mr. Porter."

"Could you move the camp?"

"No, this is the best there is. It's got the only real thick-rooted prairie grass and all the rest. They wrote up some bullshit about keeping the natural habitat, but that's bullshit. That just means the plastic and concrete is going to be green and brown."

"I think I'll work on the boats," Charlie says. He can see that talking about it doesn't help Mag at all. His eyes recede to a faraway gleam like the eyes of a hawk. Charlie starts to walk away.

"You know that Oates at all that your mother sees?" Mag asks.

"No, I've never seen him clear."

"He used to work on the dam," Mag says. "Now I hear he is going to be the cat man who's going to dig up the place, the son-of-a-bitch."

"I've never seen him clear," Charlie says.

"It's no good to talk about it," Mag says. "You go and do your work."

"Sure," Charlie says.

At noon heavy black clouds scud in over the river and Charlie hurries to get the rest of the boat dock in, pulling sections of it up under the trees with the little orange tractor Mag has borrowed somewhere. He wonders where Mag has gone and then he sees him cleaning up the camp area with a rake and a shovel. But he's not there, Charlie thinks. He's somewhere looking in his mind for somebody to fight so they won't come here.

"Hello!"

She's bright with a blue jacket and levis and the incredible red-gold abundance of hair. Behind her, the front door of the big gray car swings shut. He turns off the tractor and looks at her. She wiggles her new, carved western boots into the track made by the dock sections.

"He's going to be all right!" she announces.

"What?"

"Jock. He's going to be all right."

"Oh." Dismounting from the tractor he hates his own grease filth, but she touches his jacket and smiles. "You're dry," she says. Her mouth is a violet rich bud of flesh. "Is he your father?" She's pointing toward Mag, who has stopped to watch only for a moment.

"That's Magnuson. He owns this place."

"What do you do?"

"I'm the official assistant guide during the season."

She laughs—hard and tight, but wonderful just the same.

"Where do you eat?"

"Mag fixes it about one or so."

"In there?"

"Sure?"

"Can you take a break for lunch and go with me?"

"Sure, if I want to."

"Do you want to?"

He does. "Sure," he says. "I've got clean stuff in the dugout."

He hurries. Changes. Dashes on shaving lotion—even on his socks. That's not enough. He sponge bathes. Hurries outside to Mag.

"I pulled her dog out of Cheyenne Creek," he says to Mag. Mag doesn't stop raking. "She's from Pierre. I used to know her. She wants to buy me lunch. I'll be back in an hour."

"No you won't," Mag says, not turning or even lifting his head as he works over the little pile of debris.

"Is it all right?"

"It's all right with me, but you better damn well watch out it's all right with you. I think I've seen that caddie before and I sure as hell have seen that look before." He turns. "But you don't know what that look is, do you?"

He's a little angry with Mag. "What's that mean?" he asks.

"It's a look that says 'I'm going to try something new,' is what it means, but you won't believe a thing I'm saying and you are thinking with your cock so go ahead."

"Bullshit!" he says.

"Go on. She hears the call of the wild," Mag says. "I'm not really all that mean. I'd go too if I were you."

"She's a minister's daughter," he says, thinking, God, I feel foolish saying that.

"Well," says Mag, "he'll never marry you, I can tell you that. This is a special kind of missionary work."

"Well, nuts to you," he says.

"Nuts is right," Mag says, "but I got no right to get on you. Go ahead."

Walking toward her car he sees that she is taking photos with a little slim black camera—lots of pictures—snapping them in quick sequences. "I wonder what that is?" he asks himself aloud.

"It's beautiful out here," she says. "I took photography last year."

"Where was that?"

"In Minnesota at a private school in Minneapolis."

"Are you in 12th?"

"No. I'm going to college next year."

He doesn't like it when she sits in on the driver's side, but he goes around and gets in and she drives away, the big car rocking and pitching with silent, deep power up the incline to the road that winds up and over the road that crosses the dam.

"Where you going? There's a drive-in two miles the other way?"

"I'm going where we met first."

"We gonna eat grass or squirrels or what?"

She reaches over into the back seat and sweeps the blanket off the basket. "Corned beef and dills and potato salad and good stuff from home . . ."

"A picnic," he says.

"Kind of," she says.

When she stops the car in the grass along the creek he can see the other tire tracks running in and he wonders, Who else? and When? But the long tapering of her legs, the high tight breasts under the T-shirt under the jacket, the mouth . . .

"It's a little cool," he says, "—for a picnic I mean."

"I remember you."

"What?"

"I remember the awful trouble we got into with my mother." She giggles then. "My mother whacked me hard on my bare seat all the way back to the house."

"I don't remember details," he says. He is hungry and wonders how to get some food without asking because he doesn't quite like the whole business.

"That's good. There are details I'd rather you wouldn't remember."

"Sure," he says. There's a ticking somewhere in the deep, quiet steel and upholstery of the car and a faint odor of cigars.

"Do you want a sandwich?"

"If you are."

She twists up and over the front seat and bumps him with her leg. He sweats a little looking at her, smelling her. She smell like the department store in Pierre with the perfume counter somewhere. Somewhere.

"These are kosher half-dills," she says. "I love them." She hands him a thick, knobby pickle in a napkin and then a sandwich rich and opened wide with corned beef. He sweats a little. "Coke?" she asks. He nods.

She watches him eat and he doesn't like it. It's too much like curiosity. People—especially rich and cool people—did it to him fishing, handing him things to eat as if they were bait to see if he . . . He eats slowly. The corned beef is tangy-rich and good, but he's careful eating.

"You're quiet, aren't you? I'm used to guys talking all the time to get your attention. Is your school like that?"

"Sure, but maybe quieter. I get quiet in the summer because I have to listen to so much. People I take out fishing talk all the time to me."

"I bet they tell you a lot sometimes, like confession."

"Once in awhile."

"Girls?"

"Not many—not any, but once an older lady."

"Oh?"

"She was—sad, I guess."

"What did she say."

"I wouldn't say."

"No, you wouldn't." She is leaning back, her eyes closed like she is waiting for somebody. "Are you going to college?" she asks.

"I don't know."

"Aren't there special scholarships and things for you?"

"You mean Indians?" He laughs.

"I don't know what I mean. I'm always going away someplace —St. Margaret's, St. Anne's, Breck. My mother has a high G.E. factor or something."

"Oh?"

"Great expectations. Next year I go to Carlton College. I just made it with my G.P.A. If I go there I could get into a good grad school and become a college teacher or something."

"Whew! So many people are hurrying up to become somebody else," he says.

"We live in a house that's not ours and I've always gone away to school so maybe it fits that I'm going to try to become somebody else." She stops and touches his shoulder. "You have a girl, don't you?"

"No," he says, bending away from her touch.

"You don't like me, do you?"

"No—I mean no I don't dislike you." The hand moves to his hair and his head thrills in tingly electrostatic pulses. "Your eye is gray," she says. "You're a funny Indian."

"Your eyes are teal blue," he says trying to make up things, "and brighter than sky."

"A teal is a duck."

"Yes," he says. "The wings have bright blue flags on them."

"A duck." She is thinking it over.

"Where's your dog?" he asks.

"My what? Oh . . ." She leans back again.

He wraps everything up carefully when he's done. When he turns around to put the wad of paper in the back, her face is there close, her eyes and breath close and her mouth moist as she presses her tongue on the upper lip. He sweats and holds back. And then, poised over the seat, he trembles and hates himself. It's too quick, he thinks. I am not the man, he thinks.

"Do you want to walk out on the sand finger?" he asks hoarsely.

"Do you think I'm an older woman?"

"What?"

"I am. I'm eighteen and I've had older friends."

"I'll be eighteen next January, but those are man years."

"You don't like this do you?"

"No. All summer I take people out in boats—a lot of time their boats. And they hand me things and talk to me as if it was 1876 or something. They don't know where they are on the river or where to go, but inside the boat they always talk to me the same way like they know things I'll never know."

"Do you have a car?"

"I can use Mag's old pickup."

"It's silly, but maybe we should start over. I'll come out tomorrow afternoon if you like. I won't be so serious then."

"Serious? Well, sure. But I could come in."

"No, I'll come out. You can come over here in your pickup and we can sit in it. We can start over."

"Sure."

"I'm not used to this. If you don't like me, please don't come over here. I'll be here at two."

"I'll come. Do you want to drive back?"

"Sure." He gets out, feeling stronger and better, and gets in on the driver's side. The car drives swiftly and smoothly. She sits a little stiffly next to him but not touching him. She doesn't say anything at first when he gets out, but then she says it, sitting there a little grim-jawed and sullen: "You're welcome!"

"Thank you and you're not too serious," he says.

"Sure!" The car careens and dips up out of the camp in a clicking of gravel and dust.

"At least you got ahold of the steering wheel," Mag says, standing there behind him.

"Maybe it's not so bad."

"Maybe," Mag says.

Charlie works hard and hurries the week away, working, surprising but not surprising Mag. Charlie thinks, Saturday. Don't think too much about Saturday.

Charlie is nervous as he drives the pickup toward the little road that runs along the north side of the creek. It's Saturday—a gift day, another Indian summer day. A few leaves flutter down on the hood of the pickup as he turns down the road. There's nobody there, but he parks and in the rear view mirror he sees the big gray car floating down toward him with its sad blonde angel at the wheel.

In the tall grass they talk about small things. Then he kisses her, pressing down on her. She rolls out and then, out of swift motions he will never remember, she is there above him, lowering on him, eyes widening as she feels him, her eyes going out of focus and she rocks, rocks, rocks on him, yelping up from the deep thrusts.

Sun springs burst in his back and loins and he bucks at her, trying to rise, to push but not to push her away. He cries out sadly. They lie forehead to forehead on the blanket, hands crossed to hips, tongues tippling at tongues. "You are so big," she sighs, "but wait a little longer."

"O.k.," he says. He thinks, She knows so much. This is what she means by "older." Thinks too, Her eyes are like the sky and her skin is as white as the clouds under her fur. She's not going to stay; she's going to go away and take some of me with her.

It is two weeks or so before he realizes that she doesn't want to go anyplace where anyone she knows would see them. But he meets her anytime she wants to come out. He talks to her before and after, sometimes with his head on her lap. He wonders if there could be a child because he never uses anything. He loves the feel of her: the wet rasping of her tongue in his ear, the glide of her belly, and the flight of her fingers on the small of his back.

But he knows in his heart that she can never fill the broken circle of need inside him and that she will go away sometime as suddenly as the white geese on the river.

14

Lover and Hunter

Fall passes—a browning of grass and a dry voice of wind, little whirlwind dust dancers in the streets, leaves drowning silently in the water of the river, shot geese crumpling in front of the pits where he and Mag sit watching the great blue-white hosts of their flight southward.

In the house Nancy bends over her books and papers on the kitchen table in the evening, her face grim with resolve. When she walks to her bedroom or the bathroom, her shoulders are narrowed forward under the brown sweater and her steps are not steady and even on the floor. Sometimes she turns suddenly toward him and, in a voice that sounds like it is coming from far away, says, "I give up on you sometimes, Charlie. You got too many secrets. You never open your heart to me, only your mouth when you're hungry. You're mad at me for nothing."

"No I'm not," he says. He could say, "I don't care enough to be mad," but he can see that she's very unhappy. And why hurt somebody already hurt?

"What are you chasing?" she asks him with that same voice.

"You mean, besides girls?"

"You don't even take my questions seriously anymore," she says then. "Do you know they take me seriously at the office now? I'm a very good secretary—a legal secretary. And I am learning business law by correspondence course from the University of Minnesota and I have had three raises in 18 months."

"That's good," he says.

"That's good. An echo, not a feeling. Is there another Indian lady who's done this? Mr. Porter pays all the tuition for my school and he likes me and treats me like someone to be taken seriously at the office."

"Mr. Porter likes the green frog skin," Charlie says.

"What? What is that? Some more crazy talk?"

"Green frog skin." He knows he's being cruel now because she hasn't the vaguest notion what he's talking about.

"I suppose I'm supposed to know that."

"It's a dollar bill. It's what John Lame Deer calls a dollar bill in a book I had. He says Indians chase visions and white men chase green frog skins."

"So that's what you read—about old medicine men in time gone by like the river of yesterday."

"He said everything is green frog skin business now," Charlie says.

"What did he do—sit around in a sweat lodge and smoke the weed and complain? I bet he never kept a job. Is that what you like?"

"He said being an Indian now is a full-time job."

"It's not real," she says, shaking her head. "You're not real or honest, Charlie. You're just hurting me again for trying to do something for us, that's all."

"For you," he corrected.

"Oh, Charlie!"

She runs into her bedroom and he can hear her throw herself on the bed and cry. When she comes out, she presses her hands on the bows of her glasses and stares at him. He is startled by the bruise on her cheek and he sees that the glasses have been twisted at the corner of the frames.

"Who did that?" he asks softly. "Who did that to you?"

She touches the bruise vaguely and unconsciously. Her voice is deep and bitter. "The other who likes to hurt me when I try to be somebody," she says.

"I'm sorry," he says.

"No, you're not. But maybe someday you will be—not because you're sorry you hurt me, but because you see that you're being used too, Charlie."

"What does that mean?"

"It means that when you care for somebody you're vulnerable and numb and easy and don't even know they've hurt you until afterward."

She's leaving then, her books under one arm and the dark look that says, "Hurry! Hurry!" on her face. Through the front window he can see her fixing her face under the dome light in the car. When she has finished, she sits there, looking nowhere before she turns off the light. He hears her start the car and drive away toward Pierre where she can type her school papers at Porter's office.

It depresses him to see her go. He thinks, I have two places I could call home but I'm not anyplace. I have two—maybe three—people close to me but I'm lonely. At school they don't even ever quite look at me. They say, or somebody said, I am in an OYUMNI, a wandering. Does that mean I have a place to go? He looks at his watch. It's nearly eight o'clock.

He turns off the lights in the house and walks out to the road that leads up to Mag's boat landing. But he's not going there. In a little while the big gray car will swing by him and, if there are no other cars around, it will stop on the shoulder waiting for him. He will walk to the driver's side and slide into a soft region of music and little lights. He will say, "Hi" to the face in the kerchief. She will wear the kerchief because she doesn't want her long blonde hair to be a flag somebody might notice . . .

The car passes him, nosing down, the rear brake lights flaring on the dark macadam. He walks up to the driver's side. Anger burns in his head and chest. The chrome door handle is cool in his hand when he cranks it to get in. Inside, shrieking voices on the radio insinuate making love all night, all night, all night. "Hu . . . y!" she says from the shadow on the seat. "God, she's beautiful," he thinks, the anger gone already because desire has replaced it.

They make love a long time. He tries to see her in the light of the sliver of moon above them in the sky. Even in the dark her eyes seem bright blue and her hair is a fountain of cool, fragrant sun as he kisses it or it flows over his loins. "You're big! You're big!" she cries, her eyes blurring violet blue and her tongue sweet wet stiff as he sucks it, sucks it.

Afterward she opens packages of food she's bought somewhere and she hands him a Coke and a napkin. She watches him eat very carefully, but he sees, too, that she is looking at her watch "It's over," he thinks to himself. When he's with her he talks more to himself than to her.

"We should have gone to the lilac hedge again," she says, adjusting her kerchief.

"You talk a lot about that hedge," he says.

"That's one of my fantasies. Do I say terrible dirty things about it while we're making love?"

"No," he lies. "I can only think and talk in Indian while I'm doing it."

Her face comes closer to him and she strokes his hair with her hand because she knows it soothes him. His forehead is one of his most vulnerable places. "Why do you say that?" she asks. "Why do you talk to me like that?"

"I don't know. Just being smart, I guess."

"Are you mad about something? Have I said something? I won't bother you if I have. I'll just go away."

"No," he says to everything about going away.

"Away at school it could be different," she says. "It's an awful narrow town, Charlie. I know it's terrible, but I do save this for you. I couldn't be with another man."

"Is it your parents?"

"Mostly."

"Is this your father's car?"

"No. It's an uncle's."

"What's his name? Does he know you use it to . . ."

"Oh, Charlie, please . . . I have some things to worry about. Please try to understand. Some day we'll find a place."

"I heard that line before," he says.

"Oh?" Stiffening. Edges of anger. Line. Insinuation.

"West Side Story."

She laughs a nervous laugh. "Oh, that."

They drive back because she has to be back—somewhere—by ten o'clock. Driving along the river he feels a deep tearing away inside himself again as if once a week or so he had been torn open to heal again until next time.

He turns off so she can slide over and drive. They kiss, his tongue darting to taste her again. A little silence. He thinks, this is more than I ever dreamed I could have and, still, I don't have it.

"Sometimes I feel like I'm just wandering around the night," he says finally into the warm silence between them.

"Sometimes I feel like I'm wandering around the night—even in the daytime," she says.

"Will you see me again?" Inside, his valve flutters.

"Yes? Of course. I need to see you and I need to know when so I can reach up into next week and know you'll be here. I feel insecure if I don't."

"O.k." he says, touching her again and bending down to reach under her sweater and spill a breast out to kiss the nipple.

"Oh, Charlie, I could cry," she says, petting the top of his head as he flaps the bra back over the breast.

"Oh," she says, "all my wires are tingling again!"

"I'll stop," he says. "I don't want to light a fire for somebody else."

"Somebody else?" Her eyes poise at center as she looks at him.

"It's something Mag used to joke about. He said once in awhile he had the feeling he was starting a campfire for somebody else to cook on."

"He talks to you about things like that?"

"Once in awhile when we're fishing or hunting. But he doesn't talk about us."

"Charlie?"

"Yes?" He doesn't like the seriousness on her face. He's afraid she'll say it finally.

"I'll have to go away to school in December. I'll be kind of finished with my job by then."

"Where do you work? I never quite got that straight."

"For a kind of public relations company."

"I don't get it."

"I have to go now," she says, looking at her watch again. I'll tell you about it someday—and something else too if I can."

"Sure." What else can he say?

As he watches the car glide away down the road he wonders why she hasn't waved goodbye and he knows that he'll worry about why she didn't wave goodbye and what it means that she didn't wave goodbye—will worry about it all week, will spend the week tormented on a crest of desire and worry.

For a little while the night is cold and empty, the stars tall blue and indifferent to him and all the little human lights along both sides of the river. How is it love is such a lonely thing? he asks, not really thinking *love* but thinking Why is this-thing-I-want-I-don't-know-what-it-is so lonely and tall a thing even when I am lying down with her?

There's a bright cold-sharp taste of snow on the wind, a far-off ticking like sand on tin in the wind. He has a feeling that someone or something is watching him. He thinks about talking to her—how it never touches the truth of things or the truth of the lie in things. He thinks about the glory of silence around him—of the perfect balance in the stars and on the earth. What does it know to have such lovely and perfect balance? What is the mystery off the road and in the swales of dark grass and stone? What does pain do?

He wanders far off the road and into the grass. The deep grass is moist and cool on his feet but the tall grass is dry and warm on his legs.

The stone is small—so small he shouldn't have found it perhaps. But it's there among the anthills not buried but balanced high on a large rock that is wine dark in the vague light. The stone is warm. Has a hand put it there recently? A chill tremors up through his back and flicks needles of ice into his loins. The stone fits his hand intimately. It is nearly round. It beats a small silent pulse in his hand or maybe echoes the beating of his own heart. In his heart he pushes away what his mind is saying about a silly thing like this which only children think and do. Silly. But, then, what out here would laugh at this and here he is still a child even though he has made love to a golden goddess in a silver gray car. He keeps the stone. The silence of the night is patient with him.

As he walks slowly toward the road a quick gust of wind ripples his hair and clothes. He stops, chilled deeply inside. Who is it? he asks. A coyote yips far off. Coyote, he remembers, wanted to have people die and be gone a little while and then come back to life again. But Coyote closed the door of the grass hut so the whirlwind spirits of the dead could not enter and had to wander the earth. And Coyote saw what he had done and ran from place to place looking over his shoulder to see if anyone was following him. That is not a Sioux story. That is not a Sioux story and it seems silly. He has heard it from a Caddo man who came to the school a long time ago. Why does he remember it? It's a silly story, but why does he remember it? A coyote is a selfish, thieving trickster. And yet the hills and grass take him too. Even he can't cheat the mystery. The silence is stronger than his yipping and howling. So.

Up on the road he can hear noisy voices. It's a car full of drunk Indians—older men who have been drinking in the shacks in Indian Town. He holds back afraid of them. Their car weaves along the road, rumbling and rattling when its wheels hit the shoulder. A six-pack of empty beer cans clats and clatters on the shoulder as they pass. The car has dim headlights and there are no tail lights at all. After it passes, the night shadows swallow it and the voices of the drunk people fade like coyote calls into a silence far off.

When he gets to the house Charlie hides the stone in another place in his bedroom wall, but that makes him worry because Nancy might find it and because it doesn't belong there. He sleeps fretfully, sweating and cooling, sweating and cooling. His body remembers her and aches like a half-shell for the other half, but when she appears in his dream she's looking away from him and he can't make her turn around to fit into him. And he sweats, tossing and turning. Then he cools down into the cadences of night breathing under the stars. Toward morning the wind is blowing slowly and steadily. The snow ticks and whispers against the house and puts the prairie to winter sleep in the morning.

That night he walks out to Dick Bissonette's place on the north end of Indian Town which sprawls in the snow, a mottled, crusted sore of shacks and tents nobody has been able to heal. Ahead of him and to his left he sees an old Indian woman walking up a dirt road toward a shack that seems to be settling in some terrible twisted wood agony into the earth through a ring of grass that surrounds it. Already the snow has melted off most of the roof and the black tar paper roofing gleams like a tilted tar road in the streetlight a few yards from one corner of the shack. The old woman is burly thick in her coat and she walks with a thin walking stick that punctures the ice crust and enters the wet earth underneath with a plick! plick! noise as she walks. She is wearing tennis shoes and long underwear that looks like stockings under the heavy flapping of her coat.

Boxes, Charlie thinks. These are all boxes—rotting death boxes: rusty house trailers, sagging log cabins, toppling privies. The old woman stops by one of the privies, backs in, heaves up her coat and sits down with the door only partially closed so that, even in the darkness inside Charlie can see apparition of her white long underwear. Around her, as he passes the privy, bulbous rusting fenders of old cars lie in the snow like shells of steel hearts. Dogs bark everywhere in the shadows and their barking ripples through the small, high cries of children playing in the last blue light on the snow. The lights in the windows are pale yellow when they come on and sometimes he can see the silver-gray flickering of light from a television set somewhere inside. And they can't see the stars, Charlie thinks, thinking on the children mesmerized at the little ghost boxes of the television sets.

The old woman sits in the cold privy looking eastward past Charlie's walking. Still, the old woman has poked the earth and sits crapping and breathing and watching the first stars appear while he walks out to Dick Bissonette's to hunt jack rabbits illegally at night because Dick has asked him to come out and in the little world of the school that is some kind of gesture of friendship and Charlie has no friends except Billy Whitefeather and then only when Billy is left out of other things. Charlie and Dick Bissonette have never fought again because Charlie has never tried to do anything in school except keep quiet.

Walking up the black, freezing ruts on the road bending around into the Bissonette place Charlie can see the wooden quonset hut where Dick lives with his parents and the big, galvanized sheet metal garage, now glowing white silver in the last light. Both buildings have been left behind by a bankrupt Indian implement dealer who could never collect any money from anyone because no one could really make anything grow with either the seeds or the machines sold them.

Walking up the little hill Charlie feels good about the night and the thought of hunting jackrabbits with Dick. He rattles the box of shotgun shells inside his mackinaw pocket and his heart beats faster with the climb and thoughts of the hunt. When the geese and ducks are gone there are always the jackrabbits.

Dick is working on the car—a big tan Dodge with oversized snow tires on the back wheels. The back seat has been removed and the guns lean into the back window. The old car uses so much oil that the plugs are always fowling and Dick has to clean them before they go out to hunt with it.

"You got number two or fours?" Dick asks from under the hood. The old army fatigue jacket he always wears is black with grime and rabbit blood, and smells sour even in the cool outdoors.

"Two boxes," Charlie says. "Is there a moon tonight?"

"No moon," Dick says, ratcheting the last plug into the old L-head engine. "What you want a moon for?"

"To see."

"I don't know about you," Dick says, bending stiffly back up from under the hood and slamming it. Charlie waits for the rest of "I don't know about you," and thinks. Fight! Fight! Everything's a fight so win this now!"

"You think the warden can't see if there's a moon? No moon is good because he can't run without lights and we can see lights. The snow is right. The wind will cover tracks."

"You're right, I guess," Charlie says. "The snow is already moving a little. The crust is coming off."

"I got to have some money," Dick says. "I want one of them automatic Browning pistols that shoots 11 shots before some son-of-a-bitch can hit the ground." He holds the ratchet wrench and aims it at Charlie, laughing, his eyes dark, his face man full and sullen with a meanness that's always been there.

"What are you getting apiece now?"

"Seventy-five cents mink feed price or maybe ninety if they don't have more than one or two holes in them. Shoot high on them and catch their heads with the bottom of the pattern."

Dick pauses then and the two of them look westward over the running thin veil of snow sliding with the wind over the tufts of grass and the patches of shadows on the prairie floor.

"I seen you," he says, a wide, twisted smile on his face.

"Seen me what?"

He disregards Charlie's question and goes on. "You are some jackrabbit. Your old jackrabbit ass was bobbin' and your T-shirt looked like the tail of a jackrabbit diggin' a hole with its front paws."

"You're makin' that up."

"Why, it was a nice gray Cadillac and a big mop of silky yellow hair. We though about joinin' the party, but Jimmy Red Fox was talkin' killin' the girl so I thought maybe some other time."

"It must've been somebody else," Charlie says, feeling a sick tremor of disgust down inside and hating the smirk.

"You some gold digger. You don't like the girls at school or maybe you fillin' in while one is away."

"It must've been someone else," Charlie says again to buy some time and cool his anger.

"It couldn't have been, you dumb Indian. That is the lawyer's car your mother works for—the Wasichu lawyer over in Pierre."

Charlie feels his throat tighten and his eyes bulge in his head. "You're full of shit." he says, stepping toward Dick, hating his face and wondering why he has let himself come out to hunt with the meanest bastard in school.

"Suit yourself. You want to say that tomorrow we'll fight, but you ain't as smart as you think you are in school. You think any Wasichu bitch ain't a taker? They think we like niggers. I had an old white woman behind a bar last week cryin', 'Rape me!' and crazy stuff like that! Big white belly like a sow and I got out of the car."

He nearly says, "But she's not like that," but he doesn't. He says nothing at all. He lets the hurt fly around inside him and go into a cave of secrets down in his head. He doesn't know everything, Charlie thinks to himself. He doesn't know much at all so it's still my secret and I will keep it from him or anyone else.

Dick walks past him, climbs into the driver's seat and starts the engine. It roars the shed behind it full of blue-gray smoke—acrid smoke that bites him out of his numbness.

"You shoot first!" Dick yells over the noise.

Charlie climbs into the front of the car next to Dick, crawls over the back of the front seat and stands up. He can stand up because Dick has cut a big hole in the top of the car with a welding torch and has lined the edges of the hole with bolted-on pieces of tires. Charlie loads the old Winchester 97 with six shells and braces himself over the noise and smoke.

The car shoots out of the yard and plunges out into the grass-land running between the huge coiled bales of hay and the squat, snow-mossed haystacks. The two headlight beams swing out, boring corridors of light through the night blackness over the snow. Charlie's eyes blear with tears in the cold surges of wind. He wipes them with his sleeve and sets himself to shoot.

They appear out of nowhere—big white and tan-white jackrabbits doing their spooky white arpeggios down the reach of the lights and side galloping like bent little horses across the patches of grass and snow.

Charlie shoots them in mid-stride or crouching slack-eared along the edge of light or leaning straight-eared up the edge of a ditch. His own ears ring with the whomp! whomp! of the shot-gun. Shot, the jacks leap straight up and run a yard or two before they slither kick in the snow and do convulsing ampersands of fur until they're dead.

He runs to retrieve them and throw them into the back of the car. Blood, heat and moisture. Green rich feces stink. Each shot sears a small pink torch into the darkness.

He steps on one. It screams a plaintive piercing scream so loud and human that he steps back and blows its head off. Each place a rabbit dies there is a little melted place moist with blood and urine and feces. The car trunk fills with fur and bones.

When he first sees the lights they're so far off they seem like a flashlight beam. "Turn 'em off!" he yells down at Dick. Standing there, the engine growling like a sated wolf beneath him, Char-lie's tongue is thick in his throat from all the running. Dick

turns off the engine. Silence, except for the dull, sporadic muffled kicking of rabbit feet in the trunk.

Another light beam—slender and very sharp—detaches itself
from the other light and sweeps the prairie to the east of their
car.

"They got a spotlight. It's not so good," he tells Dick, leaning
down to say it softly.

"What's not so good?"

"Doing this when it's not legal."

"What you want anyway? You want to shovel an old white
lady's walk or maybe wash dishes or something? At the station
you wash cars when it's too cold for any white man's station to
do it."

"I said hunting this way *at night.*"

"Crap! This land belongs to us at night. These ranchers come
out here and poison the prairie dogs with strychnine so they can
run one more cow out here. No prairie dogs no hawks or eagles
and maybe only a few coyotes. You see that spotlight? It's white
like a white stick. They want to beat us out of here the last
time."

"They're comin' this way." Charlie says. "We're going to get
arrested. We aren't on the reservation and it'll get us in jail for
sure."

"I ain't goin' to get arrested. That man in the big green truck
ain't goin' to touch me."

"Run it then," Charlie says, but he knows they can't outrun a
four-wheel drive conservation department truck.

"I ain't goin' to get arrested. Get your ass out and crawl in the
snow if you're afraid."

"You can't stop it if they want to arrest you," Charlie says,
holding hard against a flap of tire on the edge of the shooting
hole and hoping Dick can't see him shaking: Then when he sees
Dick has a rifle aimed over the window sill toward the lights he
begins to shake hard and has to do a little dance to try to cover it
up. He pushes himself up farther so he can't see Dick. He's a
stranger, Charlie thinks. What am I doing here? I'm afraid of
him. I don't like him.

The headlights swing away and wobble their beams eastward toward a second road.

"You know, Charlie, you got a chicken heart for a tall man who can stud a white preacher's daughter." Dick's voice sounds far away below Charlie in the hull of the car.

"I don't mind fighting, but I don't want to get arrested."

"I expect to get arrested a couple dozen times but one time I ain't goin' to get arrested without killin' a couple of the big men in the big trucks that think they own all this they took away."

Charlie leans down. "For what?" he asks.

"Pride. I got some pride that school don't take."

"Pride? In what? Are we proud of shooting rabbits so a mink can eat, so some fat lady in Sioux Falls can have a mink coat?"

"You don't get nothin', do you? You don't see nothin', do you? They say you love hawk, but you mostly love chicken. You just kind of hang around the school and come and go and sneak your nose in a book. You maybe come and live out here in the mud and shit and you see what we ain't got—except boxes. A box is death. I got to kill somebody who puts me in this place."

"I know what you're . . ."

"You know, but you don't feel nothin' because you ain't nothin'. I'm nothin' but I'm gonna get at the ones that got what was ours."

"Well, Jesus, if that's the way you feel, I'll get out and go home. I'm not taking anymore crap from you."

"Not until I get my shots," Dick says.

"You gonna shoot some more?" Charlie slides down into the front seat to drive. Dick moves up past him into the turret.

"My old man drove a thing like this in Korea," Dick says. "It had four 50-calibre machine guns on it. He could shoot a whole Korean town down. He was a sergeant. He shot up a whole company of gooks. Now he's nothin' but a drunk workin' in the back of a store cleanin' up. See if you can get me some shots."

Charlie watches the slaughter through the cracked and frosted windshield of the car as he swings the lights over on the jacks and the shot patterns catch them.

They shoot more than 30 rabbits and Dick counts them care-

fully when they get back. Lying in the snow the rabbits are stiffening, pinto things, their eyes open in gleams of wide sadness in
the lantern light.

When Dick has finished counting the rabbits he pays Charlie
$13.25 out of his own billfold.

"What's this for?"

"Seventy-five cents a rabbit and four for your shells."

"You don't have to pay me now."

"Sure I do. You're getting phoney-assed stuck up and bitch too
much. I got to play basketball with you but I don't have to hunt
with you. I got to hunt with a brother."

"See you in school," Charlie says, "—only don't flap your
mouth like that when you're not at home."

"You want to walk out there?" Dick says. His eyes blaze and
he does a little shuffle, holding a rabbit like a limp club on one
hand.

"No, I don't want to walk out there. This whole thing is
crazy."

"You sayin' I'm crazy."

"Goodbye!" Charlie says.

"Say when!"

"Save it for basketball tomorrow night."

"You get your ass out of here before I forget our center got to
star tomorrow night."

Charlie doesn't say anything; he just waves a "forget it" wave
of his hand at the rabid little form pivoting and snarling in the
snow by the car. He turns and begins the long walk home
through the snow. Looking back, he sees Dick bending over the
engine with the gas lantern. In his right hand he holds the
ratchet wrench like a pistol. The guns lean on the car by the pile
of rabbits.

Charlie avoids Indian Town, walking nearly a mile out of his
way so he doesn't have to look at it. But in his heart he can't
avoid some dark thoughts about his golden girl. "Who?" he asks
himself and then "Why?" The snow runs low over the prairie
around him and behind him he can't see his own tracks.

15

The Titans

Most of all, winter is basketball for Charlie. He has high-hunched narrow shoulders and his string-tendoned boney legs seem half again too large for his body. But he can jump, can pull down a rebound before anyone else has touched it. And he practices jumping—in the house at a spider on the ceiling, at the Mobil station where someone wants a fan belt from one of the hooks high over the oil barrels, at school where his mark in the washroom is three inches above the others. Sometimes, too, in a crazy mood and with Billy Whitefeather tagging along, he gallops down side streets in Pierre, slap-banging signs hung out of the sidewalks and striding away before the owners of the stores can do much more than slam a cash register angrily shut and mutter "Indian hoodlums!" And heaven help the jaw or rib cage that catches his levering elbows in a game.

But he can never quite run smoothly. He runs in horse gallops a little sideways. "Lord!" his basketball coach says to him after practice, "If you didn't run on the oblique so much you could really get down on a fast break!" Once, sitting on the bench after fouling out under the boards, Charlie hears someone behind him say, "That Number Ten ain't no goddamn Indian. He don't run pigeon-toed at all. He run like a jackrabbit chased by a car." Charlie is going to turn around and say something, but the coach lays an arm over his shoulder and says very quietly that the man is drunk and a little stupid and that Charlie should let it go.

Charlie leans over with a towel on the back of his head and lets
the sweat drip down on the hardwood floor and tries to not see
all of the tennis shoes of the Ft. Pierre team running by him
pigeon-toed.

And thinks, seeing Nancy sitting alone down near the door to
his left beyond the Ft. Pierre cheerleaders, Doesn't she know I
don't want her here? Doesn't she give up? Doesn't her face ever
look happy? Doesn't she know I hate her face for looking so goddamn sad? Thinks, They don't talk to me much, these guys.
They don't ask me to anything after a game. They just like my
22 points and an average of 18 rebounds. This is a team, but I'm
a guest athlete. Thinks, She'll be gone by December 15, but she's
inside me now so I'll be like a fish swimming around with a
hook in its belly. Thinks, oh God how I like to scream her name
when I come and scare her pushing too deep for her. Thinks, Mr.
Porter, are you doing it too? Then stops thinking about anything
except his shoes and the hardwood floor and the final score.

Saturday mornings after the Friday night basketball games
Charlie sometimes works for Bob Buckanaga at the Mobil station on Western Avenue in Ft. Pierre. Bob usually has Charlie do
lube and wash jobs, but if the work is caught up, he lets Charlie
do extra wax jobs and keep most of the money. This is how
Charlie and Billy started waxing hearses and funeral cars from
the funeral homes in Pierre and Ft. Pierre. Bob is really good
about seeing that the two boys make some money because he's a
barber shop jock with four basketball letters himself, a forty-
year-old barbership jock who sits in the Sun Barbershop every
Saturday morning discussing what Charlie and the others didn't
do right Friday night and Tuesday night.

But Bob won't let either Charlie or Billy drive anything. He
drives the hearses back and forth himself because the owners
don't trust the boys and because he loves to do it himself, smiling fiendishly as he wheels the big old death buggies down the
streets and jounces them into the garage and over the grease pit.

Trouble is, Old Man Engen, the owner of the Engen Mortuary,
wants a really simonize job—the old paste stuff thick as half-set
glue. Charlie finds that he can only do about a square foot at a
time with the stuff—especially if it's cold. Billy and he rub and

rub and rub on the old Packard hearse, sweating and eating candy bars and swigging Cokes. Sometimes Charlie gets a hard on leaning into a fender and thinking about Tina. Working there inside the Mobil station garage with the coal stove ticking and the doors closed against the winter cold they both feel remote from everything. The wind snaps at the window and moans on the roof as the hearse begins to shine bright black from their rubbing.

Billy loves horses and sometimes he stands looking out at the big red pegasus high on the Mobil sign banging in the flurries of wind and snow.

"When was that horse?" he asks Charlie for the hundredth time. "You said you looked somethin' up about it." Billy never looks anything up. Maybe can't.

"It was the age of myth, the encyclopedia says. It was before history it said, like when gods and stuff were running around everyplace in Greece."

"In Greece? Like a couple thousand years ago?"

"More like four thousand."

"No wonder there ain't any more around, but I want that sign if they take it down. There aren't hardly any of them signs around even any more," Billy says, his brown eyes wide with a deep, far-off mourning.

"Keep waxin'!" Charlie exclaims sensing Billy is about to descend into some mournful philosophy.

But it's no use. "Joe Gray Hawk rode in this one," Billy says, standing over the chrome rollers in the back of the hearse and shaking the can of chrome cleaner.

"Sure," says Charlie.

"You push him out of the shower room when he was acting silly ass last Friday night?'

"No, but . . ."

"He just had a jock strap on. You should've heard him out there kicking the locker room door with his bare feet.

"I did . . ."

"He was screaming and swinging like a windmill when we let him in. That was before Sunday when he was dead. Never came back to school." Billy pauses. "You didn't go to Joey Gray

Hawk's funeral, but you took the day off from school?"

Charlie doesn't answer that one. He's heard enough about it.

Billy slides himself back into the hearse head first and lies there wide-eyed. Charlie shoves the vacuum cleaner hose in with him and turns it on. Billy picks up a few flower petals and lets the vacuum suck them up, whick! zap!

"Jesus, Charlie, I'm sick!" he cries. Charlie shuts off the cleaner. His voice is dim and feeble as a ghost's. "What was it he died of, Charlie? You ain't supposed to die of that anymore."

"It was scarlet fever and you come out of there now," Charlie yells. He pulls Billy out by his legs and they sit on some oil boxes alongside the hearse. In the shining waxed surfaces their faces contract and expand in rubbery ghost-white masks. "You ate too many peanut bars," he says to Billy.

"Sure," Billy says. Then he begins to throw up on the floor between his bow legs. "We were mean to him," Billy cries between spasms of vomiting.

"That had nothin' to do with it," Charlie says, recoiling from the acrid vomit stench.

"But he wasn't supposed to die from that. A white kid wouldn't have died from that would he?"

It's no one's fault. He didn't die from what you did to him, you dumb shit! I'm sure somebody died from my being born, but I'm not sure who, but it wasn't my fault."

"Died from what?"

"Nothin'." Charlie is sick of Billy and the hearse and wants to get out of there. He wants the wind outside to cool him and numb him and make him quit thinking about things. "You get the money and hold my half and quit eatin' all that candy and crap and thinkin' about dead stuff. I got to get some fresh air!" he says to Billy as he walks out on the street that slants down toward the river.

The slabs of ice along the banks of the river curve like lost pieces of a white and gray and blue jigsaw puzzle. The middle of the stream is open and throttles by in blue-green pulsings of deep current running between the buildings. Sometimes when the wind lifts, a wisp of steam rises like a breath of vague smoke from the surface of the water.

"Bang! Bang!" Two little boys, bundled up in blue insulated snow suits are playing cops and robbers in a graying hulk of an abandoned chicken brooder house. "Bang! Bang!" One staggers, holding his stomach, his black plastic gun twisting out of his hand, his face grimacing in simulated final pain. "Bang! Bang!" He pitches on the ground and rolls over, his round blue eyes staring at the winter sky.

"Dumb little shits!" Charlie mutters.

He walks a long way along the river through the snow. Ahead of him he sees the black smoke boiling up from the city dump where tires and garbage are burning. Even though the smoke bites his throat and chokes him as it swirls around him, he pushes toward the people there: two old Indian women rummaging with their gunny sack; a proud old man sitting on a little wooden wheelbarrow out on the sand that covers deep regions of garbage. Both women wear yellow work gloves on their hands. The old man holds a thick gray blanket over his shoulders. His face is a deep interfolding of wrinkles, his nose a brown protuberant beak of a thing, a roman thing under the wide black hat. His eyes are clear and deep brown and proud. Of what? Charlie wonders.

"The last of the proud race in the city dump!" Charlie grumbles to himself. He thinks about talking to him, about baiting him, about offering him a candy bar or something—he doesn't know what. He walks closer toward the strong old eyes watching him.

"Hey!" one of the old women yells. He turns toward her without quite looking at her, not wanting to look at the brown-black dirty knot of face. "See here! See here!" She is holding up a mirror—a large medicine cabinet door from someone's bathroom. "You want for cheap?" she asks. "You want for cheap?' she asks, walking toward him with big rocking motions, the voice coming in watery vibrato from her toothless mouth.

She thrusts the mirror toward him. "Good lookin!" she laughs. "Good lookin!" He sees his own long face and good white teeth and the Trojan seed corn hat, yellow and green. She rocks closer with a horrible limp, her hands out of the gloves black claws at the edges of the mirror.

"No!" he says.

He backs away from her, stumbles and begins to run, her swearing and terrible laughter pursuing him as he lurches past the old man and up into a thick run of woods rising north and west above the river.

Inside the woods he feels better and walks slowly. In the falling light he sees a horned owl slant down into the grass at the river's edge, its ears laid back. The owl's feathers are black washed and ghost bright in its ribbed plumes. It cries softly like a lover's ghost, then slants down wing over the grass where the mice are. Then, suddenly, it circles back and perches on the dead limbs of a cottonwood across a little opening in the woods beyond. Waits. The top of Charlie's head tingles with nervous fear. Is it the claws descending silently?" Hunter. Clean hunter!" Charlie says to himself.

He lets Charlie approach to the edge of the span of cottonwoods where he has perched. Then he slips silently off the limb, gliding stiff-winged over ranges of dark grass below. Circles. Flares. Drops to take a mouse. "Hunter. Clean hunter!" Charlie says to him.

When Charlie walks back along Western Avenue through the town he aches with hunger and loneliness. The pulsing red artery of the neon sign for the Sirloin Stockade Cafe draws him into the glow of lights over booths and tables done in pink and orange plastic and thick-grained oak with local cattle brands burned into the wider surfaces of the wood.

I don't like this place, he thinks. I got a feelin', he thinks. But, oh God, I'm hungry, he thinks, pushing in through the rattling aluminum storm porch and trying to look older and bigger because he has a feeling about the place.

He slides into a booth, and digs for some quarters for some music—any music.

"Hey!" the waitress yells.

"Hey what?"

"No one person in a booth. If you want to get served you go to the counter, O.K.?"

"Why?" A *stubborn* why because he *knows* why.

"Skip the why!" the cook yells over the high counter where

the plates glow under the red-orange warming lamps.

"It's O.K.," the waitress says. She is freckled and skinny and blue-eyed. She flirts with everybody who comes into the place.

"O.K." says Charlie. When he gets up, he's afraid everyone will be watching him, but the booth is away from the main dining room and he realizes that nobody is paying any attention at all. "I'm waiting for a friend," he tells the waitress.

"Whenever!" she says.

Waiting for Billy, Charlie stands by the coat rack and wishes he wasn't alone. He has stayed away from the Stockade for a lot of reasons—especially on Saturday night, but tonight he needs company because Tina can't meet him. Billy is the only company he can find tonight. He feels up tight in his loins and head. He needs it badly. Orgasm as memory. Memory of what?

"Billy, you sad-assed hearse waxer!" he yells when the squat body on thin legs bobbles toward him in the parking lot. Billy's coat is too big so it looks like someone has dropped it over him without buttoning it. When Billy pauses at the door Charlie steps out and pulls him in.

"I was so fuckin' sick you wouldn't believe it," Billy says, "but I finished and got us four apiece."

"We celebrate," Charlie says.

"Screw that. Let's get to some serious eating."

They hang up their coats. When a white-haired man wearing a camel hair coat comes in he pushes their coats—Billy's old wool navy one and Charlie's sheepskin—way over to the end of the rack.

"Lice! Sheep lice!" Billy says. The man disappears into the big dining room, pulling his coat back on and walking with stiff, angry steps. "Hair ball!" Billy calls after him.

The two of them sit down to the counter to order. The waitress is nice. She says that the hamburger steak special at $1.95 is for noon but that she could write it up special for them, their being nice young men and all.

"Ain't she got blue eyes?" Billy asks Charlie.

"Sure!" Charlie says.

"Some say I look like Katherine Hepburn," she says, "—except I don't have all them freckles and I'm half her age."

"Number 14!" the cook yells.

"Don't forget my extra order of American fries, lovely lady," Billy says.

"Well, I couldn't ever after that," she says. A false eyelash tilts up like a tiny loose comb over her left eye and quivers with her voice. She feels it and turns away to disappear into the kitchen to adjust it.

"She likes you, tall man," Billy says. "She never wrote no hamburger steak order up for me at night like that!"

Charlie shakes his head. His voice tastes flat in his mouth because he has seen somebody in the mirror behind the counter. "More like Katherine Heartburn!" he says.

When the two of them spin around on their stools to see who's in the Stockade, Charlie sees them—Nancy and Oates. Nancy's back is toward Charlie but he knows the hair, the bent shoulders, the green knit dress she wears Saturday nights. He wonders if she can see anything clearly without her glasses. Across from her Oates butters his Texas toast with big strokes of his butter knife, spreading the slice of it over his short, thick fingers. Then he points at her face with the knife and talks, chewing on the toast. His words sound curt and thick and heavy.

"She's with that construction wasica," Billy says. "She's been drinking. They both been drinking."

Charlie can see, by the position of Nancy's left shoulder, that she is reaching under the table to squeeze the man's leg. But Oates disregards her. He salts his mashed potatoes, digs up a bulging scoop and buries it in his mouth."

"Runs a cat." Billy continues. "After they built the Oahe Dam he stuck around and digs stuff. I heard him talkin' real loud and sayin' he's gonna dig up Mag's place next spring and they are goin' to build a resort out there, the sons-a-bitches!"

"Here you are, fellas!" It's the waitress and their food—hot and pepper sprinkled greasy mounds of it. She looks at them and then beyond them and stops smiling.

Charlie forces his food down between Billy's words. The food is getting cold and Charlie is having trouble swallowing it. When he turns around to look, he looks hard at Oates' blue-whiskered wide chin as it works heavily on his food. And then he looks at his eyes and gets caught at it. Mean, Charlie thinks, feeling thin and nervous anger inside his head and stomach. "I'd like to bust his face!" he mutters at Billy.

"You can't," Billy says as he forks in the last of the greasy American fries. "I seen him pour diesel fuel right out of a forty-gallon barrel into his cat tractor and throw the barrel off like it was paper. Turn around so he don't come over here. You don't have to look for trouble with him; he brings it to you without askin'."

"Eat!" says Charlie.

"He can rabbit punch real fast with those short arms. You can ask and see."

"I don't ask you anything."

"I only said it so you wouldn't do anything." Billy has begun eating candy bars for his dessert. " I pay for the candy separate," he says, gnawing on the side of a Bit-O-Honey bar.

"You pay for teeth. Your teeth look like a worm has lived one week in each. You ever go to a dentist?"

"He chews me out."

"But you just keep on eating."

"Look, I'm almost done. Don't get mad at me. You watch you don't get mad and lose your teeth to cat man," Billy says.

"Eat!" Charlie says.

"Jesus! Charlie, Mag is comin' in here!"

They see Mag enter, his face red from the cold, his eyes glass hard. He's wearing only a thick gray sweatshirt on top.

"He don't see us," Billy says.

"He's not looking. He doesn't want to look."

"See that thumb?" Oates is saying very loudly. "See that thumb. That gets on the lever of a machine and moves a whole mountain, by God. You look up at the dam, by God, and you can see what a cat man can build, by God. And I ain't done yet, lady."

When the jukebox begins playing "Ghost Trailer Number Nine" he talks even louder.

"If that lawyer ever gets off his ass and quits shufflin' paper we could even start diggin' now there's so much sand out there, by God."

Nancy reaches over and takes the thumb. It's thick and yellow-gray and looks dead to Charlie. Oates begins to laugh. "You like that thumb, don't you lady? And this other finger finger you like too."

"Please, not so loud?"

"Shut up now, I told you!"

"Jesus!" Billy exclaims.

Oates is holding Nancy's jaw like he is holding a fish to remove a hook, holding the thumb over the top of her lower lip and the fingers under her chin.

Standing there, his knees pressing the stool, Charlie holds himself between fear and hate. Talk slows around him; voices recede and come back. A nervous voice, a woman's voice, calls out, "Why, that man; do you see that?"

Mag pushes Charlie back down on the stool and sweeps by in one ruthless motion. Or, rather it's two motions—one to smash Oates' nose when he tries to stand up the first time, a napkin under his chin; the other to pull Nancy out and over Oates on the floor, swinging her, sobbing and waving her hands, into Billy and Charlie. And then other motions blur in quick murderous ritual as Mag bobs his head and slams it into the other man's rage and helplessness. Slams it so ribs crack and the jaw whocks into itself. Oates staggers, broken on his feet. He falls in sick-grinned crooked faced wonder—falls heavily sideways to rise on all fours before a kick on the side of the head ends it. The napkin has flapped back, blotting blood spray at the nose and mouth.

A few chairs have been tipped over and some of the people at tables farther away have stood up in alarm, but the whole dining room seems miraculously untouched.

Mag's cold, blue-gray eyes soften then as he stands breathing in jerks and wheezes. He regards the three of them standing there. His mouth is bleeding and a deep, gaping slit has been opened on his forehead. Behind them Charlie can hear the waitress dialing the phone and he knows she's calling the police.

"Listen," Mag says, still diving for breath and shaking. Nancy begins sobbing again. "I've got to get out of here!" she squeals. Charlie pushes her back toward Mag. "Listen," Mag says. "I did this for you, not my boats and all the rest of it. This is got noth-

ing to do with land, do you hear? Or your goddamn lawyer", do
you hear? This is somethin' else!"

Nancy pushes violently into Charlie, her face darkly insane
with fear. "Oh, what will he think when he finds this out?" she
moans.

"The pickup's in the lot," Mag calls after them. "Charles, my
boy, you get her home now and then come back for me.

As they huddle toward the door Mag yells after them, "Nobody is going to do that to her, Charlie. What the hell is she
doing with him anyway?"

When the cold outside bites into them, Nancy cries out again,
"Oh, why did he have to do that? What will he think now? Oh,
I'll never be able to go back!"

Inside the pickup Charlie turns to Nancy, studying her grim,
silent face in the dashlight. "That's it?" he asks. "Is Mr. Porter
what it's all about? He's waiting back there for the police and
Mr. Porter is what it's all about?"

"I want to go," she says. "I don't care about anything anymore. I just want to go."

"Sure," he says.

"Jesus!" Billy says. " He was like a battering ram or something. Nobody ever done that to Oates."

"Please!" Nancy screams and begins sobbing again. Charlie
hurries the pickup down an alley toward the house. When they
get there, Billy steps out and lets Nancy go in. She hobbles like
an old, broken woman to the door and enters without turning
around toward them.

"Goodbye," Charlie says. "Goodbye!"

Back at the restaurant they can see the black and white
county sheriff's car parked in a No Parking zone behind the
kitchen.

"We gotta?" Billy asks.

"We gotta."

As they descend from the warmth of the pickup cab they can
see the sheriff's car is backing toward them and they wait to let
it come to them. The window on the driver's side rolls down.

"We took her home," Billy says. "She was sick and scared."

The voice from inside the little region of squawking radio

noises sounds weary and remote. "He's alive—won't even take an ambulance. Are you her relatives?"

"Kind of?" Charlie says.

"What do you mean, kind of? You're not in any trouble. What's the matter with you?"

"She's his stepmother," Billy says, dancing bug-eyed on his cold feet and shivering and nodding at Charlie.

"Well, let me tell you good relatives something," the voice continues, "nobody, including the cafe, is pressing charges. Now that may seem all hunky-doory to you, but to us that means trouble later, do you know what I mean? This isn't the frontier."

"Who said that?" Billy asks. "White guys are beating up Indian ladies, aren't they."

"Well, it's not the Indian ladies who are going to make trouble: it's Magnuson and Oates. Oates is going to be like Old Hugh Glass: he's going to heal up and then get his revenge later, do you understand?"

"Sure," says Charlie.

"Sure, Sure. Shit, you aren't even sure who your relatives are. But I'll tell you this: you better do what you can to stay out of trouble and to cool those two old wildcats down. There's going to be a lot more trouble here and I have to clean up, you understand?"

"Sure," Charlie says, as the car lurches into gear and roars away on Western Avenue toward Pierre.

"What else could Mag do?" Billy asks.

"Nothin'," Charlie says, "but it's not Mag that really did all this."

Mag is waiting for them just inside the door. His face is grim and pale except where the bruises are.

"Is she all right?" he asks.

"We took her home," Charlie says. "But I'm not going back."

"What?" He had expected Mag to like that but Mag is shaking his head sadly. "No, you go home. She's having a bad time. I don't like what she's doing with that lawyer son, but this is something else. She's all alone."

"I don't want to."

"Well, sure, but she's been treated badly by a lot of people, even me a little. She was lonely."

"Lonely?"

He can feel Mag's eyes now. "You ever done anything that didn't make sense because you're lonely?" he asks. "I just wonder about that."

"I don't know."

"You know. It's not so easy to say it, but you and I both know. Sometimes I think none of us ever learned how to treat a woman out here. There's a whole new bunch of women trying to do something better and they're confused and we're confused."

"I'll go back tonight, but I'm not stayin'."

"Well, you think on that a lot, will you? I'm tired out. I got to sleep and rest up . . ."

"For what?"

"Well, I have got a lot of things to get ready for."

He takes Charlie's arm. "You got a good arm," he says. "Now keep a good heart." He doesn't let go of the arm. They stand there, tall, embarrassed, doing nothing—with Billy watching. Mag's arm shaking.

"It's no wind out there now and I got to get back in case. Do you mind the walk back?" Mag asks.

"No, but I'm not staying." Charlie says as Mag walks out.

"That is some man!" the waitress says behind them. "He went around and apologized to people afterward when Oates was gone."

"He don't have anything to apologize for," Billy says.

"I never said that. I just said he did it. And now, if you don't mind we have to close."

Billy walks with Charlie about half way to Charlie's house and then walks off, wobbling as always, toward his place at the edge of Indian Town. "I never thought it would turn out like this!" he yells back at Charlie.

In the house, in the light from the TV set Nancy's face is putty gray as she sits in the chair. When Charlie starts to close his bedroom door she cries out to him. "Oh, please, Charlie. Just come and sit in here a little while! I can't bear all of this alone. Just sit in this room a little while!"

He pulls up a wooden kitchen chair and sits down across the room from her. "Come closer," she pleads. He sits rigidly upright. He doesn't move.

"Well, you see I might as well be a lawyer's hired bitch," she says, "or maybe I should say '*One* of the lawyers hired bitches.'" Her voice is brittle and her face gray stone.

"Sure," says Charlie.

16

Games

It's the Friday afternoon pep rally at Ft. Pierre High School. There are 190 students in the high school and, although some of the freshman and sophomore students never stop talking for a film or a lecture or anything else, varsity boys' basketball is too serious a matter for silliness or indifference. There is a mighty and terrible issue at hand—winning the Friday night game. To interrupt a pep talk or say stupid things is to evoke doom. "Why didn't you shut up?" a senior girl says to a silly, gopher-toothed freshman girl. "You talked, didn't you? He heard you make fun. He looked over and saw you and heard you, you know what I mean? You think he don't think about that out there?" Nobody ever sang a *Te Deum* before a South Dakota high school basketball game or did a serious ceremonial dance, but basketball in South Dakota is not to be reckoned with lightly.

Charlie stands in a line with the coach and the other eleven players facing the students and the "disciplinary" faculty members in the bleachers. "Doc" Red (Redding), the coach, stands at Charlie's right elbow, nervously scratching his thin sheaf of red hair, and wishing, as all of them do, that the pep rally would end quickly. Bea Drew, Charlie's English teacher, is standing behind the team and that makes all of them especially nervous—not because she "hawks" the bleachers looking for "uncivilized" behavior, but because she never quite enters into the seriousness of the event and is forever making low-voiced comments on the orations of Superintendent ("Sick") Wells.

And here he comes—a sturdy little man with a round, pink face and blue eyes. He wears a black suit that looks like someone has waxed it down the back. He wedges between players six and seven and raises his hands, palms out, toward the bleachers. Nervous, anxious eyes come to rest on him. Giggles trail off. The players bow their heads—except Dick Bissonette—and hold their hands behind them. Doc Red scratches his head furiously. Miss Drew laughs her tight, low ironic laugh.

"Boys!" Wells announces, laying his hands on the shoulders of Joey Redwing and Billy Whitefeather, who, like the others, are wearing black shirts and baggy tan pants. They are the shortest players on the team. Wells positions himself very carefully between them. The others lean over the little trio in the center like hawks leaning over sparrows. A pause. A cheer. In the bleachers girls wanting—something. Boys hating their wanting. Jealousy. Love. Hate. Fear. And sweating, much nervous sweating.

"Boys," chants Wells, "how do you win? *How* do you win?"

Billy Whitefeather tries it, feeling Wells' arm stiffen at his shoulder. "Score?" he asks, tucking his shirt collar up and looking down to survey his feet.

"What does it take to win?" Wells asks again, disregarding Dick Bissonette's quiet "Shit!"

"Points!" somebody yells from the railing above them. He is soaked. Mumbles something else. Cringes.

"What does to take to win?"

No answer. The crowd is silent before the mystery.

"What does it take to win? Why it takes prespiration!" Wells cries. "You got to have prespiration!" He dances, red-faced, on one foot and then another, clapping as some of the students clap.

"Pres-pi-ration is what it takes!" The ironic voice behind Charlie is barely audible. He glances furtively sideways and sees Miss Drew. She raises her eyebrows at him through the huge jeweled plastic frames of her glasses. Her eyes are full of mischief and pleasure and defiance. She pushes her wide chin out with insolent delight." "It's full court pres-pi-ration," her mouth announces with a fiendish, exaggerated lipiness. Charlie chokes down a laugh and coughs.

Well's eyes are on him then and they are full of anger. "And here's Good Thunder to tell us how we're going to win tonight," he announces to the crowd.

"But the coach . . ." Charlie begins.

"I present Charles Good Thunder," Wells says, bowing.

Cheers. Faces long and brown-eyed as collie faces. Faces seared with scars. Adenoidals. Pug faces. Wolf-eyed girl faces. Twins, geeky and shy as young deer. Clumsy, incomplete young people waiting and squirming. Charlie panicking and shambling out a step or two toward the crowd. The wind roars in the transom overhead and he wishes it would blow him away.

"You're right, Mr. Wells, " he says finally. "It does take perspi-ration to win. I know, because I sweat out every game myself." Nervous laughter somewhere. Waiting.

Charlie stalls, fumbling to open his little memory bank. He fumbles and stalls.

"My, my," says Wells," and you a good English student."

"There's one little word," Charlie says, remembering something. "I heard it in a movie. It's what Gary Cooper said in old western movies when things were tough and when he's outnumbered and facing a tough situation . . ."

"Like somebody else I know," Drew says behind him.

But they're taking him seriously. They lean over into him—all 180 of them. The wind roars in the transom. They wait. What *is* it? their eyes ask. Jesus!

"Yup!" Charlie says, "—just one big positive word—short and sweet—yup! yup!"

Cheers. The band attempts to play something. Three girls flourish blurring white pom-poms and leap into the air making quick pink-bronze A's with their legs. Charlie tries to avoid Miss Drew's eyes. It's over, but never over. Turning, Charlie sees Dick Bissonette's hard eyes. As he walks back into line, Dick mutters, "So your big hero is cowboy? Where's your hat, orator?" So nothing is ever over with.

The game that Friday night is in the town hall in Carroll, South Dakota—a white team. Most of the teams they play are white. Charlie hates playing there in the tight, undersized rattling gym. There's so little room in the bleachers there are always feet ranged along the "out" lines and sometimes some wise guy sticks a boot out or worse, a cane as you run along the side court watching for a pass. Carroll has a bad reputation as a Cowboy vs. Indian town in all sports. The regular cheerleaders don't do it, but when a game gets hot you can hear little cheering sections inside the crowd chanting "Scalp em! Scalp em!" and "Beat the Braves! Beat the Braves!" It's a tough place to play for everyone—especially the referees—school superintendents and principals usually—tight-faced men out to earn some extra money, men who live and work all week with conflict and find it again on Tuesday and Friday nights.

The Ft. Pierre Indians are wearing red uniforms with black numbers and when they wheel out on the floor to warm up, the people cheer "Redskins! Redskins!" from somewhere high up in the bleachers. On one end of the little gym and up on a raised stage behind the defensive basket a large black coal stove huffs waves of hot air—so hot that the joke is that the white players change colors on a break. They start out blue on the cold end near the big entry doors and turn rosey pink as they run into tropic regions on the other end. We got our jokes too, Charlie muses, waiting in line to gallop in for lay-ups.

"Little Big Horn—but they got *us* surrounded again," Blue Elk cries into Charlie's ear. "What you mean *us*, Indian?" Charlie yells back. It's an old joke. He's not even sure it's funny.

Charlie misses his lay-up as he tries to avoid another row of feet of standers on the wall between the two entry doors. He passes by the face of an older man—a lean, brown sinewy faced man. He focuses on his face only a second and is surprised to see warm regard. It helps. He knows that sometimes, since only the cheerleaders and team go to games as far away as Carroll (110 miles), all of them feel like they're in another hostile country, surrounded by unfriendly parents and other townspeople. "Surrounded" isn't always just a joke; it's a deep feeling—a bad one.

The whistle. Line-up. Announcements of starting line-ups. Coach Doc Red scratching his thatch of red hair and chewing a huge wad of Dentyne gum. Cheerleaders going shrieky little rubbery bouncing things. One of the Carroll cheerleaders is tall and very blonde. Leggy and very blonde like Tina. Tina has gone away.

The whistle. Blue Elk is at center because Doc Red thinks Charlie can't see behind him very well. Once, after a fake hand-off to a guard cutting across the center post, Charlie had plowed into a big string-bean center with frail wire-rimmed glasses and blue-stick legs. Both referees, who hadn't heard the center's "Cretin! Cretin!" litany, kicked Charlie out of the game. "We don't have to do that. We're not savages!" Doc Red said.

So the tip-off goes to Dick Bissonette at left forward and Charlie gallops down to the right forward slot. He fumes at the guards, Billy Whitefeather and Dick Whiteheels, because they aren't working the ball in but dribbling, dribbling and passing across the front. Charlie lays in close to the big red-faced blond forward playing him man-to-man and then slips around him so he's open for a pass, but neither guard ever seems to be in position. They pass and pass and then shoot flat-trajectory shots because the ceiling is low.

Charlie goes for the boards with hawk hunger and flailing of arms. He and Blue Elk ride the air like sinewy, lean flying horses.

It's nearly half time and Charlie has climbed through flailings of arms and elbows to collect seven field goals and two fouls for two free throws. When he goes up for a rebound on one side of the basket and Blue Elk on the other they control the board. Sometimes, for just the second when he's up a little higher than the Carroll center—a high stalled moment at the peak of the jump—Blue Elk flashes his big smile of fiendish delight before he pulls the ball down or tips it in. Blue Elk is 6'4" tall and built like a rangey ox. But his hands are small and quick and he shoots with uncanny delicacy. "Swish!" goes his shot. "Aw!" the crowd goes—not "Ah!"

None of them has ever been coached much, but most of them have been playing together for a long time. Doc Red, their coach and a math teacher, is fresh out of Northern State Teachers College. He has made them all get into shape and learn some basic plays, but mostly he lets them work out things on their own.

"You know what's not working," he says. "You know your timing is off and only you can get it back." And they do know it and they usually get it back.

Time out, the score 29–22. Doc Red, surrounded by his Indian team, struggles to say something over the din of cheering and feet stomping. "You have to triangulate the goal and converge on it more," he yells hoarsely at the two guards. He backs away as if he's trying to get to a blackboard. Blue Elk holds him from stumbling over the bleachers. "You've got to get more momentum in and more momentum out or you're not *powering* the game, don't you see?"

"What's the Doc say?" Billy Whitefeather asks. Doc Red raises his eyes to heaven and looks over at Charlie.

"You got to run in, not around—break in and pass in and work at the basket more."

"Eloquent," says Doc Red.

The "Doc" part? Well, Doc Red is always handing out free vitamins. "All I hear is coughing," he says after practices as he taps the vitamin C tablets into their palms. "The mucous passages need some help in the winter, don't you see?" They don't, but most of them take the tablets or take them home for somebody else.

"You guards stay closer together so you're ready to pass in!" Doc Red yells as the buzzer sounds and they run out on the floor again.

Hot work. The big coal stove glows up on the stage. The referees sweat and glow, blowing their whistles pink-faced. Sometimes they dance little indignant dances when bad fouls are committed.

The crowd seems far away as Charlie works into a heat, feeling it all working like a smooth-turning circle, feeling sleepy smooth as he shoots over ranges of frantically waving big hands or bats down a shot. Loves it. Feels big. Does everything right without thinking about it. Feels good. Loves the ball, hugging it and playing it on his hands. He wants the strong motion, the good heat and the beautiful simple winning to go on and on. Shoots. Shoots. Hits, swishing, swishing.

Whistle. Dick Buckanaga comes out on the floor pointing at

Charlie. Then Dick remembers he hasn't checked in at the scoring table. He paddles back there, twist-flicking his stiff black hair up over his head as he bends over to report.

"Me?" Charlie asks, glowering at him and he stands there looking past Charlie at the others, no answer in his eyes— nothing. He throws himself down, angry, his hot game motion broken. He sits down next to Joey Redwing. "Shit!" he says to Joey. "Don't shit me. You don't pass to anyone. You just hog the ball and shoot, shoot, shoot." Joey coughs and coughs. His right shoulder is misshapen and his left arm like a broken wing. They never did get a doctor when it was broken—or a medicine man or anybody else. I ought to feel sorry or something, but I don't, Charlie says to himself. Ball hog! Shit! Pride is a hard, hard thing.

In the roaring noise of the crowd the Indian cheerleaders have small, little-girl voices. Their cheers are half sad echoes of the throaty, feverish bouncy noise rhythms of the three sturdy blonde Carroll cheerleaders.

One of the Ft. Pierre cheerleaders, Buffie, is all belly—a little tub belly. Buffie has eyes like a robin and a little bird face. And Sue, tall as a heron, looks like a heron trying to lift off a sandbar in the river. Their faces look sickly green-brown. They look tired. From what? Skim milk and crackers? Potato chips? Flour fried in lard? But still we are winning? Winning what? Are my mother and the Pettigrews right? Charlie thinks about all these, thinks, sitting there on the bench.

The Ft. Pierre cheerleaders give another quick, nervous little yell out in front of the Ft. Pierre bench: "Come on, team. Come on, team. They leap up like purple-legged, red-feathered birds. The Carroll cheerleaders respond and the crowd stomps, stomps, "Get that score! Get that score! Shove 'em right down through the floor." The whole building rumbles with feet and voices.

A slap on the back and Charlie is up again, plunging at the table to report, then galloping into the right forward position after slapping Dick Buckanaga on the butt.

"Goodblunder—thunder at right forward, oh, replacing Buckanaga." Laughter rocks the bleachers and Charlie turns toward the scoring table, his eyes blazing hatred. Sees a student blushing behind his wire-rimmed glasses, but definitely enjoying it all. He thinks about going over there but then he sees that everyone is laughing—except Buffie, who sits on the bench like a red-breasted mother robin on the nest. He holds his head down and lets the anger flow into his legs to become power.

Takes the tip off from Blue Elk, climbing high, trying to fly so high he can go right over the top of them. They run, pour the passes and shots through and over the cowboys. They run the five of them into the floor, laying a smooth, fast pattern of attack and defense. They run the nice, clean-cut, had-been-laughing five of them into nervous dismay, making them miss shots, double dribble, travel, make stupid fouls and lose, lose by 20 points. "Aw!" the crowd moans. "Aw!" Some of the crowd begins leaving early. "Aw!" the crowd moans when the Carroll center misses an easy lay-up with just ten seconds to go. The blonde cheerleaders sit looking dismayed.

After the game Doc Red and the first five have malted milks and hamburgers and vitamic C on Doc Red in the truck stop on the south side of a little town 20 miles south of Carroll. They never stop in the town where they've just played—too much trouble. Blue Elk keeps bitching about the rawness of his hamburger. He has taken an enormous bite out of it and is chewing with a woeful look on his face. "Give this one to Good Thunder," he pleads mournfully. "Charlie likes raw meat and blood tonight. He makes the game a blood battle. Why do you think he gets so mad at the Cowboys so he wants to kill them?"

"Oh, my," Doc Red says. "I thought he was just hot tonight."

"Blood hot," says Joey Redwing between coughs and slurps of his malt.

Blue Elk won't let it go. Charlie feels it coming and bends over his hamburger chewing it slowly, his face sullen.

"Hates cowboys!" Blue Elk begins.

Dick Bissonette picks it up. It's going to be the two of them: "Hates cowgirls!" Dick exclaims in phoney, wooden "Indian" speech.

"Blackbird wishing to be crow hates crows maybe."

"You speak truth. See blackbirds flying at crows every day."

"O.K. you guys!" Charlie mutters.

"Good Thunder angry at fair-haired girls with pink legs."

"Can't be one," Dick says. "Something else in this fella's heart."

"Maybe wants one," Blue Elk says.

"Maybe had one," Dick says.

"Listen . . ." Charlie begins to get up.

"Oh, my!" Doc Red exclaims. "Is this going to be an internecine quarrel? What's the point of all this?" He scratches his head nervously. Dandruff flakes snow down into his malted milk.

"What's that word?" Billy Whitefeather asks. He has a cream-tan ice cream moustache on his upper lip and he is bug-eyed. Obviously he's trying to pull them off Charlie.

"I'm sorry," Doc Red says. "I hate people who do that. I just meant I hate to see you quarreling among yourselves—especially after the way you pulled together tonight."

"In the *second* half," Dick Bissonette says, "and then it was like playing with a *heyoka*, a crazy man."

"What you crazy about?" Joey Redwing asks.

"Him mad at Blue Elk for taking place of honor at center?" Blue Elk asks.

Doc Red seems ready to intrude but he looks at Charlie and shrugs his shoulders helplessly. "I don't know what to say. I can't tell you all how to think or feel, I guess."

"You speak great truth," Dick says, speaking to Blue Elk, not Doc Red.

"Him mad because he not at center, maybe. Not at center, not happy fella."

"Ho! Ho!" Charlie says, slouching a little more.

"Charlie worse in football last year." It's Dick Whiteheels. "In pile-up he go for blood. Bites."

"Ho!" Charlie says, glancing at Doc Red.

"Hole!" says Blue Elk. He lifts a huge long foot up on the table and peels back the pantleg. "Bites friend and enemy," he says, shaking his head and pressing his fingers into the little sets of white marks on the calf.

When Blue Elk brings the foot down on the floor again, he stomps it on the waitress' foot. She yelps, jumping back and spilling the glasses of ice water. "Sorry, lady," Blue Elk says, "but I was showing where my friend here bit me. He ate too many raw hamburgers!" She doesn't smile as she lays the slip for the malts and hamburgers down next to Doc Red. As usual, he sits there not saying much but nodding and smiling.

"We gave a big show in that town hall basement tonight," Joe Redwing says.

"Especially Goodthunder walking back and forth down there with only a T-shirt on."

"Girls scratching at windows to get in."

"Charlie is horse rabbit and girls know it."

"Blonde girls."

"You could be a South Dakota Jackrabbit at Brookings State," Doc Red says, trying to shift the subject. "The Carroll coach was a big jock there and he says the SDS coach has been scouting you and Blue Elk."

"College?" Joey asks. He begins to cough and cough and cough. Blue Elk hits him on the back.

"Why not college?"

"Got to read. Got to read and write and talk bullshit like a book," says Joey.

"And then college boy will get too good for us savages," Dick Bissonette says.

"No," Charlie snaps, "But maybe I can get as good as some others and maybe we all could win some things."

"My gosh, Charlie, it's not all basketball. You can't beat all of *them*. It's not healthy for any of us. I know these guys are giving us both a hard time, but the basketball and winning stuff is just a part of it, you know what I mean?"

"No," Charlie says.

"Well, we better get going," Doc Red says, spinning out nine dollar bills.

"I'm not going to any college," Blue Elk says. "It's more boxes and learning to get the frog skin. You don't feel too great about yourself in those colleges, I heard. They can make a good man feel like nobody."

"That's how you see college?" Doc's eyes are sad asking it.

"That's how I see not going. You can't play basketball all the time. You got to sit inside and forget the stars and sky and

Mother Earth while they make you feel like you got to be taken all apart and put together a different way."

"White man's way," Dick Bissonette says.

"But there's *one*—one—Indian teacher at the school," Doc Red says. "How can you let that go on and on?"

"We don't," Blue Elk says. "We ain't there most of the time. *It* is going on and on, not us."

"The whole school has got to be taken apart and put back together for us," Charlie says. They look at him, surprised or angry. He can't tell.

"Exactly," says Doc Red. "But this is too much for a tired-out coach who's been up since six o'clock. We'd better move out now."

Outside, a sheet of stars is turning back toward the east. The little town yawns sleepily around them, lights winking off. Charlie crawls into the back of the car because he wants to sleep and to avoid Doc Red's eyes and words.

"Whew!" Doc exclaims as they drive along the wide black band of Highway 14. He is trying to see through the snow running like white veil being pulled over the surface of the highway. "Whew!" he exclaims, squinting through the windshield. "The crust must've broken. It's all one big motion again."

"Ghosts now," says Blue Elk.

"College snow," says Dick Bissonette.

Driving through the Dakota winter night they lapse into postures of haggard sleep—except Charlie, who can't sleep at all. They pass little gingerbread towns that look like someone has thrown them on the prairie floor and snowed on them and forgotten them. They drive toward a glow of lights and find, usually, a string of light poles lighting a corridor that runs at right angles from the highway past a small motel or filling station and down through main streets. Trucks chortle and snort past them, slamming wind blasts into the car and powering down the tunnels of their headlights toward the West. A jackrabbit looms like a small, indecisive spectre on the edge of the road and ghosts back into infinite whiteness. The snow runs under the high, clear regions of stars and out into regions of ice—fields wide with whiteness, except that, here and there, hulking batteries of

cattle lean into straw sheds and gerry-built ranch houses drift
and sail through the protean snow with glazed window eyes.

Doc Red drops him off first and says a hoarse, tired "Good-
night." The others sleep, twisting against the frosting car windows and trying to not lean into each other too much.

The front screen door of the house is whapping in the wind
and a light is on in the kitchen. He sees the other tire tracks in
the driveway and knows whose car has been there and it angers
him, or would if he weren't so tired, so tired. Under a tilted broken window shade at the living room window he can see the silver ghost flicker of the television set.

He pushes into the kitchen. Nothing, not even a "hi." Then
he sees that Nancy has fallen asleep. Her face startles him. Her
eyes seem half open and, as she choke snores in long fluttering
breaths, her mouth looks torn and gaping. "Ung! ung!" she cries
sadly. Her blouse is unbuttoned and out at the waist. There's no
picture on the TV screen, only more bright, frantic snow. He
kneels down to turn it off.

"Leave it. I don't want the other light," the ghost voice behind
him says. When he turns to look at her, he sees that she has not
rearranged her clothes and buttoned the buttons on the blouse.

"Are you all right?" he asks.

"Oh, Charlie, that's funny, do you know that? Am I all right?
No, I'm not all right. Are you all right? No, you're not all right.
Is anybody all right? Not that I know of."

"We won the game," he says, sitting down, as he always does,
in the straightbacked kitchen chair she has put at the corne
where the living room and kitchen meet.

"You won the game. You won the game. What's that you
won?"

"Just the game." A long pause. "Charlie, I'm very, very drunk.
You know why?"

"No."

"No. Well, it's because I am a little crazy, that's why. I was
crazy to try to do so many things. . . . I'm tired, Charlie. I'm
crazy and drunk and tired old."

"You want some coffee?"

"No, I don't want any coffee."

Pause, her breath heavy.

"I want love, Charlie. Don't you want love?"

"I guess so."

"You guess. You *know*, Charlie! . . . You know what? I tried to get a man here, but it's no use."

"He's mean!"

"No, it's me. I got no way to turn. I got no way to go now . . . Even Mr. Por-ter. You know about Mr. Porter, don't you, Charlie?"

"No."

"No?" She laughs, half sobbing. "No?" *I* do. I do. . . . You men! You men you." Another laugh. He has never heard her laugh like this.

"I'm tired. I should go to bed," he says.

"To bed. I've been to bed. He said after—he said afterward that it was one of two thinks—things—he was going to do. That is why he got himself healed up, *don't you see?*"

"No."

"It was awful. I don't like it. You men, you men, you. Even Mr. Porter, even Mr. Porer. I got no place to turn, Charlie. Do you know what I mean? I am in a fish trap. I tried to go up and got caught. And I can't go back. You know what I mean?"

"A little."

"A little."

"I'm going away. You men can have it . . . all. I am going to Minneap-o-lis."

"Because of him?"

"What? Never. Because of *me*, becuz me. You goin? You can't go. You don't like it. You don't like me even."

"I do, but I don't know what to do."

"You could . . ." She waves an arm angrily. "No you couldunt! I can't ge- that from you."

"Well . . ."

"It's ter-ble, Charlie. All want to win. There's somethin' ter-ble gon' happen." She sags in the chair then and cries. He stands up and walks over to her.

"It's no use now. It's too late and you won't remember," he says to the top of her head as he pats it. And yet she takes the hand and kisses it and holds it to the side of her face. He stands there a long, long time. In the kitchen he can see the clock. Long minutes pass, before she lets go. He turns off the lights.

He slides into the blankets in his room, tosses something like a curse or a prayer off into the dark and sleeps.

17

Rapid City

As the bus rolls toward Rapid City, Tina Pierson tries very hard to not think about things. The little switch in her head has clicked off and when that happens, she always has trouble talking or thinking or making decisions—even the silliest, simplest ones. Like right now. Should she reach into her purse and take out a piece of gum? Half a piece? It all seems so heavy. Her bones are lead tubes; her head is heavy with a fuzzy impotence of thought and feeling. She wishes she were—was—dead, but thoughts about life keep coming.

The landscape rolling by through the window doesn't help much. Towns with snow-packed dirt streets, frame houses sprawled into gerry-built leantos. The people, wind-humbled and wind-bent as they stand or walk on the streets. The bus pulls into a bus stop hotel and she sees through the lobby window old men sitting there—canes at knotted hands, wrinkled faces, lensed eyes. They stare out into the wide streets. Even inside the lobby they seem wind-dried like ancient trees. The Last Hotel in South Dakota. The wind is the Alpha and Omega of the prairie.

And yet she thinks about things, talking to herself inside herself sitting in the seat alone, sinking into it, held in it like a—dear God! She tries a catalog of signs from the street: Highmore Cafe, Rumley Hardware, Larson Standard Service, Bus Stop. Who or what put her on the bus? What will it be like coming back? Why (But she knows why)—why won't her mother let

her call from the clinic at Rapid City? This is no wayward bus.
"You can't ruin your life; you have to be hard. No I can't take
you. Of course I can't take you. It's all arranged. Yes, it's a cruel
deceit. Yes we're lying to your father. But do you want to ruin
your life?" Mama, mama, you bitch you!

She has six hundred dollars in cash and a nicely modified birth
certificate—birth certificate—in her purse. Ish! The money to
get rid of too. Todd, Todd, you bastard you! It's off to Carlton
and, meanwhile back at the ranches, business as usual for you,
you bastard you, whose wife never knew, you bastard you.

It was a night extension course in Pierre—the University of
South Dakota. She could transfer credits, all three of them. Eth-
nic American literature, Ms. Murillo, instructor—liberal, but
careful to be "objective" as soon as she sensed hostility in the
class. She invited a Pierre attorney to talk to the class because
she believed that too much of the reading in the class—mostly
Black and Chicano literature—presented a negative view of the
American system of justice.

Todd Porter, attorney at law, appeared one night standing
there by the lectern and smiling with gracious self-assurance.
"Ladies and gentlemen of the jury." Was that the way he looked
at them? He spoke precisely and carefully, watching to see what
their eyes might tell him. So, what had her eyes told him? She
was 18, but it wasn't awe or admiration—not after a few clicking
phrases. Within a few minutes she had seen that property rights
were the foundations of his system of justice. Property—a bundle of rights accruing to title to land and things. It was a matter
of getting things one had coming. He smiled when he said it: "A
lawyer, quite honestly speaking, has a lot of economic opportunities and those are the amenities that compensate for the no-fee
cases." It was a matter of getting some things one had coming.
And Todd Porter obviously believed that a native son, a Duke
Law School graduate, had a lot coming to him.

And she came to him. Not for good looks either. Too neat.
Slightly portly, but smooth handsome. But too neat, the gray
suit like an impervious shell. But then she had wanted to break
the shell. She stayed afterward with him to argue. He smiled and
dodged and smiled. Then he suggested arguing at lunch in Hu-

ron. They could meet outside the big discount store in Pierre first. Discrete. And then it all began.

Why then? Why did she take a phoney job in the law office—a temporary one, school three months away—as ombudsperson for Native Americans? She didn't really know any except Charlie and she met him later. All she did was to sit at a desk or in the little law library and read and think. Once, when she talked to an Indian attorney he told her that she was doing a silly thing because she really had no real work but was being treated about as badly as a lot of women and Indians were. And the Indian woman in the office. My God how she hated her. What did she know? Thank God Mrs. Porter stayed home with kids and things!

Why then? He was a man who always saved a part of himself for something else later. As she lay with her head on his lap so nobody would see her with him driving to the rented cabin on the lake above the dam, she might say, "Could we ski back in where nobody'll see us? Or, could you walk with me after? I feel a little let down sometimes." And he would say, "I'd love to, but I have hours of case preparation ahead of me and then about a hundred calls." If she protested, he said, "Don't pout, for Christ's sake! I haven't got the patience for it."

So he was always a man who saved himself for something later. Even in lovemaking there was a haste and roughness. And he let her do things—soap and water things—love making's small ceremonies and large movements. Didn't always wait for her. Sometimes he left her hanging, not flying and gliding down. "Damn it!" he said hoarsely, trying to hold back. "It's all right," she said, but it wasn't. And he wouldn't try again until next time.

He wanted something else and he showed her what it was one bright October day when he stopped the gray Cadillac high along the eastern shore of the river. Below them (after she raised up) half a dozen boats were cutting through the waves, tracing slashes of power behind them.

"There it is," he announced. He was vibrant with excitement. His hand massaged her knee. He felt strong next to her, his words tight and muscular. Across from them where he pointed there was nothing much to see—wooden docks, an old pick-up half hidden in cottonwoods, a few chickens italicized against the brown earth. "Over there," he said, "will be the biggest resort and ski lodge and marina this side of the Great Lakes."

"There?"

"Of course."

"Do you own the land?"

"Most of it—a real estate investment trust."

"When will you do it?"

"It'll take about 10 years."

So she resented it. She found herself pushing hostile words at him. "Then you'll be even busier, won't you?"

"Too busy do you mean?"

"No." Backing down as usual.

"Listen, Tina, it's a man's world out here. To be in it you have to be able to do something—law, business, engineering—something. They don't hand it to you. You have to find the opportunities and use them and people fight you on the way. There's a tough, half- crazy old Swede over there with a lot of beat-up fishing boats and a dug-out. He's sitting on the center of the whole project, the *sina qua non* of the project and we can't move him with anything."

"Maybe he doesn't want to move."

"Well, for God's sake, that's clear and manifest."

"It's sad."

"Don't give me that elegiac, romantic stuff. This is serious."

"Please don't talk like that to me!" She cried then. He started the car.

"We're going to have to settle a few things," he said. "You pull yourself together. This isn't any classroom. Everything isn't all right. You have to do something not just talk about it. Do you want me to take you back?"

"No." Why did she say no? Afraid of losing?

Patronizing bastard. He told her to get done at Carlton and go to a good law school and come back out. Go away four years or six and then we'll pick it up again. Like a lease, and then she had to put head on his lap while they drove to the cabin.

So Charlie was so wonderful, a gift of fate. A dumb boy, a

beautiful dumb boy! And she met him in Todd's car, made love
in it, staining the seats even, so excited sometimes that she
must've forgotten the diaphragm sometime at one of the first
meetings. Charlie so delighted and grateful and long-coupling
and gentle, kissing her eyes and hair a million times afterward
and saying, as she dropped him into the darkness along the road
north of his home, "I'll miss you right away. I'm missing you
right now." And, "I'll be out here at 8:oo. I'll stand off the road a
little. If I miss you Thursday night I'll be out again Friday
night." A joke on Todd, a joke on Charlie, a joke on her. You
lank you, you sweetheart you! She had met him too soon. No.
Another joke. She really hadn't met him at all. Didn't really
know anything about him. Stud service. Revenge. Stud service—
better than the big Jewish boy at St. Paul Academy even.

She sleeps, not sure that she's sleeping. The doll is floating in
the white chasm of the toilet under a blue sky. Her father, his
eyes blue and wide and stricken, stands in the tall white doorway of the bathroom. He says nothing, but his eyes are wide and
blue and stricken with grief. The doll is floating in the white
chasm of the toilet under a blue sky. Tina's mother has a huge
face, a gray mask with a jaw like a great stone. There is something inside the medicine cabinet—a red jack-o-lantern whose
candle is out. Nothing moves except the pink rubber doll floating. Is she herself moving? Where *is* she?

There—at the Rapid City bus terminal. The bus has jounced
against the curb, jarring Tina out of the murkey vortex of her
dream. Night is blue in Rapid City. Even the lights seem blue
under the ranges of snow covered hills to the west. Or perhaps
it's the color of the glass of the jar descending over her again.

"You slept right through," the lady pushing up behind her
says as they descend from the bus. "I was sitting right across,
but you didn't want to talk I saw."

"Oh, I'm sorry," Tina says.

"Well, Jesus, honey, don't be sorry. You look like you got
troubles enough already. I leaned over twice and you was wrestling with that pink seat pillow and holding it like it was goin'
to get away."

"I'm sorry," Tina says. She is sweating and her hair is so oily that it makes her feel as if there's a film over her head. Layers. There are layers of film and things. The lady's travel bag pushes against the back of Tina's legs and the lady's breath is rich with a sweetly nauseating smell of chewing gum. She stares at Tina, her brown eyes blinking with curiosity and secret knowledge.

"You better see somebody," she says as she turns to take an enormous blue bag from the pile of luggage alongside the bus. The bag looks like it has been made from the skin of a blue elephant. The lady is very fat and the two of them—the lady and the bag—bump against one another as she waddles into the bus terminal "Two axe handles!" one of the men passengers comments, tilting a gray Stetson back on his head. "Two times two," another says. A little girl is screaming at her mother, pulling at the straps of her suitcase and wailing, "I don't want to. I want to go home." Her mother kneels down beside her on one knee and slaps her face with a quick little flick of her fingers. There's no crying after that, just sniffling.

She has read in *Cosmopolitan* or someplace, or perhaps her mother had told her, that she should always try to look confident—as if she knew exactly where she was going—if she traveled. She's a tall girl and taller yet on the high winter boots under the camelhair coat. She walks directly to a small liquor store to buy a small bottle. No questions asked as she pays out the $5.35 and puts the bottle in her little green valise.

"Hey, little lady," the man standing behind her by the cash register says, "You goin' to enjoy that all alone on a winter night? She can feel his eyes searching her from under the Air Force officer's cap. She begins to feel chewed a little, as if something has climbed on her and is chewing her. Behind her as she crosses the street to get a cab she can see him waver at the door of the liquor store. She hears the car start, feels the lights swing across her and hears the soft rolling of tires toward her. She wants to scream, "You meat-scanning bastard!" but she hurries inside the depot.

After she calls a cab she stays inside the depot. There are a number of Air Force enlisted men waiting there, lounging by the pop machine or sitting talking or reading on the pewlike benches beneath the long stretching blue greyhound on the sign over their heads. She sits by an old man, feeling comforted by his quiet indifference. He stares into a nervous clatter where noisy kids are playing pinball on machines with painted girls in bikinis or skimpy space suits on the lighted back panels. The girls smile and smile, promising winning. The kids jiggle the machines against their thighs and stomachs. Scream. Shake the machines angrily. Dig for change.

You bastard! she cries inside herself when she sees the car outside the depot just behind the cab stand. The officer's bars make little twin silver reflections on his shoulders inside the big tan car. She pulls her coat tightly over her knees and looks away at nothing as she tries to watch for the cab.

It comes, winging around the other car. She grabs her bag and runs, yelping a little as it hits her shin. As she hurries by the tan car, he slides over, cranking the window down and putting his smiling blue eyes and even white teeth at her. She swings the bag up toward the face, clanking it dangerously close to him as it hits the door sill. He recoils, startled. She hurries, yanks the rear cab door open and pitches the bag into the seat.

"Wow!" the cabbie says. "You just shot down the lech air force!"

"Wow!" she says. "You just drive me to the Holiday Inn and make sure we're not followed."

When her eyes have adjusted to the darkness inside the cab she sees that the driver is very dark and has braided his long black hair very carefully in two braids at the back of his head. He pulls the meter lever and drives away very fast, pulling her backward in the seat.

"You're Indian, aren't you?" she says at the motel after handing him $3.20 and a tip." In the front seat he's a tall man, bent stiffly in the middle as if there's a steel rod bent inside him.

"Santee Sioux," he replies. "I have my own cab and a few bucks and an ulcer I'm getting over. I don't give no ladies any trouble except my wife."

"Thank you," she says.

"Nobody followed. Nobody could catch us."

On her way to her room after checking in she punches two cans of Seven-up out of the pop machine. Then she remembers:

no food or drink after eight o'clock. She hurries to the elevator. The room is on the second floor. Inside on the dresser, she opens a can of pop, foams it into a glass and pours the vodka in. She turns the lights off. When she opens the drapes she can see beyond and above the ramshackle of wires and rooftops in the city the great thick concrete dinosaurs standing on the gray-white foothills above the west limits of the city. There are four of them.

She begins to drink slowly and steadily. A few stars string in wide orbits beyond the nimbus of the lighted city, but the concrete dinosaurs loom over the west end above her. Under the belly of one of them—one that looks like a giant Iguana—she sees the small pink one. She laughs. "What a bad joke you are!" she tells them, ". . . you and the blue-eyed All-American Air Force bastard." The dinosaurs seem to lean toward her out of the darkness under the range of stars beyond them. She closes the drapes and sits in the darkness, trying to not think of anything much and sipping the vodka and 7-Up.

Then, feeling a little sleepy and soft from the drink, she fills the tub, undresses and sits in it, lying back until her long blonde hair dips in it. She touches the darker hair of her mons in the water. Her stomach is flat, hard. Nothing shows. If nothing shows, nothing will be changed afterward.

She gets up, rubs herself sleepily and carelessly with a thick towel, pulls on her panties and bra, sets the electric alarm on the night stand, and plunges into the floating whiteness of the bed, letting the covers slide up over her head for warmth and comfort.

In the morning she fights the nausea as she washes and dries her hair and hurries out into the street below toward the Swinston Clinic three blocks away. Hurries so fast that events blur for her: the fumbling with birth certificate and releases, the questionnaire form, the little bag with her watch, the deposit (Cash—the nurse and receptionist not surprised by the six one-hundred dollar bills), a doctor with a ragged brown moustache asking again and again, "Are you certain, now, this is what you want? We are going to terminate a pregnancy and abort the fetus."

"Yes, I'm sure."

"As far as we can determine the fetus is 70 days old. Does that change your feeling about this?"

"No."

Injections, finally. Feeling vulnerable and cold in the loins under the white sheets on the cart outside the operating room. Her hair under an aqua cap, her pubic hair shaved, the stubble prickly.

"Well," Dr. Swan, the man with the blue, sad eyes says, leaning over her there and touching her arm before he walks away on rubber-silent shoes toward O.R., the operating room. "Well, well," he says, patting her arm.

"I hope so," she says drowsily.

In that sleep she doesn't dream at all. She goes away while they work on her body.

When she awakens she is alone in a room even though there are two other beds there. The room is very clean and white. It is full of chrome and cloth, but she's alone in it and they have worked on her. She begins to sob and cry in little bleats. Then she sleeps again.

When she awakens again a nurse is holding her left arm as she takes the blood pressure and pulse. She jots down some things and leaves, hanging a clip board at the foot of the bed.

Dr. Swan comes in then. He smiles weakly at her. "How are you today?" He looks worried—young and yet fatherly.

"I'm all right, aren't I?" She presses her hands over her abdomen, moves a little, feeling the packing—if that is what it is—between her legs.

"Everything is fine from a medical point of view. You're going home today if you like."

Her mouth is very dry. "What do you mean, medical point of view?"

"You came through nicely, but there is a high residual alcohol content in the blood, which surprises us."

"I couldn't sleep in the motel last night."

"You sure that's it?"

"Yes."

"It was a 60-day term," he says, patting her arm again. "There was always the possibility of aborting under stress anyway. Do you know what I'm saying. You're very healthy and can have many babies if you wish."

"Oh!" She's crying again, crying helplessly.

"I would like to have you stay another day if you could and talk to Jack Gernsback the other doctor. There's a let down from this and you should have someone to talk to. Do you?"

"I have to go to school."

"You have to look out for yourself," he says very sternly.

She makes up a smile. "I want to go. I'm fine."

"All right, but be careful."

She gathers all of her clothes and everything. She tries to make very sure that nothing is missing. She has given a phoney address at Carlton College, but you never know. They might mail something and it might come back to Pierre and her father would know it then. It's like checking out of a motel you're not supposed to be in and hoping to God they don't try to mail anything to you.

Riding in the cab and on the bus, she feels very empty and hollow even though she knows she looks the same. She sits alone on the bus again for the three-hour trip and holds her stomach against the jiggling. When the bus crosses the Missouri River lying below her flowing blue and clean between its ice banks she knows she's back again. She closes her eyes. What torment places can be! There's a wet snow falling and she can't see north to the places where she met the two of them. She laughs to herself, remembering the ending of a short story they read in Honors English at St. Paul Academy. "Well, you'd better not think about it." Yes, and "I'm going to get out of this town." Definitely. It was a very short story.

18

Blue Saturday

Something wakes Charlie up early—a vague knocking some-where on the blurred edge of sleep. He lies in bed listening. Nothing. He sits up on the edge of his bed, the hard-on swelling his shorts. Smells himself under the arms. Yawns and falls back on the bed, his legs bent over the edge. Stretches luxuriously and then pulls his arms in over his stomach.

It's Saturday morning—a blazing bright—cold January Satur-day morning. Through the space between the window frame and the shade he can see the white frost and blue-cold radiances of the sun reflecting off the snow—winter light, a hard day full of hard, cold light.

Another knocking—this time at his bedroom door. Startled, he pulls his jeans on to cover himself. "Get dressed," Nancy calls through the door.

"What for?"

"Just get dressed. There's someone out here to see you."

"About what?"

"Get dressed. I'm too tired this morning to argue with you."

He hurries then, pulling on the wool crew socks and the boots and the blue sweatshirt. When he pushes through his bedroom door he's surprised to see that Nancy has gone back into her own room.

"Good morning."

"What?" Turning toward the kitchen he sees him standing

there—a short man frail looking even in the thick brown wool coat. Behind the steel-rimmed glasses his eyes are gentle but steady. His thick black hair is braided back over both shoulders and he is smoking a little pipe, puffing soft little puffs of smoke up into the ceiling as he stands there on the little rug waiting. "I'm sorry to burst into your house like this," he continues between puffs. "I would ordinarily wait outside on the lawn until you're ready to come out, but it's 15 below and I have no headgear except this big old scarf."

"What's wrong?" Something has to be wrong. He has the look of someone with a message, Charlie says to himself.

"I don't mean to rush you, but I would like to have you come with me. Do you want to wash up or something?"

"It'll just be a second."

He hurries into the bathroom, relieves himself and washes his hands and face.

Outside, in the kitchen, he asks his question again: "Is something wrong?"

"Yes there is. It's Magnuson and another man, but don't you want your mother here?"

"I'm staying out of it! I don't even want to *hear* it," Nancy cries through her bedroom door.

He turns, angrily, walks back to the door and stands there. "Aren't you coming?" he asks again.

Her voice is low and mournful through the closed door. "I told you last night: I'm going away. I'm through. Today I'm putting this house up for sale."

"But you have to go with me. I don't know what's out there."

He leans his head into the door then turns to look at the man. He has turned away and seems to be looking out of the kitchen window.

"I don't have to go. I can guess everything. They all have to win, I told you. I don't have to go and I'm not. Leave me alone. And I don't want to hear any more about it."

"Just like that after everything?"

"Just like that—*especially* after everything. I'm done here. I'm going away."

"I suppose I have to go alone."

"Just go, will you please?"

"Sure. Sure. I'll go." He turns and walks back to the kitchen. "She doesn't want to go," he says, pulling on his sheepskin jacket.

The man turns to face him then. "I can wait outside," he says very quietly. His voice is so gentle that it soothes Charlie and he answers quietly himself even though he's very angry with Nancy. "It's all right," Charlie says. "We can go now."

"I must tell you who I am first. I'm Gray Deer of Autumn. I'm Oglala Sioux and a friend of Magnuson's. Of course, I know who you are and I'm sorry to have to drag you out like this. Do you need to call anybody to let them know where you're going?"

"No."

"Then we should hurry, I guess."

The morning light blazes in Charlie's eyes as they step out—hard, cold morning light.

"Your eyes will have other shocks, I'm afraid. Can I just say that to you? You'll have to prepare yourself for a bad sight—worse than anything you might expect. Here's my car; it's warm."

It's an old Chevrolet and the man drives badly, letting the car wander back and forth across the road in long, rocking motions that have the effect of making Charlie sleepy—so sleepy he has to fight it in the warmth inside the car.

"I've known Magnuson a long, long time," Gray Deer says through the heater fan noise and the clicking of gravel on the bottom of the car. "This morning a trapper, Adam Red Bear, called me from a pay phone out here someplace and said there had been a bad shooting between two wild *wasicun* men and it was bad, very bad. He called me to let me know before the sheriff found out, but as soon as I see it I have to call. I'm very sorry. I think there was great suffering for Magnuson."

"Why is that?"

"Because the trapper said they had both been shot and . . ." His voice is so soft Charlie can barely hear him. He leans toward him. The eyes are kind, the voice firm and gentle. "They are both dead."

"Both dead?"

"Yes, Adam Red Bear knows death when he sees it."

"Can we hurry?"

"I think we are, Charlie—maybe too much even."

"Whew it's bright out! It's hard on the eyes." He begins to stare ahead of them as the car rolls along the river toward the ice-locked boat landing. The snow lies on the ribbed hills like the white bones of a sleeping giant. The car hits a few drifts that have ribboned across the road. The river is frozen solid in wide stretches, but here and there blue black water ripples in oval-shaped open spaces.

He sees the chickens first—gaunt, gray feathered birds that roost in the boat sheds during winter nights and run wild as pheasants during the day. His throat gags, remembering the dead fish they scavenge—and the fish guts they clean up.

He pushes the door handle, fighting it until it finally opens and he steps out into the cold. Oates' big red Oldsmobile is about 50 yards from the brown hump of the dugout. Its left front door leans over a dark hulk half under the snow.

He approaches it, afraid of it. Oates lies there with his head under the door sill. His belly arches through the open sheepskin coat. There's a hole in it big as a man's head and fringed with blue-white ragged edges of skin. Charlie freezes in horror and awe. Chickens squawk and go back to the dead man in quick, tentative hobblings of their yellow feet. Their eyes poise above the face, looking at something and nothing. One stands on the barrel of the shotgun waiting. Steps off. They peck at the ribs and flesh. Charlie bends over vomiting in strangling dry heavings of throat and stomach.

When he stops, finally, he sees Gray Deer has looked away again. He talks to Charlie over his shoulder. "Do you want to go? There's worse to see."

But in turning toward Gray Deer he sees Mag or something that had been Mag sitting at the foot of a cottonwood tree, his head back against the trunk, a blue hand laid over the barrel of his gun, a pink halo in the snow that is like a diadem around his face. He vomits again, turning away from the sight.

Gray Deer has turned the car around so that it faces away

from the carnage. Charlie limps toward it holding his hand at his stomach. He sits in the car bent over so his head is below the window level and seeks the shadow inside the car. When he hears the trunk open and the canvas slither out, he knows Gray Deer is covering them both up.

After awhile he raises up and sees two chickens circle in front of the car. He gets out of the car, walks to the dugout and gets the other gun and shells. It doesn't take him very long to shoot them and carry them past the dugout to a deep arroyo beyond a thick of willows. They are wild birds but perhaps the cold has made them a little numb so they can't run or fly very well.

When he finishes, there is a stillness about the place except for the hum of the turbines north of him and under the dam. A little breeze hums in the cottonwoods and willows. The snow begins to move again, to smooth out the low places and to cover the tracks of the cars and men and chickens.

He walks a few paces toward Mag's body. Gray Deer has bound the head in canvas but the arms are clear and covered with a thick layer of ice. If he could say goodbye to Mag it would be like saying goodbye to a frozen fish or something. But he doesn't say goodbye.

"There was no way to prepare you for this," Gray Deer says as they drive away.

"It was all stupid," Charlie says. "Nancy saw Oates again when he came over."

"That's not it, is it? Do you think that's it?"

"I don't know, but it was stupid."

"But he suffered much to get to the cottonwood and sit there until the cold . . . He tried to keep something and to help people around him. Isn't it somewhat good, under the senseless killing of course, that he tried to look after some things he cherished even through pain and death? Nothing was very cheap for him. He must have known that it might come to this."

"I don't know. It was stupid in some ways."

"Yes, but that's the way—good and bad together."

"What now?"

"I'll call the sheriff and the coroner."

"Is he a murderer?"

"No. Oates came to him to take his life. He defended himself. Why do you ask?"

"I just wondered."

"Sometime next week I'll come over to your house in the evening and talk to you, but if you need my help you call me at this number." He hands Charlie a little square of paper with a number on it.

"There'll be a funeral?"

"Yes. Why?"

"Not at Engen. All right?"

"Sure."

"A friend and I wax hearses for Mr. Engen."

"Not at Engen."

"I didn't even go to a funeral of a schoolmate that died of scarlet fever, but I better go." He pauses, seeing the house coming up toward them. "Nancy won't go. She's afraid." Ahead of him, he sees that her car is gone. "But I'll go," he says.

"I'll come to get you or could you call me this afternoon so I can let you know when the ceremony is?"

"Sure," Charlie says.

Inside the house there is nothing on the kitchen table. He washes his hands and drinks some milk and watches TV. There are cartoons on—Tom and Jerry and others. He watches them all, but he doesn't laugh at all. Then there are the Saturday afternoon movies and then early dark. In the early dark he gets up and goes to the kitchen door. There is a deep ache inside him—a deep ache of love and grief. He pulls on his jacket and walks toward Ft. Pierre. Along the south side of Western Avenue he enters a phone booth. In the Scully County directory he finds a listing for Pierson, Carl A., St. Matthew's Episcopal Church, Rectory at 419 Fast Avenue.

His heart is beating so hard and his hands are shaking so much he wants to cry but he dials the number after dropping the dime once. A car pulls up; a man's face leans toward him. Wants to use it too. Points at his watch. "You son-of-a-bitch, I'll kick your face in!" he yells at the car, pushing the accordian door open. The car squeals away.

The number rings. "Hello," a woman's silver, brittle voice says.

"Tina?" He hates his own hoarse, adolescent voice in the wire then—and the heart in his throat.

"She's not here right now. Who's calling."

"Jeff Thomas," he lies. "I met her at school in Minnesota and we're driving through. She said to call."

"Oh, but she's away at Carlton now."

"Where?"

"Carlton. Did you meet her when she was a student at Shattuck?"

"Yes," he says. When he says it he knows he's been trapped.

"Who are you?" she asks. "I don't think this is funny. If you call again I'll call the police and have it traced."

"But . . ."

The buzzing on the phone is infinitely final, like the buzzing of those machines used in surgery—the buzzing when the person is dead. He wants to bawl. He walks toward the station. Billy Whitefeather will be there drinking pop and eating peanuts. He hurries.

Billy is there, sitting on the pop cooler and eating peanuts and reading "Gala Girls," which he shoves under some newspapers.

"Hi, Billy!" he says. "You want to play cards?"

"Where you been?" Billy asks. "Old Mag and Oates killed each other out there and they brought them back frozen stiff."

"Yes, I had to go out there," he says, pressing his hands over his half-frozen ears.

"What was it like?" Billy asks as he pulls a soiled pack of round cornered cards out from a little pile of candy wrappers.

"I just want to play some cards and not talk," Charlie says.

"Sure," Billy says. "There's hardly nobody around it's so fuckin' cold. So how is five hundred?"

I9

The Heart Knows

When he awakens late—very late—Sunday morning, he can feel the emptiness of the house in his head and he knows that he's alone again. He gets up and showers and dresses slowly, avoiding the kitchen because there, especially, he feels the inner coldness and hollowness of the house. And he knows, too, that there is another note from Nancy on the kitchen table.

Before he goes into the kitchen he pulls an old army duffel bag out of the livingroom closet and drags it into his room. There's not much to pack and he can't leave until Monday anyway but he wants to get packed, to get ready, to get it over with. He puts the boxes of shotgun shells in the bottom, then socks and underwear and then the little bright trophies for basketball and track, which he wraps in a towel. Tennis shoes and two copies of *Sports Illustrated.* The little clock radio. There are some old school things—little dumb things he made from paper and paste—but he leaves them on the little varnished shelf he made in eighth grade shop. He takes the double-barreled shotgun apart and thrusts the parts of it down the sides of the bag. He has one pair of dress slacks—brown ones. He lays them on top of the dresser with his green tie, a shirt and his tan sweater. They are funeral clothes. He has no suit or sport coat he can fit into anymore.

In a way it's disappointing to see how little there is. He thinks about the picture too—the Indian woman's picture he bought for a dollar at Buckanaga's Photography Studio. And yet, what's to think? Dead people. That's over too. You can't keep anything alive in a picture.

The furnace comes on—a hot, dust breath for the heat vents, a machine breathing. The vents are galvanized steel and the pipes uncovered through the insulation in his room. The whole place was never finished after all the years. Why? The picture can stay, too. Nancy was hurt by it. He hurt Nancy and she hurt Mag and he hurt Oates and Oates and he killed each other. And Porter was trying to do something that hurt Mag and Nancy was helping him do it and Porter was doing something that hurt Nancy and so on. It makes him sick to think about it because it goes nowhere. Somebody has to to stop it. Some people aren't good for some people. Some people aren't good for each other. What was it that happened to Nancy and to him that makes them both hollow for each other? And when did it happen, because it's impossible to remember just when? It all makes him a little sick to think about it so he tries to not think about it.

There is something else—the stone. He lies face down on the bed and reaches behind the insulation to find it. It's round and smooth and oval-shaped like a pullet egg. It fits his hand, its smoothness comforting him. It has no season, no summers or winters. It abides. He puts it in his pocket feeling both silly and good about something so little.

He swings the duffel bag up on its strap over his shoulder and takes it into the kitchen, where he dumps it on the floor next to the outside door. The note is there all right—between the salt and pepper shakers as usual. He pushes the checkered curtains aside and sees through the curtain of fine snowfall outside that her car is gone. So, something to eat.

"God damn it!" He spits the cereal out into the sink. The milk has soured and is bitter sharp in his mouth. He washes it out of his mouth with water and eats two crusty doughnuts and a hard green banana. There is barely anything else in the refrigerator. That is hollow too.

He plucks the note up angrily from between the shakers and reads it:

Charlie,

I am gone to Minneapolis to find another job. I couldn't look
Mr. Porter in the face. Saturday when I went to the office to get
my things, he came in and asked me what I was doing and I felt
like a thief.

I told him I was ashamed because of Mag and Mr. Oates and
some other things. He asked what other things. I said it was
things about myself but you know now, don't you, Charlie?
She's only 18 too.

He said it was silly to do it, but I said it was a time to go away.
He asked me if it was my former husband. I told him it was myself. I been used by too many people, too many.

He asked me to think it over, but when he left, I took my
things. I been thinking it over for a long time, my whole life.
Even if no other woman wants to be somebody, I have to. It
started a long time ago. Now that I am doing this I have to keep
doing it.

I gave you my mother's milk when they brought you to me
and I gave you all the love I could. You might think because I
chose you my husband went away, but I wanted him to go away
anyway. I don't like men, I think. Now you're almost a man.
Maybe it's good you find another family or start one. I took care
of you for 18 years, but you can go on now. You have past
through me. I can't have a man in an apartment in Minneapolis
when I'm a legal secretary.

The house is going to be sold. Two people want it in a couple
weeks. I'm sorry. But people will take you—good people.

I'll be back and we can talk if you want. Between Mag and me
you are torn down the middle. You got to heal now and make up
your mind about something. You know what I mean.

I'm sorry about the deaths. I'm tired of being sorry too. Nobody had to kill anybody. I couldn't face it. I have nobody. I am a
stranger in my own land and I made you one too. I am farther
away. I can't go back. You can go back if you want, but be somebody, not just a crazy man or a wino or something like that. I'm
too tired to write anymore. Was it horrible out there? Oh, I'm so
sorry. But men—they have to win all the time and then they
lose.

Oh, I'm so tired already today. I will take a bus at Huron. I'm afraid, but I'm going to do it.

Love,
Nancy

He puts his head down on his arms. When he raises up he sees the white lettering on the duffel bag: Sgt. Eddy A. White Cloud, US-55-145-231. He takes it back into his room, empties it into a blanket, ties the ends of the blanket up and hurries out of the house, pulling his sheepskin jacket on and fighting tears with everything he's got.

He dials the number on the square of paper Gray Deer has given him and looks down Western Avenue south toward Indian Town, vague and barely visible through the descending snow. It looks far away. There are little wisps of smoke rising from chimneys through the falling snow and children play outside the shacks.

The voice on the other end is soft and assuring. "Is this Charlie?" he asks right away.

"Yes."

"Can you come to the Smith Mortuary tomorrow at one o'clock?"

"Yes."

"Are you alone at the house?"

"Yes, but I'm going to the station to play cards with Billy Whitefeather."

"You sure?"

"Yes."

"And tonight?"

"It's all right. I don't mind."

The snow ticks on the glass of the phone booth like fine sand falling. "You're *not* lonely, are you—at least you aren't afraid of being alone. You have something or you've learned something."

"I guess so."

"Well, I'll pick you up at 12:30 tomorrow. I'll call the school. Do you want to leave from school?"

"No, I'll be at the house."

"All right. It'll be short tomorrow—just a few friends. Did you

want anything special. It's a Lutheran minister. Of course, he
never has seen Mag in church, but he's been fishing with him. I
wasn't sure what to do."

"It's o.k., I guess. It doesn't matter. Nancy is gone to Minneapolis."

"Well, I'll pick you up at 12:30 then. If you want to call me
anytime, I'll be here. And I'll need to talk to you tomorrow afterward. There are some papers and things Mag left for you."

"Papers and things?"

"Just a few you have to see. But it can wait if you like."

"It's o.k. Thanks." When he hangs up, Charlie feels the cold in
his feet and legs. He hurries toward the Mobil Station dancing
and running to get the circulation back into his feet.

Above him, as he walks hunching under the snow into the station, the red pegasus rocks silently in the gentle wind.

Billy is reading *Gala Girls* again, his mind worlds away in a
bed where one of them, a seductive frozen smile on her face, is
pulling her knees up and spreading her legs, forever available and
yet forever remote in a thin paper unreality. He is surprised to
see Dick Bissonette there too reading *Sports Afield.* Dick's eyes
rise from the page in quick, dark hostility. "Cowboy. Here's our
cowboy!" he exclaims. "Yup! Yup! Here's Cowboy Cooper."

"You want to play buck euchre?" Billy asks.

"He wants to play poker," Dick says throwing his magazine
over the little glass candy and cigarette counter into a bucket
which contains other magazines.

"I'll play whatever you want," Charlie says.

"New deck!" Billy exclaims, bug-eyed and holding it up.

"They gonna bury them two next week?" Dick asks.

"Mag's funeral is tomorrow. . ."

"Engen?" Billy asks.

"No, at Smith."

"You never went to Joey Gray Hawk's," Dick says.

"Neither did you or Billy. I was scared too a little."

"Scared?" Dick asks. "But not scared to walk out there Saturday with them chickens?

"No."

They settle down to play cards, board whacking the cards on the old wooden table and stopping only when a car runs over the pneumatic bell tube and Billy has to run out to the pumps.

"Is Nancy gone?" Billy asks after the third game.

"She's gone to Minneapolis. She'll be back to sell the house and then she'll go back."

"She don't like it here." Dick says. "Us savages made her nervous and then there was the shoot-out . . ."

"Sure, now she's afraid of everything."

"Where you goin'?" Dick asks.

"I don't have any place. I didn't ask Gray Deer about that. I can't go out to Mag's place now. It's got to wash awhile."

Dick stops his nervous card shuffling. "Gray Deer is an Indian lawyer who helps Indian drunks and stuff. What you doin' with him?"

"He took me out there Saturday. He said he's a friend of Mag's. He's taking care of the funeral and everything."

"That's funny. He doesn't work for no *wasicun* anytime. That don't sound like him."

"I don't know. It's for damn sure Porter's not the one."

They play a couple of hours before Charlie says it, half asking something. "I got no place to go now. I'm sure not going to Minneapolis."

"You got a place in my brother's old room if you want. My parents already said it." Billy says, pursing his mouth over his cards.

"You sure?"

"Sure. They was kind of expecting you."

"Jesus Christ!" Dick throws his cards down and pulls his coat on. "Jesus Christ, you cowboy horse rabbit you. Now you not too good for us poor Indians. Now you gonna go and live in the box reservation with the rest. You piss me off, you do!" The door swings open in a breath of sharp cold air and Dick is gone.

"He don't like you," Billy says. "He never did like you, but he thought he figured you out. Now he don't like you and he don't understand you."

"It's o.k."

"You sure you want to come with us? You sure as hell better like oatmeal and macaroni because that's what we eat mostly. And my parents are old as Sitting Bull!"

"But they don't mind?"

"Shit no. They probably celebrate you as *heyoka* crazy man who does everything backward."

"It'll be tomorrow night."

"I'll kill a few bugs to get your bed ready. You shower at school and pound off outside in the snow. Take turns." He laughs.

"Fine."

"You're a funny guy, Charlie. You been funny a long time. You're a wandering man."

"You gonna play cards?"

"Sure. You want an orange?"

"Sure."

When Charlie goes back to the house there are stars out and a great calm has settled over the snow-covered prairie. There's no wind, but over the snow a blue noise without sound—a wolf call infinitely sad and final—echoes into his head and stays there in his sleep through the night and while he lies on his back in bed in the morning.

"It's mostly his old friends from Rex's Bar," Gray Deer says as they stand looking into the little chapel at the Smith Mortuary. "It wasn't easy for them to come here."

"I've never seen them before," Charlie says, "or maybe I forgot."

They sit in the front row on the hard steel chairs that have been put in the chapel. The walls are a silver gray, the floor black tile. Charlie hunches over a little trying to not see any of it—especially the pine casket with the flag draped over it and a bouquet of pink flowers perched precariously on top at one shiny end. From somewhere behind them an organ plays soft, plaintive music that makes Charlie want to cry. He fights it, pinching the inside of his leg under the funeral announcement someone handed both of them. He's dead now, he says to himself.

The minister begins as soon as he comes in and sees Charlie

and Gray Deer. Out of the corner of his eye Charlie can see the
ravaged faces of seven or eight older men and women. Most of
the men sit heavily and quietly, their arms folded. A moustached old woman mews and sniffles under a tiny black hat,
dabbing at her eyes with a huge green handerchief and turning
her head from left to right to see what the others are doing. The
others are doing nothing. One nods sleepily, his head jerking up
in spasms as he trips on the edge of sleep. Somebody farts softly
and then coughs to cover it.

Mercifully it's over quickly. The minister reads several passages from a large, black Bible—things about nothing separating
anyone from the love of Christ and God's mercy and the Lord as
shepherd. Charlie realizes he doesn't know anything about this
either.

The minister steps forward. He's a tall, lank Lincolnesque
man with dark brown eyes and a long face with sunken cheeks.
He rocks up and down on his feet as he talks.

"Dear friends of Magnus Magnuson," he begins, "...and relatives, this is no place for a funeral for this man. We should have
had it on the shores of the river he loved so much—on a clear
day in spring when he would've gone out to try the river. (A little laugh. Stifled.)

"Magnus Magnuson was confirmed in the Lutheran
Church—as some of you were—about 30 years ago over in
Minnesota. Both he and his mother, who was widowed early,
had to wash dishes in a restaurant in that little town on both
Saturday and Sunday, or , at least do some work to keep things
going. Because of that and some other things he didn't see much
of the church or its sacraments after that. I used to kid him
about coming to church and he would say, 'Jesus would've come
out to see me and not nagged me to death about sitting on an
oak bench to let you put me to sleep.'" Laughter. The moustached lady sobbing.

"Still, he never forgot. He did the hardest thing there is to
do—to think on the words of Jesus when everything about you is
tough and maybe a little mean and not quite what you intended
at all. He had this thing about fishing and about stewardship for
the land. Sometimes I think he believed Jesus would come out

to South Dakota and walk out to the boat dock one afternoon
when Mag was casting out for a walleye or something. I think he
believed, down deep, that Jesus might come out and say, 'You
come with me now, Mag, and quit that. You've done a good job,
but I need you for something else.

"But He didn't, so Mag followed his vocation as best he could.
He fished, he gave joy to people on the water, and he tried to
take care of all his responsibilities. Mag never forgot his stewardship, his responsibility for the land he got on the river. He
wanted to keep it simple and good; he just wanted to make
enough money to live.

"Mag knew what he was doing and what he had to do. He
knew sin was a human condition. He knew he was a sinner. He
faced that and accepted it every day of his life. That's not a bad
thing. It redeems us and keeps us free from ignorance about the
essential truth about ourselves. And remember that Mag never
forgot some things he learned as a boy even though everything
in this tough life our here seemed to contradict it. That is a kind
of faith.

"He suffered at the end and so did a few other people around
him. It was violent and terrible as so much of life is. That in-
volves a kind of faith too.

"In this world one could do a lot worse than have this Mag as
a guide. He knew the territory; he tried the river first himself
each spring. To anyone who might criticize him I guess I would
have to say he did the best he could. I spent a couple of days on
the river in a boat with him and those were good days after he
stopped apologizing for swearing so much. The river could be a
big, dangerous place for people like me. Mag knew that.

"Mag's body goes back to a little family cemetery in Minnesota, but we remember out here and we know, too, that being
the best fishing guide on the Missouri River is an honorable
thing. That is the priesthood of all believers and Mag was one of
them.

"Amen.

"Will you stand up a moment, please?

"Dear Heavenly Father, we commend to you this man of faith.

Bless him with your Holy Spirit, now and forever, and let us all forgive one another so that each day can be good and new. Amen."

When he finishes, he smiles at Charlie and the others and begins shaking hands with all of them, saying very little. Then he's gone. The others linger only a little while, some of them looking nervously over at Charlie and Gray Deer, but not coming over to shake hands or talk.

"I got to have a drink," someone says.

"Shhh, for God's sake. He'll hear you, the boy will," the moustached lady says.

"I don't care. I got to get back. It's over, ain't it."

"Well come on then. Get out of here, now, then. Rex is having free drinks for a couple hours."

"That don't do Mag any good!" someone says.

When the rag-tag, clumsy group of them passes, and Gray Deer and Charlie follow, the moustached lady swaggers toward Charlie with a flirtatious waggle of thick body under a wide patch of black dress.

"My, you are the handsome one!" she giggles pinching his cheek with a fat warm hand. "Ain't he? Ain't he?" she says over her shoulder to the others. Nobody answers. Gray Deer smiles, but a flicker of worry also crosses his face.

When he and Gray Deer leave the chapel, Charlie fights an impulse to look back. Gray Deer's hand is on his shoulder but not pushing. Outside, Gray Deer pauses by his car. "It can be an empty afternoon now," he says, his brown eyes very serious. "I have to show you some things. Do you want to come to my office now?"

"Are you a lawyer?"

"Well, I'm an Indian first and then a lawyer."

"Where's your office."

He laughs. "It's in the low-rent district along the river. I live there too. It's a terrible mess and I have irregular hours, I'm afraid."

"I suppose I better," Charlie says.

They walk up a long flight of worn, creaking stairs to get to

the office. The door is unlocked and an Indian woman sits inside
the door nursing a child. She covers herself quickly as Charlie
and Gray Deer enter.

"Did you want to see me, Grace?" Gray Deer's voice is kind
and gentle, but she has turned away from them and won't turn
back.

"My husband will be back in half hour maybe," she says.
Charlie can hear the baby sucking noisily under the shawl and
blanket.

"Fine," Gray Deer says. "I'm going to talk to this young man,
but you can have him knock on my office door when he gets
back."

No answer. They enter the office through high yellow oak
doors, entering into regions of stacked books and papers. Charlie
can see a cot in a little adjoining room and in another a sink
bowl and the dark rim of a toilet seat. The linoleum on the floor
is a dark green obscured by layers of thick, aging brown varnish.

"Corpus Juris. What's that?" Charlie asks as Gray Deer motions him into a chair and sits down himself.

"The body of the law—the written or printed law. It's Latin.
It's really white man's law. Goes back several couple hundred
years."

"Do you know all that?"

"No. I use different ones for different cases."

Gray Deer leans back in his swivel chair looking at a folder
full of papers. Charlie guesses that he must be about 30 or so,
but his face looks serious and old and his eyes look tired under
the silver-rimmed glasses. In the outer office beyond the high
oak doors Gray Deer has closed behind them Charlie can hear
the mother crooning a soft Indian lullaby. The words are indis-
tinct but the mother's joy and love are not. The two of them are
in a warm little world of their own out there. It makes Charlie
sad as hell.

"I really don't know where or how to begin," Gray Deer says.
"There's not much here and it won't take long, but I just don't
know how to begin."

"What is all that stuff?" Charlie asks.

"It's Mag's will and a trust arrangement, but that's not what

I'm concerned about." He stands up and goes to the window—
the grimy, brown-curtained window that overlooks Cooper Avenue that runs along the river on the west side of Pierre. Then he
turns and takes off the glasses as if to see or be seen better.
"How do you feel about all this—Mag, Nancy and all of it?"

"I don't know."

"You're not quite 18 but you're already on your own in a way.
And you know the problems Mag was having with the so-called
Oahe Region Recreational Resources Council. And you're going
to have to fight just as Mag did."

"You mean Porter's hot shot resort thing?

"What do you think of it? Your mother talked to you about it,
I believe, didn't she?"

"I think it stinks. It's not that it will ruin the river and everything. It's just that it won't be the same place again. It'll be making all the people from other places renters so they kind of own
it one after another. And it's all like a big custard stand and cars
and noise."

"But you could have had a piece of it," Gray Deer says.

"No, I couldn't in a million years. I'm not going to have a
piece of, no—any plastic grave box."

Gray Deer sits down again and holds the sides of the folder up
like the pages of a menu. "That wasn't fair of me, Charlie. I'm
sorry about that, but I've got feelings about that too—and the
Black Hills and so much of the land that was once our own people's land."

"Why do you say sorry?"

"Because this is Mag's will and I asked you some unfair questions when I know things."

"Like what?"

"You can read this after awhile. He left all of it to you to be
held in trust for you until you're 21 by the First National Bank
of Aberdeen, which gets it away from Porter and Associates and
the banks here in Pierre."

"The whole place?"

"Everything—boats and truck and all."

"Why?"

"Why not?"

"He said Minneapolis was full of his relatives."

"Relatives." Gray Deer removes the glasses again. "And what are you, do you think?"

"I don't know."

"In a way I think that's true, but I think that you know that in a way you do know."

Hearing it, hearing it finally makes something fearful tingle high in Charlie's head and he doesn't like the feeling.

"Do you mean Mag?" he asks finally.

"I do mean Mag. What else can I say?"

"He never once said it to me." The heart—why does it beat on the truth so hard?

"Did he have to?"

"I don't know. He could have done something. He never once said it to me, not once."

"Well, you have to reflect on that yourself in your own way, I guess. But I think he gave you all he could while he lived and now he's given you everything he could in his death. There's G.I. insurance money for school or whatever you want it for. That will be up to you."

"Dead stuff!"

"Oh, come on, Charlie, it's not dead at all. You'll have a real fight on your hands with Porter and if you go to school you'll have to work your buns off to make up for what you didn't or couldn't learn at the Indian school. Believe me, it's not dead stuff unless you're going to be dead in your own soul."

Gray Deer has said all of this very quietly and steadily and yet it makes Charlie angry. He lays one arm down on the desk toward Gray Deer and leans toward the kind, but determined face.

"Was it because I was an Indian?"

"No, it was because the only woman he ever loved—in his own way—was dead and he had nothing but a dug-out along the river, so what else was there to do? And what's this stuff about your being an Indian? You've been living in a house away from Indians and where a woman wanted you to forsake all the old ways. In a way, her vision for you was a journey to Minneapolis and a blue suit and a job in an office."

"I didn't want it," Charlie snaps. "I never said I wanted that. And I'm only half Indian."

"Sure," Gray Deer says. "You're half Indian one-fourth by one-fourth. You were born of an Indian woman. And there's something much deeper. You don't have to be half or quarter blood or live on government trust land. You have to have something so deep in your heart that you feel the whole earth is a part of you and you a part of it. It is a relationship with Mother Earth and Father Sky. I can't define it for you. Have you ever had a vision?"

"What?" A vision—what is it. Kim Pettigrew asked him too. The thunder, but then Mag's truck honking.

"It might be thunder or something. You would know it if it happened. It would suggest to you your purpose in life. I believe that if you disregard it or resist it for whatever reason there is no peace. If you follow it as best you can, there is a peace and strength beyond all human understanding."

"I don't know," Charlie says.

"Maybe it has happened but other things distracted you."

"I don't know," he says.

"But to be an Indian is to know your own history too. Otherwise it's like having amnesia." He pauses then, looking very tired—gray green in the face. "I could never be a very good trial lawyer. I'm giving you a cross-examination and I find the questions fly back at me and bother me. Am I a lawyer—just a white man's law brain inside my Oglala head? But still at least two lawyers in this town are Indians. That's something, isn't it?"

"I don't know," Charlie says.

"That may be great wisdom," Gray Deer says. "I don't know much either except that I am trying to be true to what I think I'm supposed to do."

"I'm going to Billy Whitefeather's tonight," Charlie says.

"Do you know that when they take you in, you won't be part this or that. You'll be all Oglala. Blood runs the heart. The heart knows what it is."

"Yes."

"That won't be so easy either. They haven't got much. Can you run the boat landing next summer?"

"Yes. I hate to think of all that paint scraping again. Can Billy work with me?"

"Sure."

"But I'm not going to hire him or anything. We can share things."

"That's good."

"We should get those outboard motors out of there and put them someplace so they're not stolen. The boats will be all right."

"Use the old truck and store them at the Pierre Marine Store on Front. The old truck is yours and whatever else. The keys are out there someplace."

"Later this week. Are you going to be helping me?"

"If you want. There'll be plenty of headaches. Even there on the river there's always business and books."

"But I'm not changing much, except to maybe put some things underground so . . . well."

"And there's Porter. We could lose. He's got a lot of momentum."

"Sure," says Charlie.

Gray Deer is standing up then because there's a soft knocking at the door. "Do you mind taking a cab out to the house? Here's some money. I've got people waiting already. My hours are very irregular."

"No, I don't mind," Charlie says, "but I'll pay you back."

"All right. You do what you have to out there."

"Sure."

As he opens the door to the outer office he sees the father standing there waiting quietly. He is tall and very thin and he holds some papers in his fist, hitting the palm of his other hand with them. Behind him, the mother's face is smooth and round and very beautiful as she holds the child.

"Charlie?" He turns back toward Gray Deer's voice. "The heart knows what it is! Will you remember that?"

Charlie nods and smiles at him as the doors close on the two of them—Gray Deer and the tall thin man with trouble in his eyes.

For a moment Charlie is alone with the woman and child. She is, as so often Indian mothers are, very shy and she doesn't look up at him as he looks at her. But she is smiling a soft beatific smile and he feels that it is for him too.